14

· Miranda's Album ·

To my mother Jean, my sister Alison and my daughter Sophie.

· *Miranda's Album* ·

HELEN TOWNSEND

SIMON & SCHUSTER

AUSTRALIA

J-1

MIRANDA'S ALBUM

First published in Australasia in 1989 by
Simon & Schuster Australia
7 Grosvenor Place, Brookvale NSW 2100

A division of Gulf+Western

© Helen Townsend

National Library of Australia
Cataloguing in Publication data

Townsend, Helen.
  Miranda's album.

  ISBN 0 7318 0070 2.

  I. Title.

A823'.3

Designed by Helen Semmler
Cover illustration by Gillian Bennett
Cover designed by Pam Brewster

Typeset in Hong Kong by Setrite Typesetters
Printed in Australia by Australian Print Group

·Chapter One·

Miranda walked into her parents' bedroom. Over the walnut veneer bed hung a huge clock, mounted on a shimmering picture of Elvis Presley. His eyes seemed to scan the room and he made a hip-swivelling turn as you walked across it. Pauline, Miranda's mother, had emptied the clothes basket onto the floor and was energetically rifling through the contents. Miranda looked at the familiar scene. "Hi ya, Mum."

Pauline Darnley was a small, wiry woman, dishevelled and worn looking. But her face was still pretty, with big blue eyes that moved expressively, in an almost childlike way. Her small mouth often contracted in worry, but, now, as she saw Miranda, grinning at her from the doorway, her face lit up. "Mandy!" she yelled. "Oh lovey, how gorgeous to see you." She vaulted across the bed and hugged Miranda tightly. "You shoulda told me you were coming. I woulda cancelled netball, but Sally's broke her arm and we're playing the Tigers. If we win, we're in the semis. I reckon we got a chance at winning the comp—only the district mind you, but Roy reckons if we win he'll get a band down for the finals." She jumped back over the bed again and picked up the yellow and white netball uniform, which had spilled out of the basket. She smoothed it down, eyed it critically, then bundled it under her arm and led the way down the hall to the kitchen. "Lovey, you should see Roy's new house—geez, don't reckon he could've found a better spot and he's built it beautiful. But he spends half his time round here coaching the kids—suppose he's lonely since his divorce. I like to see him—always good for a laugh..." She trailed off tentatively as they walked into the kitchen... "Kevin, Miranda's here," her fingers nervously twisting the chain round her neck. Her husband had a beer and was adjusting the black and white TV on top of the fridge.

1

"I know," he replied with a grunt and threw a derisive look at Miranda. His bulky, muscled body and close shaven head repulsed her.

"He's thrilled to bits I'm home," said Miranda.

"Jesus!" Kevin got up and walked out the back door, slamming it behind him.

"Did you have to say that?" said Pauline irritably. "He'll be like that for the rest of the weekend now."

"You mean otherwise he'd be cracking jokes and handing out lollies?" said Miranda sulkily.

"You know what I mean." Her mother dropped the netball uniform onto the table, hauled a pot off the stove and strained an enormous, steaming mass of grey, overcooked potato into the colander. Without waiting for it to drain properly, she put it back into the saucepan and added a slurp of milk and a dollop of half-melted margarine. "How's uni?" she asked stiffly.

"I'm doing OK, Mum," said Miranda. "Pretty good in fact."

"Too brainy for your own good," said Pauline crossly but with a touch of pride, looking through the window to where Kevin was viciously attacking the overgrown vegetable garden. "God, look at him. Always on about the state of the house or not having clean overalls." She sighed. "That garden used to be a picture when you kids were little." She watched as Kevin threw down the mattock, cracking it against the wall of the aluminium shed. He strode across the yard and out the gate. They heard the sound of his truck starting and Pauline relaxed. "He's off to the club. What are you up for, love?"

"Linda asked me to come up. But I just want to come home sometimes. I miss you...and the kids...and I wanted to ask you..." Miranda trailed off hesitantly, looking longingly at her mother.

"You take him too seriously."

"He hates me," said Miranda fiercely.

"Don't talk about your father like that," snapped Pauline automatically, vigorously beating at the potatoes. Then she brightened. "Lots on this weekend. Louis is playing in the under-thirteens tomorrow, you can come to netball and you must see Roy's house. Of course Shirley's after it, but there's nothing she can do because the divorce's final." Pauline chuckled. "He's a cagey bugger. Must've kept it under the bed." Miranda sat back, tuning into the familiar chatter, her

2

mother's irrepressible, sometimes nonsensical, sometimes sensible view of the world. It was only broken by a tortured shriek from Kerry. Pauline took off down the hall. "Those two!" As Kerry's screams rose to a pitch, Miranda began mechanically mashing the mass of potatoes with the bent fork.

Miranda and Linda sat on the seat under the old plum tree. There was only two years' difference in their ages, but Linda often made Miranda feel older than her nineteen years. Always, she'd felt the oldest, sensible and responsible, Linda the carefree child. Linda looked nervously at the swarm of bees, which hung at the end of a branch, only two metres away. "I hate them things," she said angrily. "Always out of their hives."

"Why did you want me home?" asked Miranda. It was always a struggle to get anything out of Linda. Now, she became silent, like a small child, rubbing her shoe in the dust. "Why?" asked Miranda again.

Linda looked down at the dirt.

"Why?"

Linda let her breath out in a rush. "To tell Mum and Dad I'm up the duff," she said defensively.

"Linda! You can't be!"

Linda turned and looked at her for the first time in the conversation. "I can be," she said defiantly.

"Aren't you on the pill?"

"Oh the pill," said Linda scornfully. "It doesn't work."

"Not if you don't take it," said Miranda.

"Yeah, well, I didn't. I forgot, so you've got to tell them."

"How pregnant are you?"

Linda's hands went to her head. She started twisting her curly red hair nervously. "Three or four months. It's beginning to stick out." She looked down at her flat stomach.

"Are you getting married?"

"Who to?" There was the defiance again.

Miranda struggled to grasp the situation. "Danny, of course." Danny Anderson and Linda had been a couple since year eight, Uwalla High.

Linda shrugged. "He went away. Worked up the coast. I got lonely."

3

"Jesus!"

Miranda looked at Linda and took her hand. Linda pulled away savagely.

"Danny forgave me and everything. It's telling Mum and Dad. Danny still loves me. Everything's all right between us. It's just the baby."

"Just the baby?" said Miranda incredulously. She noticed the swarm of bees seemed to be moving along the branch towards them. She got up and walked over to the overgrown vegetable garden, the weeds so thick they were matted. She remembered the garden as it had once been, neatly laid out, in precise troughs in the damp, brown dirt, fresh green shoots sprouting through the earth. Her father had always been hard, but over the years she had felt his resentment growing steadily. He had supported them, she thought bitterly, but he obviously felt he owed them nothing more. "I'm not telling them," said Miranda. "You know how Dad is with me. You're the one that's pregnant." She paused and softened a little. "Tell Mum. She'll tell Dad."

"He'd scream his head off at me. I gotta tell them both at once."

Miranda looked at her sister, trying to shame her, to force an admission of guilt. Linda refused to look at her, grabbed the clothes line, pulled herself up and swung on it. Her legs drawn up under her, she looked like a child. "I'll tell them tomorrow night." There was a hint of desperation in her voice. "But I need you there... please..."

"OK, I will be." Miranda gave the clothes line a shove, sending Linda spinning round, and went inside.

"Sister Miranda fell off the verandah, her sister Linda fell out the windah." Miranda had walked up to the Andersons with a half-formed intention of talking to Danny Anderson about Linda's pregnancy. He was standing on the verandah, grinning good-naturedly, hoping he had embarrassed her with the old childhood taunt. She waved at him, realising the futility of trying to talk to him. He shouted back at her. "See ya tomorrow. I'll be down for Linda." She walked on past the Andersons' place, its front yard littered with cars in various stages of repair, one pushing over the remnants of the old picket fence.

The Andersons' house was typically Uwalla: weathered fibro, with built on sleep-outs and an old peppercorn tree at the back.

Idly, she kicked a stone onto the road and then turned to the laneway that led to her family's house. Home for the weekend, she felt for a moment as she had when she was a small child, when home was still the centre of existence. She was a small, slight girl and her clothes were the nondescript uniform of a student, loose jeans and a baggy cotton jumper. The most notable thing about her was her long auburn hair which fell in a thick plait down her back.

Down the laneway were more run-down cottages with their windswept tea-tree hedges, lazy dogs and an occasional touch of flamboyance: a gnome or a concrete Aborigine proferring a boomerang. At the end of the lane there was a glimpse of the dunes and, where the scrub thinned, of the sea. The breeze blew in gusts, as it did each afternoon, breaking the hot stillness of the township. Miranda relished the taste of salt on the wind: the salt from the sea, not the oily waters of Sydney Harbour.

She arrived home and walked slowly up the cracked concrete path. The house was neat outside, just on the edge of shabbiness. The lawn was scruffy, mown too frequently on her father's orders. The hibiscus bushes, planted to form a hedge, had long straggly branches, hungry for nourishment, bearing thinning, yellowish foliage and sticky, unopened buds.

"Hi Mandy!" yelled eight-year-old Kerry, shooting past her. Louis followed her, acknowledging Miranda by jumping his bike impressively across the gutter. Linda's pregnancy still weighed on her mind, but she felt good to be home.

"Murder in the dark," whispered Miranda. "I'm coming to get you." Kerry, the youngest sister, squealed in delight and scrambled to the top bunk, out of the way of Miranda who was writhing menacingly under the chenille bedspread, making sudden grabs through the rips in the cover. "Murder in the dark," she yelled. Kerry dropped suddenly onto Natalie, who screamed and retaliated with a slap.

"Hey, get out of it. That hurt."

"I was murdering you."

"Not that hard or I won't play."

"Mandy, give me a go, give me a go," begged Kerry. "I haven't had a turn." The older ones played, as they had when they were children, half aware they were too old for the game, but falling unconsciously into the old family pattern. Miranda drew Kerry under the bedspread. "We'll get them both at once," she whispered. "You go that way, I'll get Linda." They made a sudden grab out into the darkness and landed on Linda. Natalie jumped down off the bunk and soon all four of them were writhing on the floor, clutching and grabbing at each other, giggling helplessly.

"The girls are making too much noise," yelled Louis self-righteously from his room. "I can't go to sleep." The girls went quiet as they heard Pauline coming down the hall. She opened the door, framed by the light.

"Into bed, the lot of you. It's almost eleven. You'll be exhausted tomorrow." She came in, closed the door and started tucking Kerry in. "Miranda, you're old enough to know better." But once they were in bed, she snuggled into bed with Natalie, one of them, as she loved to be, more sister than mother.

Miranda lay under her thin eiderdown. She had been given the old one with the holes, since she was so rarely home. She lay quietly, listening to her mother's chatter, still familiar after a year and a half away from home. Other students complained about the poverty of the old Glebe terraces—to Miranda, the privacy of her own room there, sharing a bathroom with three other people rather than her four siblings and her parents, was a luxury. She smelt Natalie's cheap perfume, her mother's setting lotion, the stale smell of dust and the salt breeze wafting in across the verandah. Sleepily, she picked at an old piece of blutac on the wall, shaping it into a flat circle, finally rolling it into a ball and dropping it onto the floor.

"Pauline, come 'ere!" Kevin's voice barked out from the main bedroom and her mother scuttled out of the girls' room like a frightened rabbit. Miranda heard muttered, hostile exchanges between her parents, then Pauline quietly padding around switching off the lights, first in the kitchen, then the front verandah, the hall and finally the bedroom. She heard the squeak of springs as her mother got into bed. Then, silence through the house.

She lay awake, feeling strange to be back in this bed, to have

6

the feelings of family, the old pull, the old hurts, the old fears. She started to drift off to sleep, thinking as she always did of the sea, the beach, a great expanse of peaceful sand, her mother walking towards her, away from her, then not her mother, another, undefined woman. She was not quite asleep, still dimly aware of the images in her mind, aware of the feelings of confusion and need that went with them. She was becoming engulfed in them as she was drawn into sleep, when she became aware of a sound from the bed below. Through years of practice, she knew how to lower herself noiselessly and Linda automatically moved across the narrow bed to make room for her. Miranda lay against her, her arms around her and Linda snuggled into her embrace, reassured. Miranda held her, stroking her hair as she drifted into sleep.

Miranda led a rousing cheer from the Darnley family as Natalie triumphantly pulled herself from the pool. Who won, who lost, who played had always been a family preoccupation, with Saturday sport a strict family ritual. Linda had refused to come this morning, but the rest of them, except Miranda, were in tracksuits, ready for events later in the day. Unlike the others, Miranda had never been naturally athletic. Her body was small and strong, but she never developed the co-ordination or endurance to excel. She made up for it in her fierce support of the others. Roy was here too, as supporter and barracker. Towheaded, zinc-nosed, he looked like one of the family. He wore a Uwalla Colts jersey and there was a wide grin spread across his battered face, under the baseball-style cap proclaiming: "Roy's Pest Service—dead cert."

"Natalie's really good, isn't she, Mum?" said Miranda enthusiastically. Out of the water, Natalie was shy, ungainly, with the heavily muscled shoulders and legs of a swimmer, but as she collected the trophy it was obvious that winning, even against this mediocre field, satisfied her. She saw them looking at her and wrapped her towel around her, embarrassed.

"Trains too," said Pauline proudly. "Roy got her training. She's a real terror to get up in the morning. Every morning, I drag her out kicking and screaming. But she complains like hell if I miss the alarm."

"Look, there's Mr Rogers," yelled Louis. "He'll be up at

cricket. He coaches us," he added proudly to Miranda. Miranda looked across at David Rogers, not wanting to, but forcing herself, glad he couldn't see her with her zinc nose and thongs. He was squinting at the divers. Then Miranda noticed Lyn, his wife, come from behind and take his arm. She was obviously pregnant. Miranda quickly turned back to Roy.

Roy had removed one thong and was thoughtfully picking at the dead skin on the sole of his foot. "Nat could make the state championships, you know. Real water baby." He grinned and nudged Miranda. "Not like you." Roy, stolid and good-natured, with the persistence of a bulldog, had taken three seasons to get Miranda dogpaddling. Now, he had the same determination to make Natalie a champion.

Pauline was busily collecting thongs and towels, shepherding the children together, as Natalie, still wet and shivering, joined them, silent as always. When Miranda was young, Kevin had always come to Saturday sport, cheering his children with a mixture of admiration at their prowess and fury at their in-adequacies. Then, after one particularly bitter row with Pauline, he had stopped coming. Roy, genial and easy-going, gradually took his place, providing the battered ute that took them from the pool up to the oval and the courts.

Pauline sat in the front of the ute, chatting at Roy, while the rest of them packed in the back tried to avoid the wind-sprayed spit of Kip, Roy's kelpie, who barked hysterically at the rush of wind over the ute. The oval was swarming with children and parents, in the ritual of Saturday morning sport. There were shouts of the boys at practice, the thud of balls, and the cheers, chatter and laughter of parents on the sidelines.

Miranda walked over and leaned on the fence, looking down on Uwalla, the expanse of tin and tile roofs, like a gash through the tea-tree and mangroves. Back beyond was the river, snaking its way through the hills, the great rock bluffs, backwaters creating lagoons, then finally making its way up to the sea through a mass of sandbanks and complicated forks of land. In parts the river was blue, then, shaded by the hills, a dark green, the sea itself almost white in the glare of the morning sun.

"David!" David Rogers had come from behind her and touched her on the arm.

"Saw you at the pool," he said.

"Congratulations on the baby," she said brightly.

"It wasn't planned," he said gloomily.

"Surely that doesn't matter," she said, brisk and brittle. She wanted to get away.

"You got a boyfriend in Sydney?" he asked.

"I'll have to go. I want to watch Mum play."

She retreated and ran back across the oval to where Pauline was organising the kids. Natalie was dispatched to netball, Kerry to a coaching clinic. Louis found the under-thirteen side. Free of children, Pauline tore off her tracksuit, glanced at her watch and sprinted full speed to the netball courts.

Pauline played with the tenacity of a cattle dog, endlessly circling, darting in for the ball, jumping to challenge women who seemed twice her height, appearing again through the huddle of players, intercepting the ball, passing it to her team-mates, shouting encouragement. Her red hair came untied from the little girl pony tail and her face lost its freckles in its increasing redness. Miranda grinned at Roy as they watched from the sidelines.

Roy didn't take his eyes off Pauline. "And they reckon football's violent. She's going to kill someone one day." He winked at Miranda. "And I'll be here to see it."

Pauline came out from the shower, her towel hitched around her, awkwardly but modestly putting on bra and pants, only letting the towel fall when she donned her T-shirt. Miranda picked up the damp towel from the concrete floor of the change-room.

"Mum, I still want that album," she said tentatively.

"Jesus Christ, Miranda, you never bloody give up do you?" Pauline was usually careful not to swear, but her victory at netball had released her inhibitions.

"Please, Mum..."

"Is that why you came up? Just for that?" Pauline angrily pulled up her tracksuit pants, catching them uncomfortably on her wet legs. She sat down and started to brush her hair back fiercely. Miranda started towelling her mother's hair and Pauline relaxed, leaning back on her. "Don't tangle it, Mandy... rub just over here love." Obediently, Miranda towelled Pauline's hair, massaging her head the way she knew Pauline loved it.

"Mum, that album's important to me. I want to find out who I am. At least let me see my birth certificate."

"It won't help you." Pauline looked up at Miranda. "Adopted or not, I'm your Mum." Miranda tried to smile, but Pauline saw the anxious plea in her face. "Ask me tomorrow," she said briskly. "I'll think about it." Miranda was about to hug her, but just in time, caught her look of exasperation.

When Miranda came back, Linda was sitting in front of the bedroom mirror, doing her hair, teasing Danny into admiration and laughter. Linda had the sort of lively prettiness that made people want to watch her, each movement and gesture revealing her in a different and attractive way. When her hair came loose, it curled casually against her neck. When she brushed it back, she was suddenly endowed with an innocent, madonna-like quality. But Miranda watched her impatiently as the afternoon wore on and she showed no sign of sending Danny home. She clung to him, laughing, giggling, flattering him, until Miranda hissed at her. "Is he staying?"

"He's OK," said Linda blankly.

"Yes, but they'll think..." Miranda gave up. She felt angry with Linda, the way nothing ever touched her, nothing ever made her lose her equanimity. Perhaps a baby would finally force her to grow up. But probably Linda would stay at home, trading on being her father's favourite, using her mother's love of babies. She'd marry Danny or some other boy and float through life untouched.

Miranda, not Linda, was tense all through dinner. They sat in the tiny kitchen which was dominated by the smell of burning fat. Pauline kept sausages coming, burnt or underdone, overloaded with tomato sauce. Miranda barely noticed the food, concentrating on her father, making sure he had the best sausages, a can of beer at hand. She fed the younger ones quickly, stopping their fights and squabbles. As she sat down, her hands were shaking uncontrollably and she dumped her dinner onto the leftover plate for the dog. As soon as the meal was over, she slipped Louis ten dollars. "You and Nat take Kerry down to the pinball parlour. Don't come back till eight thirty!" she whispered at him fiercely. He grabbed the money sullenly and she turned him round to face her. "You got it,

Lou?" He looked blankly at her. "Please." He ran out, the others after him demanding their share.

She walked back into the kitchen. Linda was leaning against Danny, her arms around his neck as Pauline wiped down the table, with broad side swipes, transferring most of the crumbs to the floor. Kevin sat hunched forward over the table, one hand clutching his beer, a cigarette in the other. He didn't move as Pauline wiped round him. Miranda felt her stomach knot as she looked at them. It had to be got over with.

"Linda's got something to tell you," she said.

Kevin looked up briefly, then grunted an assent. Pauline started clattering dishes in the sink.

"Sit down, Mum," said Miranda desperately. Pauline caught her tone and perched on the stool.

"What is it?" she said to Miranda.

Miranda looked at her sister. Linda took a cigarette from Danny's pocket. "Light it, darl," she said. Danny lit it and Linda lay back on him, looking up at him.

"Tell them!" said Miranda.

Linda looked pleadingly at Danny. He looked at her, his brown eyes innocently delighted by her, unaware of the tensions in the room. "Linda's pregnant," he said, "but it's not . . ." He had no time to finish. Kevin jumped around the table and seemed to shake Linda from Danny's lap onto the floor. Pauline recoiled in terror, but with a presence of mind born of experience, grabbed the saucepan as she moved behind the table.

"Fucking bastard, you bastard!" Kevin bounced the red-faced Danny up and down in the chair, dragged him to his feet and threw him against the sink. There was the sound of metal crushing as the sink gave, a yell of pain and protest from Danny. Linda crawled under the table, behind Miranda. Kevin reached for Danny again and landed a punch across his face. Only a last minute duck stopped the full impact of the blow. Danny was no fighter. Escape was his only thought as he struggled to free himself.

The women watched in horror, Pauline raising the saucepan as Miranda screamed, "It's not Danny's. It's not his. Leave him alone, leave him." Pauline threw the saucepan, missing, but dislodging the remains of the mashed potato which sprayed all over Kevin's face and shirt. He let go of Danny, who had the presence of mind to stumble out the door.

11

Kevin stopped. "What do you mean it's not his? Who the fuck's is it?"

Linda cowered behind Miranda. Miranda faced her father. "She doesn't know. That's why she couldn't tell you."

"I don't know, I don't know," Linda screamed hysterically.

Kevin looked at Linda, for a moment, stunned, then an ugly expression came across his face as he turned to Miranda. "You bitch, you bloody little bitch." He looked at the three women, white-faced and scared. Their terrified passivity infuriated him further. "Get out, the lot of you. Ya molls."

"Get out!" Pauline echoed him. "We gotta get out." They turned, too scared to go past him, through the back door, across the prickly lawn, silently down the drive, then scampered out onto the road and ran breathlessly down towards the beach. They ran along the narrow sandy path through the tea-tree and collapsed on the damp sand. Pauline grabbed Linda. "Why didn't you tell me?" She turned to Miranda. "You should have had more sense! You know what he's like."

"I thought it'd be all right," said Linda lamely.

"You screwed it," said Pauline angrily. "What do you think it's like for me? Why can't you let me handle him?"

"Sorry, Mum," said Linda. Miranda was silent.

"He'll be OK in the morning," said Linda hopefully. "He'll come round."

"Can't you see? This is real serious." Pauline stood up, angry. "I'm going to get the kids. I'll take them home later. You two aren't to come. No way!"

"Mum," whined Linda.

"No," said Pauline furiously. "I can't take any more tonight. I'll try and sort it out with him tomorrow." She started walking towards the track.

"Can we see you at church tomorrow, Mum?" asked Miranda. "Please!"

"I'll be there. If you come too, that's your business." Pauline disappeared into the tea-trees.

Miranda shouted after her desperately. "Mum! The album."

Pauline reappeared briefly from the tea-tree.

"Forget it, Miranda."

Miranda and Linda lay on the sand, Linda, expressionless, looked up at the stars. After a while, Miranda took Linda's hand. "We could build a fire and stay here the night."

12

It was dark and they could just see the white of the breakers against the inky blackness of the sea. Linda raised herself onto her elbows, and stared out at the sea. She smiled dreamily. "Gary's having a turn. Let's go there."

Miranda spent the night in the Andersons' caravan which had been parked in the back yard for ten years in preparation for Mr Anderson's trip around Australia. "See yer own country first," was his catchcry, but he'd never got further than Uwalla Station Hotel. Over the years, the caravan had been used for the sexual exploits of the Anderson boys and it smelt of stale male sweat and old beer. Tonight the heat intensified the odours, but Miranda locked the door to keep the Anderson boys out. She spent the night drifting in and out of sleep, interrupted by the screams of the party, interspersed with memories of both parents' anger and sickening anger at herself. She thought of the old green photo album somewhere in the house, of which she had once had a glimpse and which she knew, contained her original birth certificate. She had a vague memory of a pressed flower, some cards. Pauline had allowed her a brief glance six years ago, then denied its existence. Finally, after years of pestering, she had conceded she had it, that she might even let Miranda have a look one day.

"You don't even belong in this family. You got no right to shove in your twenty cents' worth. Little bitch!"

It had been the first time she'd ever dared to stand up to her father. She'd always sensed a particular hostility lurked below the surface. When she was younger, he'd sometimes been indulgent and affectionate, but her mother had often had to protect her from his badgering anger. This time, Pauline had gone to hospital and Kevin, furious at her absence, had started picking on Louis. Miranda had stood up to her father, but got back more than she'd bargained for.

"Your real mother, some little whore, couldn't even name your father. Bloody Pauline talked me into adopting you. I never wanted no one else's bastard. Whore's kid. And I was right!"

Miranda, barely fourteen, with all the rawness of a turbulent pubescence, had run out of the house. Her face was swelling with tears she couldn't cry, her stomach a tight knot, her throat so constricted she felt as if she was choking as she ran. She ran all the way to the cottage hospital at the other end of town, and there, as the nurse was bustling visitors out of the ward, she had burst into tears on her mother's bed. Pauline had pulled the curtain round the bed as Miranda blurted out what Kevin had said to her. The late train, with the lighted rectangles of windows, had drowned out the last of her words, but her mother had hugged her and rocked her. Pauline simultaneously tried to deny the truth and explain it away. Miranda's heart ached, powerfully, physically, as she'd pressed desperately against her mother. "Mum, Mum, Mum," she'd moaned, unable to stop saying the word.

Later, when Pauline had come home from hospital, she'd shown Miranda the album. Miranda had even doubted her mother's love for a time and the incident confirmed her knowledge of her father's dislike for her. Pauline had tried to heal the breach, but without success. "He's your father," she told Miranda.

"Not any more." She hated him with an unforgiving passion. Kevin would never admit he was wrong and his sullen, angry moods became more oppressive.

"We're still a family." Pauline tried to make it true by cajoling and humouring Kevin and pretending to Miranda that nothing had really happened. But ever since she'd left home, Miranda had desperately wanted the green album. She couldn't explain why and Pauline wouldn't explain her resistance.

Miranda dozed off, and it was after midnight when she became aware of someone banging on the door. Miranda ignored it, then sleepily shouted, "Piss off!" but the banging continued and she gradually became aware it was Linda. She got up, turned on the light and pulled her jeans on.

"Is anyone with you?" she asked.

"Nope," sniffed Linda.

Miranda opened the door and Linda stepped up into the caravan, holding her face. "Oh Jesus, Mandy. I've really stuffed this up good and proper." She was slightly drunk. "I hope Mum lets us home tomorrow. I had this awful fight with Danny. Says I'm a slut. I can't make him love me any more." She burst into tears as Miranda pulled her hand away from her face and examined it. As she suspected, Danny had done no more than slap Linda.

"We'll sort it out tomorrow. Sensibly." Miranda was exhausted. "Now for heaven's sake, just lie down and go to sleep." She turned out the light, lay down on the hard, grey blanket and turned her back on Linda.

Linda felt sulky and upset by Miranda's high-handedness. "And stuff you too," she whispered loudly at Miranda, now inert on the bunk.

They waited outside the church. Miranda's dark red hair was pulled back from her face which was blotchy from the previous day's sun. Her brown eyes, usually lively and intense, looked drawn and tired. Her mouth and chin were set determinedly. She looked at Linda, sitting on the seat under the tree, her curly hair somehow messily fashionable with the few pins she'd salvaged from the floor of the caravan, her shirt tied above her shorts, her face relaxed, almost blissful as her head rested against the back of the bench.

"And give us eternal life. . . ." The voices faded and the organ quavered, grinding out the last few chords, then neatly changing to a more upbeat tune which was the signal for the congregation to leave church. First out was Mrs Jeffcott, her pink face and frock perfectly co-ordinated, the dress pulled up over her dowager's hump, causing it to curve inward and upward at the back of her skinny legs. Her face was set in a look of resigned complaint at the ineptitude and general half-heartedness of Sim Jeffcot who followed her like a resentful old dog. Miranda smiled politely at them, but Pauline wasn't there and for a moment she felt like a little kid about to cry. She started to walk back towards the seat where Linda was lying, fully stretched out, with her eyes closed. It seemed unfair—Linda would go home and eventually settle back comfortably into family life. She had to go back to Sydney, unsettled and scared for months.

"Hey! Good-looking!" She turned to see Roy leaning out of the ute, Kip, the kelpie, barking relentlessly as he jumped automatically and uselessly towards any car which passed. "You two, come here. I got something for you." Linda stretched sleepily as Miranda ran to the truck. "Get in," said Roy. "Hey," he yelled to Linda. "Yeah, the ugly sister too."

Linda walked over to the truck, sulky it was Roy and not her

15

mother. "Where are we going?" she asked, well aware she was not Roy's favourite. He had always preferred Miranda and Natalie, a discomforting experience for Linda, who, all her life, had been adored by the opposite sex.

"Sailing club," said Roy. "Get a beer, discuss the facts of life." He drove up the main street of Uwalla and drew up at the wharf. On one side was a huge shed, a bustle of activity as kids pulled their sabots into and out of the water. Roy went into the shed, emerging a minute later with three cans of beer. Kip's pathetic whines turned to a yowl as they walked out along the wharf, past a couple of kids fishing.

"God, you're cruel to that dog," said Linda spitefully. "Tied up in that truck all day."

"He likes it," said Roy. "It's his territory. He gets depressed on the ground."

"Yeah, why do you have to tie him up then?"

"It comes with the territory, smarty."

Miranda sat on the end of the wharf and Roy sat beside her and handed her a can. Linda sat apart from them and put her hand out for hers. For a few moments there was silence as they sucked on the beer. Miranda felt light-headed and realised they'd had nothing to eat all day.

Roy cleared his throat then put his can down on the wharf. He put his hand out, extending it palm upwards, using his other hand to tick off points. "One," he said, bending back the little finger. "You can't go home. Your father won't have it and your mother won't have it either, believe it or not." He looked at them sternly. "She's had enough. She can't cope with any more. And I don't want you pushing." He looked at Miranda. "I got your things in the car. Yours too," he added to Linda.

"You're OK, Miranda." He pushed down the second finger. "Where's Linda going to live?"

"I got no money," said Linda. "And I don't get the dole till Tuesday week. She'll have to let me home."

"Linda," roared Roy. "Somebody ought to give you a bloody hiding. Your mother can't cope. She won't have you home. Either of you. Final. Your father won't allow you in the house. Got it?"

"Where can she go?" asked Miranda. "Danny won't have her." She'd spoken to Danny that morning. He'd finally realised that Linda's pregnancy had made a fool of him and was all the more angry and set against her for not seeing it sooner.

"I'll float you a couple of hundred," said Roy. "But you'll have to find somewhere to live. You might be better off in Sydney."

"She can live with me," said Miranda, then immediately regretted it. Until now, life in Uwalla and life at university had been separate. She wanted it that way. Linda wouldn't fit in with her life, her friends. She'd be a nuisance, she'd make a mess and she'd try and stop her studying as she'd always done at school. But Linda was her sister, pregnant, thrown out of home and incapable of looking after herself. Miranda took a swig of beer. The sun was white in the brilliant blue sky. Her head swam. She took another swig, then, her eyes still smarting, looked into the green oily water, past her grimy, shoeless feet. "We've got an extra room."

"Oh," gasped Linda. Miranda had never even allowed her to visit before. Sydney promised new excitement. Her self-pity and fear dissipated and she looked at her sister with gratitude. She leaned past Roy and tried to hug her. "I promise I'll be good. We'll have a terrific time. I won't be a nuisance. Gee thanks, Mandy."

Roy looked at Miranda and shook his head doubtfully. "May the best man win."

Linda looked at him coyly. "You still float me a loan?"

Roy got out his wallet and handed two hundred-dollar notes to Miranda. "You dole it out." He caught her look of vulnerability and hugged her. "Keep in touch. Don't worry. She'll be sweet." He stood up and looked at his watch. "You'll get the two o'clock."

Silently, they walked back to the ute. Roy handed Miranda her bag and two shopping bags. "Linda's stuff's in there."

"Thanks," said Miranda. She hugged Roy casually. "See ya," she said breezily.

She passed two of the bags to Linda. "Come on," she said impatiently. "We've got to get tickets."

"Your Mum said she'd put in an album or something for you," said Roy.

"What she say about it?" Miranda asked quickly. She could see the outline of the album pressing against the bag.

Roy grinned and shrugged. "That you were welcome to it for all she cared."

·Chapter Two·

The old diesel stood chugging asthmatically at the tiny, sun-baked station. Finally, it pulled out, but continued its stop-start locomotion throughout the hot afternoon. In the airless, sticky carriage, the sporadic chatter between the two sisters gradually wound down, as Linda's excitement at going to Sydney degenerated into boredom and Miranda lost the energy to entertain her sister.

By the time they reached Central, it was late afternoon and the station was thronging with groups of loud teenagers out of a concert, hysterical and shouting. Linda followed Miranda, dog-like, through the long underground tunnel, both of them pushed and jostled, their bags seeming heavier and bulkier. At the bus stop, there was a large group of people waiting, disconsolate and irritated. "Sunday arvo," complained a woman. "Never any bloody buses." Linda had somehow got a seat on the bench. Miranda stood, exhausted by the events of the weekend. Back in Sydney, everything seemed unpleasantly gritty and grimy. She wanted to get home, away from people, away from activity, to lose herself in sleep.

"Why don't we get a taxi?" asked Linda after two buses had passed.

"It's five bucks from here," said Miranda primly.

"We've got two hundred," said Linda. "Come on."

"Two hundred goes nowhere in Sydney," said Miranda fiercely. "It'll cost that to get you set up."

"Mandy . . ."

"Don't hassle me, Linda."

Linda sat and sulked. Miranda leaned against the bus sign. The next bus that came along didn't go down Glebe Point Road, but she didn't care. She had to get home. She got on, paid her own fare and walked to the back of the bus. Linda

18

looked at her resentfully as the driver asked her for the fare. She sat at the front and began an animated conversation with the woman next to her. When Miranda got off, Linda said goodbye brightly to her acquaintance and followed Miranda off the bus, pointedly ignoring her. Miranda felt depressed by Linda's presence, and the feeling increased as they walked across the park, its artificial lake bordered with sodden chip packets and bottles. One of the semi-comatose drunks lying on the grass roused himself to mutter angrily at them as they walked past. As Miranda led the way across Parramatta Road, the Glebe Point bus roared past. She was aware of Linda dawdling despite her own purposeful briskness. Suddenly, Linda's resolve not to speak to Miranda dissolved.

"Mandy, look at that!" She caught hold of her sister's arm and dragged her back to a shop window with a big poster of a puppy with enormous soulful eyes. Very non-Glebe, very Uwalla. "Isn't it gorgeous!" Linda exclaimed.

Miranda grinned at her. "You're a sook." She nudged her. "You're going to have to toughen up here, you know."

"Look at its eyes," said Linda breathlessly.

"Cute." Miranda took her arm. "Come on. Let's get home. I've had it."

Linda trailed after her reluctantly. "Yeah, me too."

Miranda slowed down. "Sorry about before," she said. "But money's my biggest worry. I watch it all the time and I'm always broke."

"You'll have to watch me all the time. I'm hopeless."

Miranda knew, but she also realised it wasn't her most important concern. As they walked along Glebe Point Road, past the houses painted baked ochre with their hunting green trim, past the exotic restaurants and coffee houses, the second-hand shops, the craft and the antique shops, she came to the unpleasant realisation that she was ashamed of Linda.

"I'm a terrible snob," she'd once told Hazel, her housemate. "That's why I don't allow any of my family here. I couldn't bear it." It had been a joke, but walking down Glebe Point Road, Miranda realised she had spoken the exact truth to Hazel. She was a snob. She didn't want to take Linda home. She didn't want her to open her mouth to say "youse" and "thems", slouch round the house in high-heel slippers and talk about *Police Academy* movies.

They walked past an outdoor restaurant where people sat laughing and drinking, past the laundromat where people stared mesmerised into the tumble dryers. It was getting dark but the street was alive and buzzing. Linda was silent, trying to take it all in. All she really knew of Sydney was the Easter show and Luna Park, both of which she'd shared with Danny. She'd been shocked at Kings Cross, where they'd gone one New Year's Eve, but she'd expected to be shocked. Glebe, however, was completely foreign to her. It seemed shabby, slightly distasteful. She'd always imagined Miranda's life as exciting and glamorous. Her belief had been based on the fact that Miranda talked so much about her studies that Linda believed it must be a cover up for something exotic and slightly wicked. Now, she began to fear Miranda had told the truth.

As they walked up towards the traffic lights at the top of the hill, a man, stripped to the waist, wearing Hawaiian shorts, a lei around his neck and a Walkman on his head, jumped into the middle of the road, dancing to the music on his headphones. He combined his dancer's movements with those of a traffic policeman: pirouettes and stop signals, pas de deux and right-hand turns, leaps and bounds with a frenzied come-on to the approaching cars.

"That jerk'd be off his bloody head, wouldn't he?" said Linda scornfully.

"That's Twist," said Miranda. "He lives round here. He gets funny about the traffic."

"Looks like a perve to me. They should lock people like that up."

Miranda was relieved when they arrived at the house to find no one there. She didn't want to explain Linda's presence yet.

"Hey, this is quite nice," yelled Linda as Miranda came out of the bathroom. "You've got some nice stuff here." Miranda rushed downstairs and found Linda examining the objects in Hazel's room carefully, one by one. The room, by any standards, was extraordinary, a combination of Hazel's baroque tastes, indulged by two generous allowances, one from each parent. She had painted the wood gold and the walls deep red, traced with the outline of plants, which, when combined with numerous real plants, gave the effect of a jungle. Amongst the plants were shop dummies, painted black and gold, wearing Hazel's antique clothes and jewellery. The circular Tiffany lamp and an enormous world globe were echoed by the collection of glass paperweights. An old headstone from a grave, laid across two sawn off trestles, served as a coffee table.

As Miranda walked in, Linda was examining the inscription. "This is really gas," she said enthusiastically. Miranda firmly led her out into the hall and down to the kitchen. The kitchen was a more ordinary room, dominated by a large picture of the Queen. Under it was a hatstand on which hung various kitchen implements. Miranda put the kettle on and turned to face Linda, her arms folded across her chest.

"This isn't like home," she said. "We all have our own rooms and you can't just wander in or out like we do at home. The kitchen's communal, and so is the hall and the bathroom. The rest is private, out of bounds."

"The bathroom?" said Linda incredulously. At home, the bathroom was the only place that was private, scrupulously so.

"Well, for the girls anyway," said Miranda. "Obviously the blokes don't barge in when you're on the loo."

"Men live here?"

"I didn't tell Mum because I knew what she'd think and I didn't tell you because I knew you'd tell Mum." Linda grinned in acknowledgment. "They're just friends. One's a doctor—we hardly ever see him."

"A doctor?" Linda was incredulous.

"He works at the hospital. He's got a room there but he likes to come here sometimes."

"Where am I going to sleep?" Linda was suddenly frightened and suspicious.

"We've got a little spare room," said Miranda. "But I'll have to ask Hazel if you can have it. Her Dad owns the house and she chooses who she wants here."

"How old is she?" asked Linda suspiciously.

"Twenty one." Miranda remembered her own incredulity on discovering life outside Uwalla. "Her old man's loaded." She carefully poured out the two coffees and sat down at the table. "We'll have to share my bed tonight. Get you fixed up with one tomorrow."

21

Linda had gone to bed early. Miranda had waited in the kitchen until eleven, wanting the chance to talk over Linda's arrival with Hazel. But Hazel had rung, very drunk, very stoned, with a long and complicated message for a possible caller. Miranda didn't mention Linda.

She walked into her bedroom where Linda was asleep, curled up down one end of the bed. The room was a contrast to the rest of the house. Its bareness and austerity were not of Miranda's choosing—she simply could not afford much. She undressed down to her T-shirt and pants and rummaged through her bag for a pair of socks, her hand touching the old green album for a moment. She debated with herself whether to pull it out. Her old longing, her need to know, reasserted itself. But she also felt Pauline's painful rejection and she threw the bag carelessly on top of the old wardrobe. Linda stirred, moving uneasily in her sleep and Miranda made soothing noises, tiptoed to the door and turned out the light. Normally, she slept with a light on, in an attempt to curb her dreams, but tonight, pressed up against the warm, familiar body of her sister, she felt safe and secure in the dark. As she drifted off to sleep, she imagined she could hear the surf of Uwalla and went into her dream: the beach, the two mothers . . .

Linda woke early the next morning. She had hardly slept as Miranda tossed and turned, muttering and mumbling incoherently throughout the night. But now, Linda was glad Miranda was still asleep. She had always had two distinct feelings about her sister. On one hand, Miranda was her protector and benefactor, who'd stand up for her, fight tooth and nail, sell the shirt off her back for her. Linda was vaguely aware she wouldn't do the same in return; she'd grown up with the notion that that was the way things should be. But Miranda's protection had its disadvantages—she was bossy, dictatorial and always knew best.

Linda crawled out of bed without disturbing Miranda and quickly got dressed, fluffing her hair round her face and wiping off her smudged, black eyeliner. She searched round for a towel, and, as she expected, found a plain white towel hanging behind the door. The room seemed to her to personify Miranda: tidy, sparse, no frills or fripperies. The walls were almost covered by the wardrobe and bookshelves, but down one end, over the desk, was a large travel poster, a seascape, its colours reminiscent of Uwalla. Linda looked at it only fleetingly, then started rifling through Miranda's drawers in search of shampoo, soap and make-up. She collected what she could and quietly made her way up the stairs to the landing, knocking tentatively on the bathroom door. There was no answer and cautiously, she tried the door. There was no resistance and she went in, still scared she'd find one of the strange men of the house there. She breathed a sigh of relief and immediately latched the door behind her. Seeing a pair of scales, she hopped on. She shut her eyes and then opened them. Fifty eight kilos. Suddenly, she felt furious. Bloody preggers. God, why did it have to be her? She turned the adjustment knob on the scales and hopped on again. She'd dropped to fifty six. Feeling better, she turned on the water, lit the gas heater and took off her clothes.

Linda had always liked her body. She liked others to like it. She flaunted it and teased with it. Until recently, she had liked to look at herself, but now, she was glad that the little mirror had steamed up so fast. She washed herself, avoiding looking at her breasts, the nipples enlarged and darker, blue veins now tracing the white surface, below them, the growing bulge of her stomach, the golden hairline thicker and more pronounced. She pushed aside the thought of the pregnancy. Another five or six months and she'd be herself again.

She finished her shower and went downstairs.

The scene in the kitchen had changed since the previous night. On the table were full ashtrays, empty bottles and a pair of pantihose draped over the back of one of the chairs. From the back toilet came the sounds of someone vomiting. It reminded Linda of the Andersons and she thought of Danny, briefly and regretfully. Linda filled up the kettle, then searched through the fridge. There was a chicken breast off which she ate the skin, and a carton of yoghurt. She opened it, dipped her finger in, then put it back. Finally, she took out a packet of crumpets, the butter, honey and milk. As she put the crumpets into the toaster, and turned on the kettle, a girl walked into the kitchen from the laundry.

"Hi," said Linda, looking at her uncertainly. Hazel Johns was unlike anyone Linda had ever seen. Even with a hangover, she was stunningly beautiful: high cheekbones, big, dark blue eyes, a beautiful full mouth and flawless tawny skin. Her long dark hair was drawn up into a pony tail which sprouted from the top of her head, held in place by a piece of red silk wound round and round it. She wore an extravagantly embroidered jade and black Chinese coat, belted loosely to reveal most of her breasts and a glimpse of red silk knickers. On her feet were football socks striped in the exact shades of the Chinese jacket. She looked at Linda uncertainly.

"Were you here last night?"

"Well yes, I'm Miranda's sister."

Hazel looked at her appraisingly. "Fancy that. That girl's so secretive you'd think the whole family had two heads. Does she know you're here?"

Linda grinned. "Of course. We came down yesterday."

"Let's have a coffee. I feel vile. I'm going to swear off chemicals of any kind. Stick to reality. You know, your sister's good at that. Love her dearly, but she can be a prude. I don't think she approves of my habits. She gets drunk as a skunk once in a blue moon. I inflict it on myself every second night. That's why she's doing vet science two and I'm still failing social work one. I promise you, when I graduate, I'll be my own first case. Get this girl in line." She looked down and adjusted her dressing gown.

Linda giggled. Hazel was like an extravagant version of her mother, ineptly tripping round the kitchen, saying whatever came into her mind, pouring the coffee, too impatient to wait till the water boiled.

"And what brings you to the city? Business or pleasure? Man or woman? Friend or foe? Bird or beast?"

"I'm pregnant," said Linda simply. "And I got chucked out of home." But Hazel didn't look up from the toaster, fixedly observing the crumpets turn black. As smoke started to rise, she took them out and expertly sliced off the charred bottoms. "You'll stay here, won't you?" She buttered the crumpet and bit into it. "We'll fix up the spare room and you can be confined in comfort. Social worker, vet, sometime doctor and one layabout engineer, on tap. Do you want to do that?"

The arrangement seemed amazingly casual to Linda. "It'd be great, but I haven't got much money."

"Do the housework or something. I'd rather that than cash. How would that suit?" For the first time she really looked at Linda.

"Fine," said Linda.

"Sure?" asked Hazel. "You know your big soeur is always telling me I push people into things, so I have to be careful. That'd really be OK?"

Linda giggled. "I'm not much good at housework."

Hazel swept her arm up in an extravagant gesture. "Any housekeeper who doesn't lie in bed all day drinking gin would be an improvement on what we haven't got at the moment." She scraped Vegemite onto her crumpet, eyeing it distastefully. "We need someone to keep the Vegemite clean, remove crumbs and butter once a week." She leaned across and looked at Linda, fixing her with seductive blue eyes. "If you'd just do that. By the way, how old are you?"

"Seventeen."

"Lovely," said Hazel. "That's settled then." She looked up to see Miranda at the door, already dressed for university, but with her hair still wet. Miranda smiled at her uncertainly.

"You've met Linda?"

"Not only met her, but let her the spare room in exchange for services of housekeeping and general light duties."

"Very kind of you, Haze," Miranda frowned as she made a coffee.

"I did ask her," said Hazel.

"I'll really try, Mandy," chipped in Linda.

"Mandy! Do they really call you that?"

"She does," said Miranda, her privacy already invaded.

"Well, well," said Hazel. "I know I'm too curious, but you can't blame me if your sister lets your secrets out."

"It's just a family name," said Miranda defensively, then relaxed a little. "You know, I wanted to seem grown up at uni, not just another country kid. Miranda's got more class." She gulped down the rest of her coffee and stood up. "I'm off to chemistry. I'll see you about six."

"Can I have some money?" asked Linda. She had checked Miranda's purse earlier. The only money left was Roy's two hundred-dollar notes.

"Buy yourself a bed," said Miranda blithely, taking a hundred-dollar note out of her purse. "Haze'll tell you where to go. And get them to deliver today. I don't think we'd last another night together."

Linda flashed a big, insincere smile at her sister. "Have a nice day."

Miranda was running late and she pedalled furiously down Glebe Point Road and in the front gates of the university. She loved the place: the expansive green lawns, the spreading trees, the old stone buildings. Even more she loved the feeling that she actually belonged here. She flew down Science Road, hastily chained up the bike and rushed over to the biochemistry lecture room, walking in just as the tutor was pulling down the blackboard. In a few seconds she was totally absorbed, making a mental note of what she understood and what she didn't. Her intelligence, combined with her determination and intellectual insecurity, made her an excellent student. But she also had a genuine curiosity and once hooked by a topic would pursue it relentlessly. After biochemistry she had genetics, then a break from eleven to twelve, but she remembered to race down to the library and photocopy fifty pages from a text and track down a journal article. Thoughts of Linda kept coming to her and by the time she got to the nutrition lecture, she had decided that not only was she a snob, but she was also jealous and bitter. It had taken her months to feel at ease living in Hazel's house; months before she really felt part of the household; months before she could really call herself Hazel's friend. Linda seemed to have achieved a greater degree of intimacy and ease over a single cup of coffee than she had in a year.

"Coming to lunch?" called Geoff Harris as she came out of genetics. Geoff had been one of her tutors the previous year. He was friendly, helpful and whether she wanted to or not, she ran into him almost every day. He gave her the feeling she was being stalked.

"Thanks, but I've got to track something down at the library."

Geoff made his way to her through the crowd and stood tentatively in front of her. "What are you after?"

"The article by Stein on environmental control," said Miranda primly, exasperated by his helpfulness.

Geoff nodded enthusiastically towards the tutors' room. "I've got it. I'll copy it for you. So let's have lunch."

"All right." Miranda was resigned to capture.

They made their way up through the lunch-time crowds to the cafeteria and got into the queue moving slowly past the glass cases.

Miranda stood behind Geoff, looking at the almost permanent boil on his neck. She felt resentful that she had to sit with him through lunch, with his annoying habit of pulling at his already scraggly beard. Glumly, she remembered how Hazel had categorised him the first time he'd called round to the house. "He's the sort of man who asks you to sleep with him and means just that. Be careful, Miranda, or he'll tuck you up with a hot-water bottle and boast about his sexual conquest."

Geoff piled their food onto one tray and smiled at the cashier. "I'll pay."

Miranda protested but he took the tray and carried it out onto the lawn. They sat down and Geoff leaned over to her. "Now tell me your troubles."

Miranda took a chip and dipped it into his gravy. "Sorry to disappoint you. I haven't got any."

Miranda walked into the kitchen with a wilted bunch of flowers and put them down next to Hazel, who was standing at the sink emptying tins of curry into a large saucepan.

"From an admirer with bad taste?"

"Valentino."

"I don't know why they say Italians have style. Why does he have to dye perfectly good carnations that awful blue?"

"They never were perfectly good carnations. Actually Valentino sells things like this because he thinks Australians like them."

"Well, you work for him, darling, you'd know." She looked into a recipe book, then shut it impatiently and filled a saucepan with water and put it onto the stove. "Curry and rice for a . change. But, to celebrate the arrival of your sister, we're also having salad and wine. She's down the road with Patrick getting it."

A man appeared in the kitchen doorway. He was as good looking as Hazel, blond and wearing Hazel's Chinese dressing gown. He wore nothing underneath it. Hazel smiled at him and then looked at Miranda. "The latest flame: Phillip. Phillip, this is Miranda. You know, Linda's sister."

"Family resemblance. Red hair."

Hazel sat down at the table and lit a cigarette. "Linda's pretty young, isn't she?" she asked Miranda casually.

"Seventeen. Why?"

"Very young seventeen."

"I guess she is. Country kid really."

"Too young for a baby."

Miranda tensed. "We just have to deal with it."

"She's only three months, four at the most."

"So?"

"It's not too late to deal with it." She sensed Miranda's tension. "They can do an abortion," she said gently.

Miranda looked at Hazel, sitting there, so cool, casually stubbing out her cigarette, her legs crossed, Phillip standing behind her, beautiful, his hand draped across her shoulders. She felt the blood drain from her face. "No!" she shouted. "They can't do that." She walked out of the kitchen, slamming the door behind her.

Hazel twined her arms round Phillip's neck as he slid his hands down her jumper. "See why I keep failing social work?"

Miranda was drinking to get drunk as quickly as possible. Her outburst to Hazel had scared her, heightening her insecurity about her place in the household.

"Haze, I didn't mean to shout at you," she said fuzzily.

"It's OK," said Hazel.

"I just don't think abortion's right. But I don't mean you're wrong." She collapsed crying in Hazel's arms. "I think it's because I'm adopted," she sobbed.

"I didn't know you were adopted...that big family."

"I'm the only adopted one." She paused and took a swig of her drink. "I don't even like it for puppies." Her words were indistinct, thickened by drink, muffled by sobs.

"Adoption or abortion for puppies?" asked Hazel, taking the joint from Phillip.

"I don't mind adoption. I can't stand abortion," said Miranda. She paused, moved her head off Hazel's shoulder and swigged some wine out of the bottle. "I don't even think I like adoption much."

She looked over to Linda who was showing her double-jointed thumb to one of Hazel's ex-boyfriends who had just arrived. "I've got a double-jointed dick I'd like to show you," he kept saying and bursting into giggles. Patrick, the only one who wasn't drunk, looked at him with contempt. Patrick was a final-year engineering student. He always joined in the house parties but he never got drunk and seemed to watch the others with wry disdain. He was tall, good looking, invariably good humoured, but always slightly distant.

"You're very decadent," he said to Phillip lightly. Phillip looked at him, slightly hurt. Patrick walked over to where Hazel was cradling Miranda. "That new one's very degenerate, Hazel. He'll bring out the worst in you."

Hazel smiled her dazzling smile. "I hope so. But you're wrong. He's very moral. He's engaged, to someone else, of course. And he's in the army."

"The army," snorted Patrick. "He's not in the army!"

"He is so," said Hazel. "He's going to be head of it soon. This is low life to him." She looked down at Miranda who was lying in her lap, drinking out of the bottle. "Now that is degenerate," she said. "Miranda, it doesn't suit. I was born to it." She looked up at Patrick. "But not this one. She'll feel terrible tomorrow and then the next day she'll start a year of penance. Rescue her."

"I will," said Patrick. He took the wine bottle from Miranda and pulled her gently to her feet. "Come on, time for bed." Miranda collapsed on his shoulder.

"Patrick, I'm so drunk I won't be able to get up in the morning. I'll miss a whole day. I don't know what I'll do."

"Self-flagellation has begun," said Hazel. Patrick half carried, half dragged Miranda down the hallway to her bedroom. He turned on the light.

"Oh Jesus, don't turn on the light," squealed Miranda, covering her eyes. Patrick lay her down on her bed. She kept her hands over her eyes as he took off her shoes and then turned off the light. He went back and found a blanket to cover her. As he laid it over her, he found she was sobbing into her pillow, long, painful, drawn-out sobs, not just the maudlin crying of a drunk. He sat down on the bed and rubbed her shaking body. The sobbing continued and he lay down next to her and gingerly put his arms around her, stroking her hair on the pillow.

"Hey, Miranda," he tried to soothe her, without effect. "Tell me, what's wrong?"

She threw her arms round him and her sobs became less intense. "I wish I was really plastered," she cried. "I tried, but I couldn't get properly drunk even."

"You're not doing too badly. You want a fag?" She shook her head. "Is it your sister? I mean not just pregnant, but being here, mates with us all, all that."

Even in her drunken state, Miranda was surprised by his perception. "I didn't think you noticed things like that," she said defensively.

He was silent, waiting for her to speak.

"Well, I'll tell you. OK, Linda's pregnant, we're both thrown out of home. Mum's in a mess, I think. I didn't realise and I did a lot of stupid things on the weekend, one of which—oh God I feel ill. Don't worry, I won't be—one of which was asking for my baby book. Just a photo album, my birth certificate and mementos. Mum kept them for all of us, for when we got married. But when I found out I was adopted, she let me see it, just once to prove she loved me as much as the rest. Then she wouldn't give it to me, even though I kept asking. I let it go, then I asked her again on the weekend and she said she would. But then we were chucked out and she gave it to me, it was sort of like the end of everything."

"How?" asked Patrick.

"Like saying, 'Miranda, we don't want you back in this house and here's the album about where you really came from.' Get it?"

"Yeah," said Patrick.

"Things happened before that ended up with Dad and me hardly speaking, for years now. So now I don't know if Mum will ever speak to me again. And I've got this album. I've always had this idea I might find my real mother, not because I don't love Mum, just because... and I'm too scared to look. And I think if I look, Mum really won't want me back, but I'd really like to know where I came from. Oh Jesus." She sat up and looked down at Patrick lying at the foot of the bed. She collapsed back into his arms sobbing. He held her, stroking her hair and running his fingers down her spine. The door opened and Linda put her head round.

"Oh, I'm sorry," and promptly shut it again. Miranda drew away from Patrick and they both giggled.

"*En flagrante*," he said.

"Well I don't feel drunk any more. I know I am, but thanks for listening to all that drivel." She wiped her eyes with the sheet and smiled brightly. He didn't return the smile.

"Miranda, where's the album?"

"I shoved it up on top of the wardrobe. I'll look at it some day."

"Do you want to find your real mother?"

Miranda's smile disappeared and her eyes filled with tears. He took her hand. "Do you?" he asked.

"Yes... but..."

He hugged her, stroking her gently, like a child. "All we're going to do now, is look at the album. That's all. It may hurt, but it won't bite."

"Don't worry," said Miranda. "I'll get it down some other time."

"Now. If you don't do it, you're going to go crazy or neck yourself."

"I'm not that silly."

"Miranda, do it while I'm here." She nodded mutely and lay down, eyes tightly closed, fists clenched. He got up and felt along the top of the wardrobe. He found the bag, got it down and took out the old green plastic album. It had "Photo Album" embossed across it in gold Gothic letters and then, in texta pen, in a poor attempt to copy the Gothic print, "Miranda". He sat down on the bed and opened it. On the first page was a proof size photo of an indistinguishable baby, fast asleep, tiny fists clenched. Underneath, in the same amateur, elaborate lettering as on the cover, was "Miranda Darnley, born 1st Sept, 1966. Beloved first child of Kevin and Pauline Darnley. 34 Anderson St, Uwalla, N.S.W."

"Hey, Miranda, look at this. You haven't changed a bit." Miranda opened her eyes and looked at the photo.

"Yeah, this is it."

"We keep looking?" He looked at Miranda carefully.

Yes," said Miranda. "Thanks, Patrick."

He turned the page. On one side was the birth certificate.

On the other, at the top, was a small, pink card, marked 'Sex: F. Weight: 5lb 7oz. Feeds: 3 hrs. Lactogen.' Underneath was a pressed pansy. A handwritten sticker proclaimed, "From cot at hospital". Miranda ran her finger over the plastic cover. "I wonder if my real mother put it there."

"Probably, don't you think?"

"But it would've been Mum who cut my hair and put it in here. I remember her doing that with all the little ones." She ran her finger down the page. "And she was a stickler for first ribbons, that sort of stuff. She had my first shoes plated, but she couldn't afford it after Natalie. You know, all that sort of silly stuff mothers do." Patrick smiled at her.

"Look at the birth certificate, Miranda. Queen Elizabeth Home for Mothers and Babies. That's where they got you." Patrick watched as Miranda flicked over the pages of the album. It was only photos, family shots: Miranda with Linda as a baby, Miranda with Linda and Natalie, first day at school, with Natalie and new baby Louis, with Kerry, at the beach, at her first dance, with her dying great grandmother, in her white confirmation dress outside the church. She turned back to the birth certificate.

"Of course I don't know if I could find her," said Miranda slowly. "I know some people get so hung up about it that it ruins their life. But she might want to find me as much as I want to find her, mightn't she?" She looked to Patrick for confirmation. He nodded. She leaned over and hugged him. "I think it'll work out with Mum. I am going to try. I've been thinking about it for years." Her voice was optimistic, excited and as he held her, he could feel her body trembling.

32

·Chapter Three·

It was the third time she had tried to read the magazine and found herself turning the pages over aimlessly. She looked up at the digital clock on the wall which silently clicked over to 2.54. She made herself stare at it until 2.59. She'd only been five minutes late, twenty past instead of quarter past, but now she was frightened she'd missed her appointment. She'd waited a month for it and she didn't believe she could go through another month's waiting. She went over her movements to see if there was anything she'd missed. The girl at reception had directed her here and it definitely said "Social Work Department" over the door. She had already checked that twice, but there was no one here and Miranda was afraid to go back to the reception in case someone came while she was away. She went and stared blankly at the Japanese camellia picture.

Steeled for disappointment, the important thing now seemed to be to get it over with. All their possible negative responses ran through her head: "No...don't be silly...of course we can't find her...the law won't allow it...all birth records are destroyed...only where medical information is vital...no contact possible...adoption is a legal process...why do you want to find her anyway?...what's wrong with your adoptive mother?...don't you love her?"

"Miranda Darnley?"

Miranda turned to see a small, fair woman with a big smile. Miranda had expected someone tall, imposing and in uniform, but this woman was young, dressed in a Hungarian peasant blouse and a cotton skirt. She looked eager, wide-eyed and friendly. Miranda was instantly suspicious. "I'm Petunia Andrews. I'm so sorry I'm late," she said. "I know it's really nerve-wracking coming in the first time. I do hope I can help you." Her voice was breathless, enthusiastic and Miranda drew back from the familiarity and instant friendliness. She thought Petunia was a ridiculous name but she found herself tongue-tied as Petunia led her along the hospital corridor to an office off a landing, half way between floors. It was small, crammed with books, and overheated with a little two-bar radiator. There was a photo on the bookshelf of two women, obviously mother and daughter, arms around each other, smiling. It was inscribed in thick pen. "Thanks Petunia, love from Jan and Maree." Miranda realised she was staring at it and looked away.

"You're supposed to look at it. It's there to make you feel hopeful," said Petunia. "They were one of my first successes. And I'm much better at it now. You sit down there, fill out this form for me and I'll just buzz up to the common room and get us some coffee." She almost skipped out of the room. Miranda suspected her of silliness, one of those perennially childish women, always courting a new enthusiasm. She felt ill at ease, at Petunia's mercy, and wished she hadn't come.

"Natural mother's name, natural father's name, knowledge of siblings, half-siblings, anecdotal information on family background." Miranda chewed on the pen and looked at the blank spaces on the form. But when Petunia came back, she seemed pleased. "You know where you were born, age at adoption—that's all encouraging. I don't think there'll be too many problems actually finding out who your mother is." Her tone became businesslike, sensible. "I'm going to tell you something that may make you very angry. I can find out who your mother is, because I'm sitting this side of the desk. But I can't actually give you the information, except under particular circumstances." Miranda, brought up on the side of authority, was not angry. It seemed obvious. Someone had always known. She simply wanted to know too.

"There may be some things I can tell you about her: age, medical details, but nothing to identify her, unless she has registered here, notifying us that she wants to make contact. I can't do it right now but I'll check in the next few weeks."

"If she hasn't registered, is there any other way of finding her?" asked Miranda tentatively.

"You were adopted pre-1967, so your adoptive parents were probably given her name. Do you think they'd tell you?"

"I doubt it," said Miranda. "Is there any other way?"

34

"It depends how persistent you are," said Petunia briskly. "Getting the name's a very big hurdle. But it's possible. And then, with luck, she may have an uncommon name. But sometimes, of course, people have died. Sometimes, they may move interstate, overseas, can't be contacted. They've married a couple of times, but even so, people trace them. But often, they just disappear: not in the phone book or on the electoral rolls. Still, it's early days, so let's look on the bright side." She leaned forward, confidentially. "Tell me, why do you want to find your mother?"

"I don't know," said Miranda. "I just do." She realised she sounded hostile.

"That's OK," said Petunia, sipping on her coffee. "You don't need a reason. It's a natural thing to want. It doesn't mean you hate your adoptive parents. It's just you want to know—right?"

Miranda nodded.

"So how do you get on with your parents?"

"Fine," said Miranda, deciding she didn't want to talk about her father.

"Have you told them you're looking for your mother?"

"Yes."

"So how do they feel about it?"

"Mum doesn't like it," said Miranda. "She thinks it's disloyal."

"Your father?"

"Doesn't care."

"I'm only asking all this for your benefit. They haven't got any right to stop you. And, probably, if you get on well with them, they'll get over being worried about it. In fact, I guarantee if you find your birth mother, you'll all get on better."

"Why?" asked Miranda.

"Because in your head, you have an idealised picture of your natural mother. True?"

"Probably," admitted Miranda.

"And your adoptive parents think that blood's thicker than water and that you'll throw them over once you find the real thing." She paused and nibbled her biscuit, looking closely at Miranda. Miranda began to realise Petunia knew her business.

"What usually happens is that you find your natural mother and you have a great sense of 'Ah ha, so that's where I came from.' Then, you may find it goes deeper, that you have a lot in common, that you want to remain in contact, that it fulfils a need in you both. Or you may think, 'OK, that was that, but blood actually isn't that much thicker than water and I'm not crazy about her as a person."

"That'd please Mum," grinned Miranda, leaning forward onto Petunia's desk.

"Miranda, whatever happens will please your mother. What you and she will both find out is that the person who brings you up is your mother. It'll be more solid, more clear to you and to her than at any other time in your life. Adoption is full of insecurities for everyone: 'Is this a good enough child for us? Are we good enough parents? Would her natural parents have been better? Does she really love us? Do we really love her? How could I have given up my child if I really loved her?' Reunions resolve all that or should if they're done properly." Petunia talked a lot, and much of it, Miranda missed. But she began to like her. Absorbed, drawn in, she began to feel warm and enthusiastic.

She wasn't at all surprised at the end of the interview that Petunia gave her a hug. In two hours, they'd talked over her relationship with her father, her feelings about her natural mother, her relationship with her mother and her attitude to Linda's pregnancy. She'd also found out that Petunia was an adopted child herself, who had looked for her mother for years. When she finally got her mother's name and tracked down an address, she found she'd died a month before. Miranda's eyes had filled with tears at the story.

"The only thing I've got against my adoptive parents," Petunia confided to Miranda as she walked her down to the hospital's foyer, "is that they called me Petunia." She gave her funny little high-pitched giggle and hugged Miranda again. "I'll be in touch really soon," she said. "News or no news."

Miranda looked outside. It was almost dark, the rain coming down in sheets. It was five thirty and the lights of the peak-hour traffic shone in the wet. She felt she couldn't sit in a crowded bus, jostling against wet commuters. She had intended to go back to the university to study at the library, but she felt fragmented and fragile. Instead of being a dream, the possibility of meeting her mother had become a reality. It seemed almost too much. She retreated into the hospital's coffee shop and ordered a black coffee. As she stood at the cash register, she fingered a small, grey, furry rabbit on the gift stand. It had a funny little face and long ears.

"How much?" she asked, taking her change.

The girl turned it over doubtfully, looking for a non-existent price tag. "Oh, I don't know, love. Only work here nights." She smiled at Miranda. "You can have it for five dollars."

"Thanks," said Miranda, smiling back. "It's for my sister. She's having a baby."

"That's nice, love." The girl took the money and Miranda took the rabbit. As she walked out into the rain, she squeezed the little rabbit in her coat pocket and felt good.

Miranda was surprised to find Hazel alone, sitting at the kitchen table, staring dolefully at the Queen's portrait. "Your darling sister and Patrick have gone up to get themselves an el cheapo Chinese at the pub," she announced. "I'm too depressed for anything." She looked at Miranda, genuinely sad. "Darling, I'm in love."

Miranda poured them both a coffee and got some chocolate out of the fridge. She broke it into pieces and pushed it in front of the despondent Hazel.

"It's supposed to make you feel good if you're in love. Who are you in love with?"

"Phillip of course." She got up and took a bottle of brandy from the top of the fridge and poured some into her coffee. "I hate straight coffee," she said.

"So what's the problem—with Phillip, I mean?" asked Miranda gently.

"He's not in love with me." Miranda noticed Hazel's eyes were teary. Hazel gulped the coffee and added more brandy. Miranda didn't know what to say. Hazel had never been so upset before. "He doesn't think I'm the type of girl you take seriously." She looked at Miranda deprecatingly. "Why can't he love me, for God's sake? What's so wrong with me?"

"Nothing," said Miranda gently. "You're really beautiful."

"Being beautiful isn't everything," said Hazel despondently. "Try beautiful and intelligent with a great personality."

"Beautiful and intelligent with a great personality isn't everything," said Hazel. She laughed and drew on her cigarette. "Integrity. Like you've got. He thinks I'm a goodtime girl. He thinks I sleep around too much. He thinks I take too many drugs and I drink too much. That's all right for men, so he thinks, but not for a woman. He can do it, but the girl he does it with is no good." She looked at Miranda and wiped her eyes. "And you know what. I've had a few guys fall in love with me. I've always let them down gently. I've never accused them of being sluts or drunkards. And, I tell you, quite a few of them have been. The irony of it. Falling in love with a moralistic prick. *Ti amo*, I love you. And he tells me he's not interested. Jesus, Miranda, you're a sensible woman—what'll I do?"

Miranda was shocked. What could Hazel do? If Hazel couldn't make a man fall in love with her, no one could. "Give him away," she said abruptly.

"I can't, I'm like a school kid. I promised I'd change but he's not impressed. He's just using me and I haven't even got the strength of character to piss him off." She put her hand on Miranda's. "Have you ever been in love?"

"Once," confessed Miranda. "Last year of high school. Had a thing about one of my teachers."

"Oh that! Not a crush. Love." said Hazel.

"It was love." Miranda was stung by her dismissiveness. "We almost had an affair. It was quite serious, especially because he was married. That bothered me terribly so I finished it. But I was glad when I came down here. I couldn't have stayed in the same town as him." She thought of David, but even with his wife pregnant, the old feelings stirred.

"Fancy that. I wouldn't have suspected you."

"No one else did either," said Miranda quickly. "Anyway, they're having a baby."

"Serves him right. But you haven't had anyone down here?"

"No."

"Don't you ever feel like just screwing? I mean don't you just want to go to bed with a guy?"

"Sort of," said Miranda. "I see you having such an uproarious time and I wish I could. But it's not like that for me."

"Love and marriage and the two horse carriage?"

Miranda laughed. "Not exactly. But I don't fall into things easily."

"Like bed?" Hazel was smiling now.

"Not only bed, just going out with people or going to the pub or inviting someone to play tennis. You just do those things. They take me a lot of effort. Like fitting into this house."

"But you were wonderful from the first day you arrived!" exclaimed Hazel.

"It took a long time to feel at home."

"Bless my soul," said Hazel. "Shy." She looked at Miranda quizzically. "I can see it now. But I've never thought it, especially since Linda came. You seem so big sisterish and grown-up."

"Too big sisterish," said Miranda, going silent as Linda walked into the kitchen. Her pregnancy was emphasised by her new winter clothes and she glowed with health, far more robust and confident than the skinny kid Miranda had brought down from Uwalla.

"Feeling better?" Linda asked Hazel. She looked at Miranda resentfully. "I thought you were studying tonight."

"I was too tired," answered Miranda. "I went to the hospital this afternoon to see the social worker. To try and trace my mother," she explained, seeing the blank look on Linda's face. "You know, I told you I was going to do it."

"Did you meet her?" asked Linda casually, peeling herself a banana.

"It takes a while to organise," said Miranda. "I've got a present for you." She fished the little rabbit out of her bag.

"Thanks," said Linda, looking at it briefly. "Are we going to thread up those Hawaiian leis tonight, Hazel?" She picked hungrily at the chocolate Miranda had put out.

"Maybe later," said Hazel despondently. "I bet the real Hawaiians didn't even have leis. I don't even want to have a Hawaiian night now. Phillip won't come. And it's a really tawdry, out of date idea anyway."

"I thought you said that was the whole point of it," said Linda, puzzled. "Something so gross that everybody would think it was wonderful?"

"Except Phillip," answered Hazel.

Miranda got up and put the milk back in the fridge and wiped down the bench top.

"What are you doing tonight, Miranda?" asked Hazel.

Miranda didn't turn round from the sink as she stacked the

dishes. She felt the tears prickling in the back of her eyes. She wasn't even quite sure why they were there. "I need an early night," she said.

The floor was highly polished wood and Miranda's shoes clip-clopped on the hard surface. She felt nervous and stopped for a moment and leant back against the wall. At the end of the corridor was a stairwell, broad with a gracefully curved cedar banister. Behind it, was a magnificent stained glass window, the afternoon sun lighting it perfectly. Miranda's eyes followed the patterns in the glass, the great red band encircling the coat of arms, the brilliant blues stretching outward, the delicate engraved lettering on the banner beneath. She remembered how she had loved it when she first came, how she had felt so uplifted by the grandeur and the antiquity of the university. It still had the same powerful effect but now, she felt, she was in danger of losing it all. Her marks were down, her papers were late and she'd actually failed a term exam in one subject. She could not believe what was happening to her. Still looking at the window, she continued walking down the corridor and timidly knocked on Dr Stone's door.

"Come in."

Miranda went in.

"Sit down."

Dr Stone finally looked up from the papers on his desk. "So it is you," he said, not unkindly. "The face and the name match. So what's the problem?"

"Well, I'm not doing terribly well," said Miranda apologetically.

"That's why I asked you to come in. Why?"

"Why what?" asked Miranda, taken off guard.

"Why aren't you doing well?"

"I've had some upsets."

"Upsets?" Dr Stone sounded surprised, slightly censorious.

"Yes," said Miranda, not knowing what else to say.

"What sort of upsets?"

Miranda sensed a hostility in his tone. It was none of his business but she didn't know how to tell him that.

"My sister's come to live with me. She's expecting a baby and we've both been thrown out of home. It's been difficult financially."

"And emotionally." Again his tone was censorious.

"Yes, it is." Miranda was hesitant, apologetic. "Very. I've found it hard to work, hard to concentrate." Dr Stone rose slowly from his chair. He walked over towards the window, sat down on the sill and looked at her. He was not an old man, but nor was he young. He was one of those men who abound in universities and research institutions who look very much the same from their thirties through to their seventies: tall, grey, intelligent, and dispassionate.

"This is not," he said with surprising passion, "arts slash wank one. This is the Faculty of Veterinary Science. We do not cater to neurotic women or malcontents. If you want to stay here, get your act together. I do not look kindly on people who fail my courses."

He looked at Miranda and Miranda stared angrily back. She hated him and despised herself for not having the guts to tell him what she thought of him. But knowing if she opened her mouth, she risked humiliating herself further, she simply nodded. He sat down at the desk and she turned and walked out the door. She paused a second, then slammed it fiercely behind her.

"Yes, he is a bastard," said Geoff. "A real born-again bastard. And he doesn't like women. He's not even all that smart."

"He led me on," said Miranda bitterly. "He led me right into it. He asked me what my problem was. But the worst thing is that he's right. This is serious and I've been stuffing around."

Miranda had gone to the library after her encounter with Stone. Geoff had come across her, leaning against the journal shelves, her head resting on her arms.

"He was awful," said Miranda. "You can't imagine what he's like."

"Don't forget he's my supervisor," he whispered. "I don't like him, but he's there. I have to live with him or forget it."

"So how do you live with him?"

"I excel. It's your only defence." He nudged Miranda encouragingly. "And you're terrific at it. You really are." He smiled at her, pulling nervously at his depleted beard. She forgave him. She needed sympathy.

41

"Geoff, it's not only his stuff I'm behind in, it's everything. I never thought this would happen to me. You know, if I fail, I'm out. I'd lose my allowance and I'd have to go to work."

"Well, don't fail." Geoff moved closer towards her and lowered his voice even further, to an urgent whisper. "Listen, last year you got high distinctions and distinctions in everything. Fact number one, Miranda Darnley can do it. OK?"

Miranda nodded.

"This year is a bad year. All that stuff with your sister. I understand." He blushed and spoke even lower. "Of course I've never had anything like that, but it would be hard, I can see that."

"So what do I do?"

"I had a bad year in second year too." He smiled at this bond linking them. "Dad just couldn't make a living on the farm any more and we had to sell up. I failed and it was horrible because Dad had to borrow the money to put me through again. I did fine that year and then in fourth year, I had this dream I was going to marry this girl. I found out she thought I was an idiot. She just wanted my notes." Miranda looked at the floor, feeling vaguely guilty by association. "I'd learnt my lesson though. I made a decision just to pass, not to try for anything better. That's what you have to do."

"I don't understand."

"You just aim at keeping up, doing well enough to pass. Don't try for anything spectacular. Don't panic when your marks go down. Pass every time. Got it?"

"I think so." Miranda was thoughtful. "But I've always wanted more."

"Just pass until things get better." He looked at her longingly. "You coming over the road for a coffee?" She looked back blankly.

"Thanks, but I've got to stay here to get some articles, so I can pass."

"OK. I'm going." He looked at her as if he was about to say something more, then pulling at his beard, disappeared behind the shelves.

"Hawaii, Hawaii, straight to Hawaii. Do you want to come along with me?" The music of the Beach Boys echoed round the house. The hallway was festooned with garlands of plastic hibiscus and in the kitchen, someone had painted over the Queen's portrait, so she was now holding a large slice of watermelon. Dancers in grass skirts streamed through.

In the back yard, Phillip stood tall and erect, silhouetted against the flames of the fire. He wore a grass skirt, made from a green plastic garbage bag and a feather in his hair. A girl was painting him with tribal markings from a tube of black paint. Around them people in identical plastic skirts, sang along loudly to the music, stopping only to rescue sausages from the fire or swig on their beers.

"Hey, Phillip, what do you think of this?" Hazel yelled, pushing Linda into the yard in front of her.

"Fantastic," Phillip shouted back. Linda wore a Hawaiian shirt, tied neatly above her expanded stomach. A matching sarong was tied beneath the bulge. Hazel was bare-breasted, with a grass skirt and elaborate headdress of fruit and flowers. "Come here," Phillip yelled. "I've got an idea." Hazel and Linda walked across the yard, under the Hills Hoist, to the enormous fire which lit up the entire yard, making a strange contrast with the terrace houses crowded behind the back lane. Phillip put his arm around Hazel and kissed her. "You're really good at parties, Haze."

"But do you love me?" she whispered desperately.

He laughed at her and looked at Linda. "You need just one more thing. Come here."

Linda stood obediently in front of him. He began sketching with the tube of paint on her protruding stomach and, gradually, an X-ray picture of a baby began to emerge. The spine was made up of blobs of paint and below he drew a head which was skeletal, but somehow baby-like. Legs and arms pressed in neatly against the confines of the womb. Linda watched as he drew, as if it was being revealed to her, for the first time what was inside her. Phillip stood back to admire it, his arm around Hazel. "I think it needs just a bit more detail on the foot," he said. He dabbed a smudge of paint onto his finger and began to delicately trace out a tiny foot on Linda's stomach. Linda watched, as if the baby was coming alive before her eyes. Hazel looked admiringly at Phillip.

"Feel it," said Phillip excitedly. "It moved. It kicked." He pressed Hazel's hand onto Linda's belly. "Feel it, Haze."

"It's the first time it's done that," said Linda. "It just fluttered before. This is like a wave moving across. I can really feel it."

"All this primitive stuff—brings out the best in women and children," said Phillip, resuming his usual dry manner. "Great, isn't it, Haze?"

Hazel looked at him, reassured by his niceness. But she hoped that if he did really fall in love with her, he wouldn't expect her to have a baby. "It's lovely, Linda. It really is." She turned to Phillip. "I wouldn't have expected an army person to be interested in pregnancy."

"Just a hobby," he said lightly.

Linda put her hands gently over the X-ray drawing, cupping her belly. "It's like a little flowerpot, isn't it? With a bulb growing inside. There's the door. I bet it's Miranda."

The music had changed to a slow Belafonte song. "My heart is down, my head is turning around, I had to leave a little girl in Kingston town . . . ," the three of them sang inanely as they danced into the kitchen, arms around each other's shoulders.

"Conga line time," shouted Phillip. "Let's take the music to the street." He put his hands on Hazel's waist, as she stamped out after Linda. The rest of the party began to fall in behind them. They proceeded down the hall and opened the door to an astounded Miranda who watched the train of dancers moving out to the street.

"I forgot," she yelled to Hazel over the music.

Linda broke away from the dancers and went over to Miranda. "Come inside," she said. "Haze and I have a costume for you."

In Miranda's room, they could still hear the music. The screams and laughter grew louder as the conga line moved into the street and there was a yell of protest from one of the neighbours. Linda held up a sarong. "We'll tie it at the shoulder," she said. "Then we'll do something with your hair."

"Thanks," said Miranda uncertainly, and started to undress. Linda stood hesitantly at the door, watching her sister.

"I've been a bitch lately, Mandy. I'm sorry. You know I really appreciate you."

Miranda wrapped the sarong around her. She looked at Linda, grateful. "Thanks. I haven't been that easy either. But I want us to be friends. I hate to come home and feel out of it." She put a plastic hibiscus in her hair and laughed at her reflection in the mirror. "I don't know that I'd really pass for an Hawaiian."

She put her arms around Linda and hugged her. "We have to look after each other." Embarrassed, she pulled away and looked down at her stomach to see a smudged image of Phillip's drawing on her sarong. She looked at the drawing on Linda's stomach with interest. "Is that your baby?" she asked tentatively.

Linda took Miranda's hand and pressed it up against her stomach. The baby seemed to be rocking, almost pressing up against her hand. She shivered in excitement and put her arm around Linda's neck. "Let's take him out dancing," she said excitedly.

Pauline sat alone in bed under the Elvis clock, its loud ticking still audible over the tape of "Love me tender". She fumbled under the bed and produced an old copy of *New Idea* that she'd pinched from the doctor's waiting room. It had a feature about Priscilla Presley which she'd read while she was waiting, but she'd pinched the magazine for its picture, one of Elvis on stage at Las Vegas, that she'd never seen before. From under the bed, she got her scrapbook, scissors and paste, cut the picture out and set about the enjoyable task of deciding where it would best fit in her book.

She had had the scrapbook since she was a teenager, always cutting and re-cutting, repasting and rearranging, making new headlines and banners. Apart from a brief flirtation with the Beatles, Elvis had been her one true love. She stopped at a favourite picture, a slightly chubby, but not yet gross, Elvis in a shining, lamé suit. There was something sad and lonely looking about him, in spite of the cocky, arrogant pose. Pauline looked at it and smiled. In some way, the photo reminded her a little of Roy.

She thought of Roy, of his sudden suggestion after the blow-up with Kevin that she and the kids should come and live with him. She hadn't taken him seriously. She was sure that it was just his way of trying to get into bed with her. Still, she couldn't help wondering what it would be like, to wake up in a nice house, with a cheerful man. But perhaps he'd turn into a mongrel like Kevin. Perhaps they all did. She'd heard some strange talk when Roy and Shirley got divorced and she meant to ask him what had really happened. But it never seemed quite right and besides, she'd never liked Shirley anyway. Still, she thought as she began cutting out the picture, even Kevin had been slightly nicer in the last few days. You could never tell with men.

It was their anniversary tomorrow. Twenty four years. He always remembered it, she gave him that, but he often used it as an opportunity for recriminations. She thought to herself that she didn't really know how to handle him in spite of what she told the kids. She tried hard but she never knew which way he'd jump. She clung to the vain hope that things would somehow get better, that the tension in the house would ease. She was always looking for signs, for small changes in his moods. Sometimes, she thought of the past nostalgically, but she knew that she was endowing it with a rosy glow. Maybe, she thought, she should stand up to him more. Eventually he'd have to let the girls come home for holidays. She turned the page and looked up to see him standing in the doorway.

From years of observing him, she knew he was stone cold sober. He threw down a plastic shopping bag onto the bed. It split open in one corner as it hit the bed and she saw an iron poking through the plastic.

"You might as well have it now you've seen it. For tomorrow."

"Yeah," she said hesitantly. "Thanks."

"We need to have a talk," he said.

"OK," she said non-committally, sliding the Elvis scrapbook under the bed. He sat down on the end of the bed.

"I've been a bit of a bastard lately," he said.

For the last twenty four years, she thought, but said nothing, waiting for him to continue.

"Piss that does it to me. No good. I'm giving it away."

"Fair enough."

"I've decided Linda can come back," he said magnanimously. "But only after she's had the kid."

"Big of you." She couldn't resist the sarcasm and she saw his body stiffen.

"Don't you forget it," he said menacingly. "But she's not bringing the kid. I'm not having no other man's bastard in this house." He waited for the effect of his words to sink in.

"Are you talking about Miranda?" Pauline asked with a cold fury.

46

He looked at her steadily. "I don't want her here. She's full of cheek. Needs to learn a bit of respect and gratitude."

Pauline took a deep breath to fortify herself against the enormity of what he was saying. "Miranda's our kid too. Same as the rest of them."

"Not mine, she isn't!"

"You signed the papers. You wanted her back then." Pauline felt her fear rising.

"You were the one that was on and on about having a family," he shouted at her. "I only did it to cut your whingeing." He slammed his fist hard into the bed and Pauline flinched. He got up and looked at himself in the mirror. He was off the booze; he'd lick the bloody family into shape; get the vegetable garden going; get them all into line, including Pauline.

Pauline lay, in sick dread, huddled against the wall. Such a bastard, she thought bitterly. She'd stayed with him all these years, just so they'd be a family. It was no use arguing with him or trying to reason with him. You had to ride it out till he forgot about it. The worst was, right now, she knew he wanted sex. And she had no way to stop him.

·*Chapter Four*·

"Ohhh, iron legs, so beautiful, so strong."

Miranda looked down from the stepladder at Valentino, eyeing him distastefully, thinking she could do as neat a job of kicking in his face as he was of looking up her skirt. "Pass me up some more ivy," she said briskly. "This lot looks very droopy."

Valentino handed her the ivy. "I am not droopy, Miranda. When you stand up there, I have the hots for you. I always have the hots for you."

Miranda draped the ivy over the nail on the wall, then jumped down from the stepladder amongst the buckets of fluorescent carnations. She was of average height, but still considerably taller than Valentino. "Stop it," she said angrily.

Valentino smiled ingratiatingly as he moved towards her. "I love you to be angry. I love it when your face go red." He followed her to the big refrigerated compartment, where she got out some long-stem red roses.

"If you don't sell these today, they'll be finished by Monday. Do you want them in the window?"

"With two green carnation each bunch. Seven dollar," he replied quickly. "You beautiful, Miranda." Valentino started rearranging the dried-flower pictures in ceramic frames. The flowers were a dreary yellow, the frames an ugly cream, inaccurately spotted with pink. "Why nobody buy these, Miranda? Look, they cost me three dollar each, I sell them for ten, then seven, then five. Nobody buy. I put them up to twenty. More exclusive."

"Make it twenty five," said Miranda dryly. "That way, you'll get tourist buses stopping off."

Valentino did not understand. "Twenty five then," he said, disconsolately writing out the price ticket. "This business is terrible. All the time my wife want more money." Miranda ignored his whining and continued to rewrap the bunches of roses with green carnations, putting them in buckets near the door. The shop, as always, looked extraordinary, with its array of dried, dyed and artificial flowers, a floral extravaganza augmented by five, larger-than-life, china dalmatians. Hazel had once delighted Valentino by buying a china stork which now stood in their outside loo, a shopping bag strung casually over one wing and a condom over its beak.

When the shop first opened, it had become instantly popular. Like blue wine or harbour bridge souvenirs, Valentino's horrendous bouquets provided instant and hilarious dinner table conversation. He had never understood this initial success, so its current decline caused him to indulge in considerable soul-searching. Costs forced him to downgrade his grandiose plans and now, some mornings, the window had only a few plastic buckets of blue carnations and green daisies. Miranda's work with the ivy was a brave attempt to recapture the old days.

"You owe me this week," said Miranda.

"I cannot fight such beautiful woman," he replied and sighed heavily.

"Sixty dollars," she demanded, holding out her hand.

"Fifty," he replied truculantly.

Miranda felt weary. She'd worked for him for over a year, ever since she came to Glebe, and she felt as if they were an old married couple, always fighting over sex and money.

"Sixty," she said fiercely, producing a piece of paper detailing her hours. Valentino threw it down contemptuously as a young couple came into the shop. He bustled forward to meet them, with an oily, greedy smile. Miranda glanced at her watch. Another five minutes and she'd be free. She stepped into the window and began watering the pot plants. She looked up to see Linda coming down the street, laden with parcels, cross and sulky. Miranda smiled, pointed at her watch, holding up five fingers.

"Thank you, thank you," said Valentino to the departing couple who had refused a bunch of the wilting roses. "Fresh on Monday, come back Monday." Then, as he too saw Linda, his face broke into a genuine smile. "Ah, la madonna," he sighed looking proudly at her swollen belly as if he were responsible.

Linda turned her most vicious face to him. "Don't say that!" she threatened.

Miranda took off her overall and put out her hand. "Money." Valentino handed her a fifty-dollar note. Miranda leant over the counter, pressed the button on the till. It rang and opened, shaking the china dalmatian sitting on the counter. She grabbed a ten-dollar note. Valentino slammed the register shut as Miranda and Linda walked out.

"I can't understand why you work for him," said Linda.

"Money," said Miranda dryly, waving the sixty dollars in front of her nose.

"Now let's have a coffee. I want to talk to you."

It was too cold to sit outside so Miranda and Linda sat inside the coffee shop, staring at the gloomy fish tanks and travel posters of the 1960s. The tables were flecked black laminex, in the currently fashionable fifties style, the chairs uncomfortably small and hard. Miranda sipped at a cappuccino. Linda, whose tastes didn't range past instant coffee, played with the cream on top of an extravagant hot chocolate.

"I know what you want to talk about," she said defensively. "Why I haven't been to the doctor's. You can't talk me into it."

"Why won't you go?"

"They stick fingers up you, all that stuff."

Miranda looked at the ugly albino goldfish opening and closing his mottled mouth against the glass. "Four or five months and a baby will be coming out. Fingers are nothing. Go to a woman doctor. You have to make sure everything's all right. And you have to start thinking about the baby."

Linda coloured. She was silent, her face stubborn, set. "I never, ever wanted this baby. You know some girls get pregnant, piss the guy off and they're quite happy to play houses, on the pension. Then they get bored and have another one and they pretend that was all a mistake too." She licked the cream off the hot chocolate and looked at the stony-faced Miranda. "I got drunk," she said virtuously, "that's how I got pregnant. But I want to get married. I want to live in a nice house. I don't want bloody kids ruining everything. And, you know what? All that stuff Mum told us about abortion was bull. Nobody dies. Hazel told me it was a hundred per cent safe." She looked at Miranda angrily. "You could have told me that. By the time Hazel told me, it was too late. I'd go to a doctor for that, but not for this." She looked down angrily at her protruding stomach.

Miranda wanted to tell her about the baby. She wanted to tell her about the tiny pups she'd once found when she'd dissected a pound dog. She wanted Linda to feel the baby, to love the baby, to care about it. Yet she could see that Linda was determined not to care, not to show, not to feel. The baby, to Linda, was not the issue. "Go to a doctor, Linda. Don't be so stupid. You have to get booked into a hospital." She played her last card. "If you don't book in down here, you'll have to go home to have it."

Linda looked at her, sulky. "All right," she answered.

"This afternoon?" asked Miranda.

"Chrissakes, it's Saturday!"

"There's a woman open down at the Point, all day. I'll come with you if you like."

"I'll go myself."

"Promise?"

"Yes!"

"OK, OK," said Miranda. "There's something else too."

"Oh God. You're worse than Mum!"

"You're supposed to be looking after the house—it's worse since you came!"

"Well Hazel never says anything!"

"She wouldn't notice."

"So what's it got to do with you?"

"I live there, Patrick too, Dr Bob sometimes. We notice. You promised you'd clean the bathroom."

"I was going to," said Linda virtuously. "Yesterday."

"But you didn't!" said Miranda furiously.

Linda scraped the last of the cream from the big mug and stood up. She thrust her stomach towards Miranda like a badge of martyrdom. "I'm going home," she said. "I don't think I'll go and see that doctor down at the Point. Haze has an aunty who's a baby doctor. I'll make an appointment Monday."

"I know you don't want to know, but in about four months, you'll be having a baby." Irene Johns, Hazel's aunt was the obstetrician and she looked down at Linda who lay, docile, on her examining table. "Has it occurred to you what you'll do with the baby?"

"It'll be all right," said Linda, smiling at her.

"Are you going to keep it?" asked Dr Johns. Even at fifty, Irene Johns was a striking looking woman, with the same deep, dark blue eyes as Hazel.

"I haven't thought," said Linda obediently.

"A few minutes a day. Wouldn't hurt," said Dr Johns. Linda did not see that she was being sent up, but she did suspect this woman didn't quite approve of her. And she wanted Hazel's aunt to like her.

"Well, I talked to Hazel," said Linda defensively. "She told me about abortion."

"She would. Too late. Thought about adoption?"

Linda smiled her most charming smile. "I might start knitting. I quite like knitting."

"Easier than thinking, I suppose." She recognised the glaze over Linda's eyes. Too young, too single, too panicked, she thought. No more today. "Come back in two weeks," she said.

"I thought I only had to come every month," said Linda desperately. She had got off the couch, disappeared behind the screen and emerged fully dressed in record time. As she made for the door, Dr Johns positioned herself casually in front of it.

"Listen, next time I just feel your tummy, try and establish dates for you a bit more accurately. After that, it's only once a month, until the last month." Linda still had the panicked look. "Please come. Make life easier for me. I don't want to be called out in mid-November when I was banking on delivering you on Christmas Day." She raised her eyebrows and smiled. Linda smiled back at her.

"OK."

"Good girl." Dr Johns opened the door and Linda bolted past her to the lift.

The back yard consisted of a small circle of concrete and a jungle of weeds beyond. A Hills Hoist was set into the concrete. It was covered with a lush choko vine. Hazel always claimed the Hills Hoist was the perfect plant support. "If you want to do some pruning, you just wind it up and spin it round." The choko had obviously not been pruned recently. In fact, it seemed to have jumped the concrete circle and rooted itself in the ground beyond and was making advances over the fence to the next door's clothes line. "That's how Hills Hoists mate," commented Hazel. "Plant-borne seed. We'll have a little Hoist springing up here when Linda drops the urchin."

They were lying on the warm concrete in the midday winter sun, on their stomachs, except for Linda who had to lie on her side. Beer cans, ashtrays and an empty chip bag lay in the middle of the circle. Linda had drunk a can and was giggly. Miranda had drunk the same amount, but was getting maudlin. Hazel and Phillip had drunk a lot more, but were showing no effect. Both Patrick and Geoff Harris were there, one on each side of Miranda, sidling closer towards her with each can they drank.

Dr Bob had just left after his first visit to his room in three months.

"Why does he rent it?" asked Linda.

"So he can get away from the hospital."

"But he never does," she protested.

"Well, he's a bit of a creep, but the perfect lodger," said Hazel. She raised her eyebrows. "He even chips in for the phone."

"I don't like him," said Linda petulantly. "He looks like the sort of person who'd judge people by the way they look."

"So that was your very first impression: that he judges people by the way they look?!" Hazel hooted with laughter and grabbed Linda and hugged her. The hilarity spread to the others, until they were all laughing—all but Linda, who looked on prim and proper.

"I don't know what you think's so funny," she remarked, as the laughter died. "He does look that sort of person."

"Don't, Linda, don't," said Hazel going off into another spasm. "I can't stand it. If I want to exercise my lungs, I'll walk round the block, thanks."

"Hey, look at this," Miranda suddenly dived into the thick weed beside the fence and produced a large lizard, which struggled to escape and then suddenly lay still, playing dead. It was almost thirty centimetres long, plump, patterned in grey and black.

"Miranda!" Linda screamed.

"What is it?" Patrick moved nervously away from Miranda and looked anxiously at the big blue-tongue lizard as Miranda held it up triumphantly.

"Just a blue-tongue—isn't he wonderful?" Miranda looked at him admiringly. He twisted in her hand again, his blue tongue darting in and out. She turned to Linda. "Lou'd love him, eh?"

"It's disgusting," said Linda. "Oh, don't put it down there." Miranda put the lizard in the middle of the circle. "I don't know how you always find these awful things, Mandy." The lizard lay still, looking nervously at the chip packet.

"Oh for God's sake, give him a drink," said Hazel.

"He's obviously a lounge lizard," said Patrick.

"Sort you'd see down in the Haymarket," said Hazel, stroking the lizard's back with her long red nail. "Selling fake lizard skin purses outside the pub. 'Hey, psst, real lizard skin. Made in Hong Kong.' He's really lovely isn't he?"

"He'd make a cute little purse," said Phillip, pulling Hazel on top of him.

"Or a cigarette case," she said lazily.

"I wish I could get him to Lou," said Miranda, picking up the lizard. "But I don't suppose you can post them."

"I'm driving up the coast tonight," said Phillip. "Party tomorrow at Port Macquarie. Want him hand delivered?"

"Really?" said Miranda. "You're driving up past Uwalla?"

"Yep, leave in half an hour."

Hazel looked at him crossly. "I didn't get an invite."

"No," said Phillip. "Boys' night. Army do. Not your scene."

Hazel pouted. "I can be military when I want to," she said.

Miranda thought of Uwalla and suddenly felt a surge of homesickness. Her mother had told her everything was all right, but that she and Linda should not come home. But their conversations always seemed stilted and unnatural. "Can I come?" she asked Phillip. "Can you give me a lift?"

"As well as, or instead of the lizard?" drawled Phillip.

"With the lizard," said Miranda breathlessly.

"Where'll you stay?" asked Linda.

"At Nanna's. And I'll see Mum at church and the kids later. You want to come too?"

"An RX only holds so many," Phillip warned. "Even the slimmest lizards..."

54

Linda looked down at her stomach, convinced he was teasing her. She didn't like Phillip, but she felt in any case she could not go home. They mustn't see her like this. "Nope," she said jauntily. "Couldn't be bothered."

"What about your biochem assignment?" Geoff asked Miranda uneasily. "It's due Monday."

"I'll do it on the train, on the way back," said Miranda breezily. Geoff gave her a reproachful glance.

"Oh come on, Geoff, you're always telling me I work too hard. Give me a break." She stuck her tongue out at the lizard and smiled delightedly. "Bird of passage. You'll just love Uwalla, my pet."

The shabbiness and cracks in Nanna Darnley's fibro cottage were emphasised by the late afternoon sunlight slanting onto the front of the house. But Linda's easy acceptance into the Glebe household had taught Miranda that her working class background carried with it a certain interest and glamour, entirely unrealistic, but nevertheless useful.

"See you next week," she yelled to Phillip as he zoomed off. She walked up the path, overgrown with weeds and pale faced pansies struggling through the tangle of wintergrass. Yellowed petunias were almost flattened by onion weed and an occasional chipped and battered gnome stared hopelessly onto the cracked concrete edging. Nanna Darnley's garden had been a Uwalla showpiece, but it had been the men of the family who'd done the hard work. Now, even Lou could no longer be induced to spend an afternoon weeding on the strength of a stale lamington and weak lemon cordial.

The half-blind, eczema-ridden Maltese terrier yapped piercingly as Nanna unlocked the door for Miranda. Miranda hugged her grandmother. The old lady kissed her dryly on the cheek and drew back. Kissing, she had always maintained, spread germs. Miranda proffered a box of jellied jubes.

Nanna looked at them doubtfully as she took them. "It's a pretty box, I suppose, but they're cheaper up the K-Mart." She turned back into the house, which smelled as musty as ever. Nanna hated open doors and windows. "Your father tells me you're not short of a bob on this allowance you get from the government. I suppose you can afford to throw your money round." She put the box of jubes into the hall cupboard.

Miranda knew better than to protest. She followed Nanna dutifully down the hall into the living room, where Nanna slumped back into the chair in front of the TV. In deference to Miranda, she turned the sound down slightly. "That woman's supposed to have had twins," she said, pointing to the soap opera star. "Figure like that. These shows aren't true to life at all." She clicked her false teeth disapprovingly.

"How's Mum?" asked Miranda.

"She got kidnapped," said Nanna, intent on the flickering screen. "They've got her holed up in Adrian's flat. Serves her right; real old tart, she is. See, that's Adrian there—bit of a devil."

"No, Nanna, my Mum, Pauline."

Nanna turned her attention briefly and unwillingly to reality. "On and on about Linda going down to Sydney with you. If you ask me, it'll do the girl good. Learn to stand on her own two feet." Obviously Nanna hadn't been told about Linda's pregnancy.

"Is Mum cross at me?" asked Miranda desperately.

"Why would she be cross with you?" Miranda had always been her favourite grandchild. She condemned the rest "a waste of time". Their faults she deemed to be from bad blood: that of her son's.

"When I ring up she doesn't really talk to me. Always says she can't. And she didn't want me home."

"Him." Nanna nodded significantly. "He's got it in for you. Nasty temper. Had a brute of a temper ever since he was a kid." Nanna often reminisced how she had warned Pauline against marrying Kevin. She was ambivalent about Pauline, despising her weakness in marrying Kevin, condemning her desire for children as "unnatural" but nevertheless sympathising with her as a victim. "He's been a real bastard lately." She nodded significantly at the dark, pained looking Adrian who had reappeared on the screen.

Miranda pressed on. "Do you think Mum'd see me?"

Nanna had lost interest in Miranda and was now watching the television with total absorption. "I rang her to tell her you were coming this afternoon," she said off-handedly. "Just after *Days of Our Lives*. She said she'd be at K-Mart in the morning—boys' wear, tennish."

"I'll cook us tea, Nan." Miranda retreated into the kitchen.

Knowing that her mother would see her, she almost danced around the kitchen. She got the blue-tongue lizard out of her bag and laid him on the counter, where he lay looking at her, his blue tongue darting in and out as she put Nanna's shrivelled chops under the griller.

In the morning Miranda crept into Nanna's darkened room, with a cup of tea and toast. She moved the glass containing Nanna's teeth and put the breakfast on the bedside table, next to the indigestion tablets. Nanna continued to snore, then suddenly started awake.

"Brekky, Nan," Miranda said, drawing the curtains. "It's nine o'clock and I have to go.

Nanna sat up, her face crumpled through sleep, her badly creamed make-up streaked in a weird swirl over one eye and her mouth closed in over toothless gums. Her leathery skin hung in folds, disappearing under the pink satin nightdress with its inappropriately low neckline revealing her flat, thin breasts. The room seemed to Miranda to smell of age and decay. Nanna sat up and popped her teeth in, her mouth resuming its normal shape. But she looked old and frail, the sunlight emphasising the almost skeletal outline of her face under her sparse grey hair. Miranda felt a pang, realising the self-opinionated indulgent Nanna of her childhood was no more.

"You off?" she asked. Miranda nodded. "Not coming back, I suppose?" she asked tartly. "None of those other bloody kids ever come up." Miranda felt a surge of pity for her.

"I'll come back if I can, Nan, before the train leaves."

"Well, not if it's any trouble to you," replied Nanna sarcastically. "I get plenty of practice keeping myself amused." Miranda kissed her and, even though Nanna stiffened disapprovingly, gave her a hug.

"See you later," she said fondly. She hurried out of the bedroom, through the kitchen where she got the lizard out of the box under the stove and went out the back door. Nanna's house backed onto the beach, a prime spot in Uwalla, but Nanna had always hated the sea and had constructed a high tin fence to block out the view. Miranda jumped the lower fence to the neighbours' back yard, almost tumbling down the dune to the beach. She looked at her watch. It was nine thirty and even though she'd be a bit late, she decided to go the long way round by the point. The sea shimmered unevenly as the sun shone brilliantly through the gathering clouds and the wind roughened the tops of the waves. Miranda kicked off her shoes and started walking along the beach, squashing little craters of sand around the thousands of tiny holes dug by the soldier crabs during the night.

"We have a little girl about three years old, blond hair with pink ribbons and blue eyes wearing an *Australia Two* tracksuit," a nasal voice whined out over the public address system, interrupted by the high-pitched screams of the distressed toddler.

Pauline, with a tracksuit over her arm, felt thankful. To come shopping alone was a rare freedom, even if she couldn't afford much. Mentally, she added up her money and finding she had two dollars over, grabbed a pair of bootees in a pretty plastic container.

"Save your money, Mum," said a voice behind her and she turned to see Miranda.

"Oh lovey," she said, hugging Miranda and the tracksuits all in one embrace. "I've really missed you." Miranda, hugging her back, noticed how tired she looked. "It's been a bit tough," Pauline said quickly, noticing the look. She looked at the bootees disconsolately and put them back. "How's Linda?" she asked, almost embarrassed. "She must be showing now."

Miranda followed her over towards the coffee lounge. "She is, and she doesn't like it."

They lined up and Miranda ordered a cappuccino and a Vienna coffee for Pauline and a slice of pavlova to share. Pauline had dumped the tracksuits on the table and still slightly ill at ease, sat down and took the coffee from Miranda. "Love, I do want you both home," she blurted out. "But he's mad as hell about Linda." She paused and then smiled with a reassurance she didn't feel. "He'll come round." Miranda remained silent. "How is Linda?" asked Pauline

"It still hasn't hit her, Mum. I don't know how she's going to cope with a baby."

Pauline sighed. "You know, last year, she asked me if we'd

let her marry Danny, under-age. I wouldn't hear of it. Little silly, but I should have."

"Mum, I don't think she cares about Danny. She hasn't mentioned him."

"Marriage isn't all about caring, Miranda—it's about getting on with it. Getting on with having a baby is a lot easier if you're married."

"Maybe you get on better if you care."

"Don't start all that, Mandy." Pauline looked angry. "All right, you want me to say your father's a bastard. Yes, he is a bastard sometimes. But he keeps a roof over our heads. He pays the bills. It isn't as if he belts me or anything."

"Everything but," muttered Miranda, then looked at Pauline and raised her hands. "OK, sorry. But listen, next school hols, why don't you come down and stay with us? Natalie and Lou would manage for a few days."

Pauline beamed. "Oh, Mandy! Really, you wouldn't mind?"

"No, Mum, it'd be great. I miss you."

Pauline's face softened and she began to think out loud. "It's so long since I been down to Sydney and never without kids. I don't know...your Dad...he makes such a fuss." Miranda looked at her. Pauline brightened and took the strawberry off the pavlova. "Well, maybe I could even talk some sense into that girl."

"If you could, you'd be the first." Miranda took a large spoonful of cream. "Let's get another slice." She went up to the counter and ordered two more coffees and another pavlova slice, realising that neither of them could afford it. Momentarily, she longed to be rich, to indulge her mother. As she sat down again, Pauline smiled at her. Miranda felt embraced by the smile, no longer banished. "Mum, I want to tell you something."

Pauline sighed and closed her eyes. "You're not pregnant too are you?" She giggled.

"No, Mum, don't be an arse. I just want to tell you I contacted the hospital. I'm trying to find my real mother." The look on Pauline's face cut her like a knife and mentally, she kicked herself for her choice of words. "I mean my natural mother. Mum, please don't take it the wrong way."

Pauline looked at her unsteadily. "I always thought that's what you'd do—the album and all. I don't understand. I know you and your Dad...but really, I tried." Her voice shook slightly. "You know I saw it on one of the 'Willesees' about a girl that did it, but I can't understand it." She looked almost pleadingly at Miranda. "Mandy, you're really my favourite. You know that."

"I do know, Mum. I don't even know why I need to do it." Miranda felt an almost physical pain. "I know it really hurts you, but I don't want to do it behind your back. I don't want anyone else for a mother. I just want to know who it was, why it happened. If all that hadn't blown up with Dad, maybe it wouldn't have mattered. But ever since then, I have this dream, almost every night, sort of about finding out. It does matter, it just does."

"I can see that," said Pauline coldly.

"Look what Miranda brought up for Louis," said Pauline as they belted along in Roy's truck. She produced the blue-tongue lizard. Roy almost ran the truck into the gravel on the side of the road. He turned the steering wheel quickly, still watching the lizard out of the corner of his eye.

"Jesus, Pauline, you nearly gave me heart failure."

"It's only a bluey."

"Do they bite?"

"Only if they know you're scared." Pauline looked sideways at him. "And you call yourself a pest exterminator."

"At least I get paid for knocking off things like that." Roy grinned at her. "I think young Louis might be getting past the pet stage. At least those sort of pets. Saw him hanging round with some girls, down the beach yesterday."

Pauline sighed. "They're much easier when they're little."

"How's Mandy?"

"She's OK." Pauline was tightlipped as Roy pulled the truck over to the side of the road.

"You want to walk from here?" Roy and Kevin were no longer on speaking terms since Roy took Kevin to task about his attitude to Miranda and Linda.

"Yeah." Pauline started to open the truck door, looking tentatively at Roy. "She wants to find her mother, her 'real mother', she said. I can tell you, Roy, that really hurts. She just doesn't seem to understand how I feel. You know the moment I saw her, that little baby, she was mine. She just was. I can't for the life of me understand why she's doing this."

"Curious, that's all."

"No, there's more to it." Pauline was defensive. "I reckon she thinks I let her down. That I should've stood up to her Dad. But it wouldn't have done no good. Nanna's right, he's a bad-tempered cow, always has been, always will be." Her eyes flashed as she looked at Roy. "He'll come round. He wanted to throw her out after the big blow up last time."

"No decent bloke treats his family like that."

Pauline frowned. "He always kept a roof over our heads. I know its hard for the kids, with his moods and that, but marriage is marriage, better or worse."

Roy slid his arm down the back of the seat and pulled Pauline towards him. He started to croon. "Love me tender, love me true, you know that I love you."

Pauline grinned. "Cut it out, Roy. See you at training." She opened the truck door and jumped out, neatly avoiding further contact. She leaned back into the truck to grab her parcels but Roy caught her under the chin.

"I mean it you know."

She smiled, then slammed the door shut. She looked at him through the window. "Yeah, but maybe you meant it when you married Shirley too." He smiled at her as if what she was saying was irrelevant. She felt she had to make herself clearer. "I heard Shirley might've had a few bad times with you. I'm not one for fooling round, Roy." The smiled left his face. He revved up the truck and sped off towards the beach, Kip barking stupidly at the wind.

The house was quiet as Pauline came in and she felt a relief at being alone. In spite of her constant and emphatic rejection of anything more than Roy's friendship, she found that her meetings with him stirred something in her. On one hand, she felt a feminine pleasure in being wanted and desired. But she hastily dismissed that from her mind as "silly stuff". On the other hand, she had a suspicion Roy might be using her, thinking she was easy or desperate because of what she'd told him about her marriage. She knew she shouldn't have opened her mouth to him but she wasn't entirely sorry.

She put Louis's new tracksuit on his bed. Remembering the lizard, she put it down one leg of the pants, giggling to herself as she went out of the room. Hearing voices at the front, she glanced out the door to see if the kids were coming. But it was only some of the younger Anderson kids horsing around. She walked into the kitchen and started, seeing Kevin, sitting at the table, his black hair slicked back, a fresh shirt, pressed trousers.

"Hi," she said, artificially bright. "Just went into town, picked up a tracksuit for Louis."

"I went over to Mum's." His voice took on a mocking tone. "Told me she'd had company."

Pauline felt her stomach muscles tighten. She got a cabbage out of a box under the stove and began to hack at it viciously. She could hear the kids coming in the front door, but she paid no attention. She vaguely heard Louis squeal first in fear, then laughing, yelling to Natalie.

"I know you reckon you can get round me." Kevin's voice was hard. " 'Just wait and he'll soften up.' I know how you scheme and carry on. Not this time. Those girls aren't coming back, not till they've learned their lesson." He sat back.

"You bastard!" she yelled. "Christ I hate you. I cook, I clean, I keep the kids out of your way. What sort of a father are you? What sort of a man are you?"

"Don't give me that!" Kevin stepped across the kitchen and grabbed Pauline as Louis walked into the room, laughing, holding the lizard. "Look at these kids," yelled Kevin. "All bloody hopeless." He swiped the cabbage off the table. "I'm sweating my guts out for you lot to buy the rig and this place is like a pigsty." He shook Pauline again. Louis was usually terrified of his father, but his adolescent maleness now asserted itself and he lunged towards Kevin and swung at him. Kevin, an experienced pub fighter, deflected his swing and efficiently pummelled him to the ground. As Louis lay winded, whimpering on the floor, Kevin wrenched the kitchen door open and strode out.

Pauline lay over Louis and hugged him. "Lou, Lou, why did you do that?" She touched his face and noticed his eyes full of tears. "It's OK. I won't let him touch you again." She looked at him tenderly. "Louis, don't ever do that again."

Louis shook himself free of his mother and sat up. He had his mother's childlike eyes, but his face was hard, masklike, as he fought to suppress the tears. He wiped his nose on the back of his sleeve and pulled himself up, away from Pauline.

He felt a searing pain where his father had punched him but he refused to be cosseted. Next time, he'd get the old man. "I'll be right, Mum," he said furiously. "Let's find the lizard."

·*Chapter Five*·

Petunia took a fistful of biscuits, put one in her mouth and guiltily shoved the rest in the large, loose pockets of her skirt. She hated her addiction to biscuits, but even more she hated the thought of getting through the morning without them. She followed her colleagues along the corridor, and caught up with Carol, the other adoption social worker.

"Have you ever heard of someone called Virginia Nathan?" Petunia asked.

One of the other women turned and looked back at her. "Is this your new way of doing reunions? Enquiries after morning tea?"

"Nope. Just friend of a friend," said Petunia quickly. But nevertheless, she felt guilty.

"I'm sure I've heard that name somewhere," replied Heather McDonald. "Fashion designer, socialite—something like that."

The others shook their heads or shrugged their shoulders. "Sounds sort of familiar," said Carol, "but I can't place it."

Petunia cut short the conversation. "It doesn't matter. Idle curiosity really."

She walked back to her office, took off an ug boot and scratched the sole of her foot. She wished she could place the name. It was a familiar name, a known name. Virginia Nathan was Miranda's mother. Fifteen years ago Virginia Nathan had contacted the home where she had given birth to Miranda to inform them that there was a history of asthma in her family, a piece of information that certainly had not been passed on to Miranda or to her parents. It had been put in the file but Petunia was sure that the approach by Virginia Nathan had not come from a detached, conscientious desire to provide medical information. She could imagine the anxiety that preceded the call to the hospital, the anticipation that maybe

64

they'd tell her something, the searing disappointment, "Yes, thank you, Miss Nathan." Perhaps Virginia had been brave enough to front the matron with the questions all adopting mothers wanted to ask: "Is she all right?" "Is she happy?" Hundreds of times, Petunia had heard the typical response: "Don't ask...it's not your business...we couldn't tell you even if we wanted to...I'm the matron...Remember you surrendered your baby." Virginia Nathan had undoubtedly been told to buzz off and forget the birth of her child five years earlier. She was just as sure that Virginia Nathan had never forgotten, that whatever happened to her since, she had a deep cocoon of hurt, buried inside.

Petunia hated to think of herself as being part of the bureaucracy that eventually extended as far as those old time matrons and their hospitals. She often stated at staff meetings that she didn't see herself as either "a red tape or a fine print person". But she trod more carefully than these public proclamations revealed. She had to be cautious. Her job was not to track down mothers and children separated by adoption. Her job was not to bring them together. Her job was to advise and help them and only assist in reunions when "clearly requested by both parties". That was the fine print and a lot of red tape went with it. She felt passionately that she had the moral right to go further. She knew she risked losing her job and her credibility if something went wrong.

She weighed up the chances of something going wrong in Miranda's case. Miranda Darnley had clearly requested her help in making contact with her natural mother. Petunia knew the real desperation that lay beneath Miranda's polite request, all the more poignant because Miranda, unlike many of the others, hadn't wept or got angry.

On the other hand, Virginia Nathan had told someone fifteen years ago that there was asthma in the family. Fifteen years ago, Virginia Nathan had wanted to know Miranda was all right. But fifteen years was a long time. She could have married, had other children. Petunia decided she had no business barging into Virginia Nathan's life. It would take time and energy and she was short of both, even for the things she was actually supposed to be doing. She dropped Miranda Darnley's file from her desk, onto the pile of folders labelled "No further action at present".

"Tunia," a voice cooed. It was her least favourite contraction of the name she had always hated and she looked up to see Heather McDonald peering round the door, her big brown, cow eyes alight and shining. Girlishly shy, she slipped into Petunia's office.

"Hi, Heather," said Petunia. "How are you?" She wasn't pleased to see Heather. Heather saw social work as a mission to fix other people's lives. Petunia had discovered that most people did not want their lives fixed. People preferred drama to serenity. But from her expression, flushed and breathless, it was clear Heather was about to fix someone.

"I remember who Virginia Nathan is," she said excitedly. She looked at Petunia, like a child expecting a gold star on the back of her hand.

"Really?" said Petunia, now trying to play down her own interest.

"Yes, she's a builder," said Heather earnestly. "I don't mean she actually goes out and builds things, but she's head of a big company. She's terribly successful and after her company crashed she built it up again." Heather looked at Petunia, waiting for the appropriate reaction. Petunia looked at her blankly. "She's a symbol," explained Heather.

"What for?" asked Petunia.

"For women," said Heather piously. She lowered her voice. "Is she one of your adoptions?"

"Nope," said Petunia casually. "Friend of a friend's old girlfriend. Just wanted the gen on her."

"Oh." Heather's face fell.

"Thanks anyway," said Petunia. She looked at the papers on her desk. "I'd better get back to work."

"You busy?"

"Yes, very." Petunia pointedly started shuffling through files.

"I'll leave you to it," said Heather beaming widely as she backed out and shut the door. Petunia grabbed the yellow pages and started looking for construction companies.

Virginia Nathan stood at the dual-screen computer workstation behind Andrew Miller, one of her engineers. To one side was an old style drawing board, but their attention was riveted on the screens in front of them. Andrew moved the digitiser back and forth on the board, rapidly clicking its buttons, creating new lines and curves on the screen. Virginia looked at the sketches on the drawing board, then back at the screen.

She was well-dressed and immaculately groomed. Her clothes were those of a successful woman. Her face was sharp and intelligent. But there was also humour and a gamin quality to her. And underneath it, almost in spite of herself, was a softness, a hungriness, more intense because it was contained.

The screen showed a three-dimensional model, a digital terrain model which gave a precise, realistic picture of a piece of land. This was the tool with which Virginia hoped to win the Corpran contract to erect transmission lines in a remote and difficult area of the state. If she won the contract, it would justify her half million dollar investment in the computer system. If she didn't win it, the firm would be in trouble. It kept her awake at night.

"You'll need to change the colour code so the access roads are more obvious, Andrew. It's Julian Hall we need to convince. If he can't see the whole thing in one glance, we've got a problem. There's no room for subtlety." Andrew caught her look, concentrated, an edge of worry.

"There's not much room for accuracy either, the way we're going," said Andrew slowly.

"The accuracy isn't so important right now," said Virginia quietly. "At this stage, we need to demonstrate the capability. Getting the numbers right is the easy part."

"Phone, Virginia." Her secretary called to her across the office.

"I'll be there in a sec, Di." She looked at Andrew and smiled encouragingly. "I think we're getting there."

Virginia walked across the office to her secretary's desk. "Who is it?" she asked.

"Petunia Rice," said Di. Noticing Virginia's look of puzzlement she added, "She said it was personal."

"Petunia Rice? Sounds like Caribbean nouvelle cuisine." She smiled at Di as she went into her office. "Probably a charity collector. But find out more. She might be a rich and eccentric client."

Virginia went into her office, sat down and lit up a cigarette. She bit at her thumb, suppressing her elation. There was no doubt it was going exceptionally well. If she won the contract, it'd be her first big job since she'd re-established the company. She found the memory of her first failure sickening, even now. To admit her failure had been painful. Coming back, trying again, was the hardest thing she had ever done in her professional career.

The phone buzzed and Virginia picked it up. "Petunia Rice said she's trying to arrange a sort of a birthday or a reunion for a mutual acquaintance born on the 1st of September 1966." Di giggled. "Is she a nut or do you have a friend born then?"

Virginia was silent, aware of the sudden, strong throbbing of the vein in her neck. She felt as if her throat was paralysed. She drew deeply on her cigarette. She felt panic rising.

"She said she'd call you at home if you'd prefer."

Virginia tried to speak, but it came out a strangled, pained sound which she managed to turn into a cough. But it freed her voice. "Get her to ring back in five minutes. I'm having a little brainstorm here. I don't know her, but the date sounds familiar. Probably one of Charlie's little jokes." Her tone became jocular, almost relaxed. Over the years, she'd fought desperately to learn the art of switching off emotionally, and having learnt it, almost despised herself for her ability to do it so completely. It made her doubt that the feelings she experienced so strongly were real at all.

She put down the phone, stubbed out her cigarette and immediately lit another. She placed the pale blue phone directly in front of her, squarely in the middle of the desk as if it were a live foe. She sat, staring at it. It rang and she picked it up.

"Hullo," she said. She realised she sounded stern.

"Your friend, Petunia," said Di.

"Put her through," said Virginia. "And don't let anyone barge in here till I've finished the call." The sound of her own voice made her feel in control again. "Hullo, yes, I'm Virginia Nathan. Yes, this line is private and I'm quite happy for you to talk to me. I'm sorry we put you through the third degree. My secretary tries to save me from people raffling Camiras and holidays in Fiji." She spoke quickly. "Maybe you can explain who you are?"

"I'm a social worker, from the Lucia Hospital Group. You contacted us a long time ago with some information about your family history. I wondered if you were interested in making contact with your daughter?"

"She's OK?" said Virginia without thinking. "She's alive?"
She felt her emotions rising again.

"Yes. She's certainly alive and OK."

"Sorry," said Virginia. "I'd always had an idea...I don't
know why. I suppose that's why I contacted the hospital all
that time ago. I wanted them to tell me..." Tears sprang into
her eyes and she found it hard to speak. "I'm glad to know
she's OK."

"She'd like to meet you and I was wondering if you'd like to
meet her? Not immediately necessarily. Maybe you could write
first or think about it for a while, talk it over with someone
close to you..." Petunia's voice was soft, reassuring and persuasive, but Virginia felt a hurt deep inside her—a remem-
brance of a pain that was deep and searing, a pain that had
once shattered and fragmented her. It sometimes came back
now, but only with a blunt edge, but it still caused a pounding
in her heart and her brain. Pain, nature's warning.

"No, thank you," she said firmly. "I don't want to. I don't
have any family and I don't feel like acquiring any. But thank
you for asking. I'm sure you had the best of intentions."

"Would you mind if I rang you in a month or so?"

There was a pause. But Virginia decided quickly, irrevocably.
"I would mind. I want to leave it here." She softened. "For
now...maybe I'll get in touch with you some time...maybe."
She immediately regretted this lapse. "I'm sure you understand
it from my point of view."

"I do," said Petunia, understanding, but unfairly angry.
"But please ring me if you change your mind, won't you?"

"Goodbye, Miss Rice." Virginia put the phone down and
walked out into the office, her face a little flushed. She went
over to Andrew. "Listen," she said excitedly. "I'm going to try
to get an informal lunch with Julian Hall at Corpran, just to
excite him about some of our ideas, and maybe charm him
into giving me a few more topographical maps. I'll show him
some of the designs we've worked out for the tower supports.
Come into the office and we'll go over the plots."

Andrew looked up, bemused. He would have been in love
with Virginia if he hadn't been intimidated by the fact that
she was a woman. He found the female sex too desirable, too
emotional, unpredictable, and therefore dangerous territory for
a young engineer on the way up.

"Are we moving too fast?" he asked.

"No," said Virginia firmly. "I'm going to get this contract. No more mucking round."

"No, Miranda, it wouldn't be a good idea. It's not even a good idea me talking to you now...Even if you stay at Nanna's again, he'll find out. Just let it simmer down." Pauline was ironing with one hand, trying to stave off her own fears and reassure Miranda at the same time. "Mandy, don't get upset. No, it's got nothing to do with the album and you going to find your mother and all that...No, I don't like it, but it's your Dad...Mandy, yes, I promise you, it won't last forever... he's as mad as a cut snake. I can't talk to you. I can hear the truck now...Yes, love, this is your home. You know I'm hopeless at writing. I'll try. I have to go. Don't be so upset, love. It's not easy this end either."

She put the phone down, her heart thudding as she heard Kevin's footsteps on the gravel path at the side. She realised the tension between them, the nastiness in the house was making her sick: the acid taste of her stomach, in the back of her throat, the tightness in the head. "He'll come round...It's not that bad..." She suddenly felt the real emptiness of her words. It scared her. He'd never come round, he'd never change, she knew that, but she could hardly think beyond it. He paid the bills, didn't bash her—surely that counted for something. She heard the screen door slam shut as he came in. "I want Miranda back home," she thought. "Just up and down on weekends. And Linda; for once in her life, Linda might actually need me." The desperation in Miranda's voice, always needing, always wanting. It had been the same right from when she was a little baby. No fuss, no bother, but always with that edge of insecurity. She wanted to make it right for them, to be together, to be happy, but the idea seemed like a far-fetched dream.

Tired and pulled apart, Pauline felt her fear as she heard Kevin in the bathroom, turning on the shower. In her mind, she saw the meanness of his face, the indifference in his eyes, the muscular hardness of his body. There was no giving in him any more, no caring. She wondered if there ever had been or whether it had all been the same cold, hard usage of her.

She realised, as a cold shiver passed through her body, that not only did she not love him, she hated him. Keeping the family together, not upsetting the kids, trying to win him round, to change him, had all been useless because she hated him, heart and soul, her heart as hard as his. For a moment, she sought to deny the monumental revolution in her feelings. But she knew—her marriage was over.

Miranda was sitting on the old cane settee Linda had put into the back yard. The ginger cat from next door sat on her lap. Each time she stroked his back and pulled on his tail, a shiver of satisfaction went through his long body. But Miranda remained white faced and tense, her feet freezing under her two pairs of socks, her body hunched.

Linda sat beside her in the unfamiliar role of comforter. "You should have told her to get stuffed," she said reassuringly. She couldn't understand why the conversation with Pauline had upset Miranda. "We'll go home for Christmas. Everything's always ace then."

"You'll have the baby."

"They'll love it, 'specially Mum. And Dad'll ignore it or come round. Geez he's a pig sometimes, isn't he?"

Miranda looked at Linda, wondering, if only she saw the world like Linda did, she'd have the world at her feet too. Linda refused to take rejection seriously. Miranda had been aware of potential rejection all her life. The reality hit her at fourteen. Since seeing Petunia, she had had nightmares that her natural mother was dead. Now, there was her mother's rejection. She knew it wasn't the same, but it felt like it.

"Dad's all right, you know," said Linda. "You just got to get on his good side."

"I didn't know he had one." Miranda pulled the cat's tail, this time savagely. The cat purred ecstatically.

"Masochist," said Miranda, tickling behind his ears. She thought briefly of her father. She knew, even when they were little, that he'd loved Linda far more than her. But he still behaved like a bastard to Linda, to Pauline, to the other kids. She felt that a great void, a deadness had always been between him and her. It had signalled her difference even before he'd told her. But she still didn't understand why the others tolerated him.

She pushed the cat off her lap and turned to Linda. "What will you do next year?" she asked casually. "Go back to Uwalla?"

"No way!" said Linda. "I'd be fighting with Mum all the time. I'll stay here. Next year, I'll be able to go out, have fun, get a fella."

"What about the boy here?" Miranda patted Linda's stomach.

Linda looked down at her pot belly and smoothed her hands over it proudly. "He'll be just the loveliest baby," she said dreamily. "He'll have big eyes and a cute little cowlick, like Lou's, and I'll take him for walks and down to the park." She looked at Miranda. "We can all share him. Haze even says she'll learn how to change a nappy."

Miranda laughed. Knowing Linda, it'd probably all be true. And she felt herself hooked by the fantasy, even though, as the oldest, she knew something of the reality of babies. She envied Linda's pregnancy, envied her her baby. At times, she felt fiercely possessive and protective of it, as if Linda didn't quite understand the child's importance. She picked up a plastic shopping bag from under her feet.

"Look," she said, pulling out a tiny blue sleeve. "I've started knitting. Do you like it?"

"Oh Mandy, it's so little." Linda stretched the tiny sleeve over her belly and sighed. "I can't really imagine me with a baby."

Linda ran her fingers along the racks of dresses. They all had something that marked them out from ordinary dresses. The pearls on the epaulettes, the slash of peacock blue silk across the shoulder, the hand-made tapestry inserts, the little red trousers peeking out from underneath.

"I'd love the job," she said shyly to Gilda. "But what would I wear?" She looked down at her stomach with an expression of bemused hopelessness.

Gilda was very short and very fat. Even from her high stiletto heels, she looked up at Linda. Gilda's total assurance made Linda feel very young. But Gilda smiled at her approvingly.

"Darling, I get the girls to run something up. New ones each month, eh? You like that?" Linda nodded, almost overpowered by Gilda. Everything from her long red nails to her tawny gold-tipped hair indicated power and money. Her short plump body was squeezed into an expensive, unflattering dress worn with a brazen confidence that made it look good. Linda had a sense that something exciting could happen to her here. She wanted the job.

"It will be hard work," went on Gilda in her fast, Hungarian accent. Her voice was like the darkness of the shop, thought Linda. It took time, but then you could understand everything she said.

"You must not be on your feet all the time." She looked at Linda sympathetically. "I ask no one to do that. No one pregnant." She grasped her back and winced. "God, I suffered when I was pregnant. I tell you, once was enough." She looked at Linda appraisingly. "You can do figures?"

"Oh yes," lied Linda. "Easy."

Gilda turned to Hazel, took her hand and squeezed it. "And you, darling, thank you for finding me someone so soon. I give you a discount. You are so beautiful, you will be good advertisement for my dresses." She picked the one with the slash of blue silk and held it admiringly up against Hazel. "Beautiful with your eyes. I give it to you for two hundred fifty."

Hazel grinned with the assurance of someone who didn't need a discount to buy her clothes and didn't need clothes to make her look good. "Not today," she said. "I'd have to think up an event to wear it to and I haven't got the energy. We have to go." She pulled Linda's arm. "Come on."

"I'll be in on Saturday," said Linda eagerly.

"Eight thirty," said Gilda. "And five on Thursday nights. And you ring if you can't come."

"Boy!" said Linda as they stepped out of the shop. "I can't believe it. Haze, you're a wonder getting me that. I'll be able to get some decent clothes and get some stuff for my room. And she said if I work out, I might be full-time next year. Just imagine."

"Not what you know, who you know," said Hazel breezily.

"But I can't understand why she calls it 'Chez Sleeze'. It's so glamorous."

"That's why, reverse psychology."

"Huh?" Linda shrugged as she trotted along beside Hazel through the city crowds. She realised that a lot of the time she had no idea what Hazel was talking about but she'd decided Hazel didn't really know either. It was just a way she had of making conversation, so it sounded good. "Have you ever thought of working in a place like that?" she asked.

"In a shop?" said Hazel. "Selling frocks? Not cut out for it." For a moment, Linda wondered why selling clothes was all right for her but not for Hazel. She dismissed the thought from her mind and linked her arm through Hazel's.

"Come on," she said. "I'll buy us one of those really gross ice-creams. Fancy me getting a job."

Miranda sat in the library cubicle, staring at the wooden partition in front of her. Even the graffiti was terrible. "Lesbians sux," was followed by a long and serious diatribe on lesbianism. On the desk in front of Miranda was the biochemistry text that she couldn't afford to buy. She couldn't borrow it and the library shut in fifteen minutes. She'd meant to take enough notes to do the assignment tonight. It was due in tomorrow.

Geoff had seen her earlier. He'd dropped a note onto her desk: "Keep passing." She'd smiled at him but she'd torn the note into little pieces and was still staring at the partition. She felt fearful but recognised an arrogance in her inability to work. She'd always been top or near the top. "Just passing" seemed barely worth the effort. Yet even just passing would take a lot of effort. She felt as if a weekend in Uwalla was the only thing that would restore her energy. Unfulfilled hope was draining her. As the weeks passed, the chance of Petunia phoning with good news seemed to recede.

She felt in her purse and got out four dollar coins. She picked up the book and walked over to the photocopy change machines and inserted the coins which rattled through to five cent pieces.

"The library will be closing in five minutes. All books to reserve now," boomed the PA system. Miranda hastily folded the photocopies, dropped her book on a trolley and walked out the door.

She walked along Glebe Point Road, trying to think about her assignment. Exams and assignments now carried with them guilt and fear, things she'd never experienced before in her academic life. Study, which had been her escape for so many years, had become a burden. It was easier to meander off into dreams of Linda's baby, of fantasies of finding her real mother, of going home to Uwalla, of discovering that her mother had left her father. The leftover change in her pocket jangled as she walked faster to avoid the wind and she remembered she had meant to buy a birthday present for Nanna. Hurriedly, she counted her remaining money and remembering Valentino's dried-flower pictures, she crossed the road and hurried up the hill towards the shop.

Valentino was talking to a customer as she walked in, but he winked at her and motioned her to wait. She stood there, the unpleasant smell of rotting daisy stems wafting through the shop. The lilies, tightly bound into bunches to hold them straight, had brown-tipped petals. The iridescent electric blue and silver wallpaper was peeling down behind the fake antique vases. As Valentino haggled with his customer over the price of a bunch of drooping miniature roses, he winked and then leered suggestively at Miranda. Miranda felt her fury rising. Valentino had been a joke but the joke had become too sordid.

The customer wandered disconsolately towards the door, his eyes roving over the fading flowers. Miranda walked over to Valentino. "I'm not working for you any more," she said.

The customer, sensing the impending row, loitered by the buckets near the doorway.

"You can't fire me," said Valentino triumphantly. "I have last week's wages."

"I'm not firing you. I'm quitting."

"I have your money." Valentino was almost dancing with excitement.

"Are you going to keep it if I don't come back?" said Miranda furiously.

"Typical bloody wog," muttered the customer.

"You gotta come back to get the money." Valentino looked at her slyly. "I love you so angry."

"Keep the money!" She walked towards the door, picked up a bucket full of green carnations and threw them at him. The flowers sprayed all over the shop, but the water was a direct hit and he stood there, wet and dripping. "Get stuffed," said Miranda and walked out.

"Good one, love," said the customer approvingly as he followed her out the door. Miranda felt vindicated.

Linda giggled. "That's fantastic. He's such a revolting little man."

"We should all go back together," said Hazel. "Throw three buckets over him at once. Multi-coloured watering."

"I'm going to feel so good every time I walk past there," said Miranda. She looked at Linda. "We'll be a bit broke though."

"I've got a job," said Linda delightedly. "A dress shop in town. It doesn't pay much, but we'll be all right." Mentally, she'd sacrificed her new wardrobe and her plans for redecorating her room. She felt an unfamiliar pleasure to be doing something for her elder sister.

"Sure you'll be able to handle it?" asked Miranda.

"Piece of cake," said Linda. She giggled. "The housework here doesn't actually take up that much time you know."

"We know," chorused Hazel and Miranda.

Linda came through the kitchen with a pile of washing and a martyred expression. She knew her martyrdom was ridiculous, but at the same time steadfastly refused to become more efficient or to succumb to guilt despite the continuing complaints.

"Poor pregnant washer woman," said Patrick as she walked past. "Life's so hard."

"Certainly is," said Linda, piling tea towels, Wettexes and dishcloths randomly together before swanning out of the kitchen. Patrick turned to Miranda.

"How's study going?"

"I'm getting there," she answered. "But you get behind and it somehow takes all the wind out of your sails."

"I've never had any wind in my sails," he said bleakly. "I've never actually been up to date. A week late with this, a day with that, months of lectures to catch up. You can see it all stretching ahead, never stretching behind. You know, every year, since I started high school, I have this recurrent dream. I dream it's the end of October, I still haven't done any work and I'm going to fail this year. It's so deep in my psyche I'll still be having it when I'm fifty."

76

"Geoff says when you feel down, you remind yourself you only have to pass."

Patrick looked depressed. "That's what I tell myself when I'm feeling really good. That's what's wrong with being at the back of the pack—there's no fall back position."

"Why on earth did you do engineering if you find it so hard?"

"I wanted to prove to my father that I could do something solid and masculine. I'm actually very good at languages and if I ever get through I'll go and work in some foreign land to prove it. You know, go to Saudi Arabia to build a skyscraper city and become a recluse, an incredible Islamic scholar. No, scrap the city but I'll do something important, study something for its own sake, get to the bottom of it."

Miranda stirred some more sugar into her coffee watching him talk. The way he ran on reminded her of David, how he'd start on something that was important and then make it sound silly, as if he was scared someone else would destroy the dream first.

"Miranda, I want to tell you something." His tone changed. The statement came from nowhere.

"What?" said Miranda.

"I want to change my relationship with you." He looked at her, embarrassed. "I was going to say I've got a crush on you but it sounds almost as silly as saying I want a date. And I've been trying to do it in a laid back way, you know, slip my arm casually round you. But the trouble is, you're never there when my arm is. You're good at avoiding close encounters of any kind." He looked at her, not wanting to stop talking. "I don't mean you're unapproachable—you're really beautiful and I'd like to have something between us but I can't find any other way to do it besides this. I've got you on a pedestal or something."

Miranda blushed, realising that it had always been there between them. But in her head, there'd always been David. She'd held back from anyone else, because that would mean what she had with David hadn't been serious. She knew now was the time to exorcise David from her mind and her heart. But she also remembered how difficult it had been with David, how anxious it had made her, always scared he might see her when she was unprepared, catch her unawares, shy, self-conscious, wanting to look right, wanting to be right for him every time. Patrick, here, sharing a house; the possibilities were like a nightmare. Her confusion paralysed her. Yet, she sensed it could be different.

"We live in the same house," she blurted out.

"That's actually an advantage." He took her anxiety as an encouraging sign.

"Yes, but, I really don't know, I like you, I feel..."

The phone rang and Patrick took Miranda's hand. "Just think about whether you'd like to come out on Saturday night," he said as he picked up the phone. "Hullo. Hang on a bit."

"I'm going down to uni now," he said hurriedly to Miranda. "I'll talk to you later. Remember, I'm a gentle romantic soul." He handed her the phone. "It's for you. See you later."

Miranda took the phone as he disappeared out the door. "Hullo."

"Hi, it's Petunia."

Miranda wished Patrick hadn't gone. "No news?" she asked tentatively.

"Not exactly," said Petunia. "But no really good news."

"Oh."

"Do you want to come in and talk about it?"

"No, please, tell me now. I've got term exams coming up, late assignments. It takes too long to come out all that way to hear bad news."

"It's not all that bad, Miranda." Petunia began to speak rapidly. "Your mother made contact with the hospital when you were about five. She was twenty then."

"So she had me when she was fourteen." She thought of Natalie, budding breasts, still a little girl.

"Yes, still at school."

"So?"

"So, she just wanted to tell them there was asthma in the family. Since then, there's been no move from her, which means officially, I should have left it at that."

"But you didn't." Miranda's warmth for Petunia came back.

"No. She wasn't too hard to find. Unusual name, not married, professional woman."

"And she didn't want to see me?"

"No, she didn't."

"Any reason?" Miranda's voice was harder.

"Not really. Past is a closed book. All that stuff. Miranda, she was scared."

"So was I," said Miranda angrily. "It doesn't have to stop you."

"I know... maybe in a year or so, we could..."

"Forget it. If she doesn't want to, she doesn't want to."

"Miranda, I think you should come in, talk it over."

Miranda wound the phone cord round her hand. She let it go and watched it spring back into shape. "Thanks, Petunia, but I think I'll let it go. Thanks for everything. I will come and see you some time. I don't want to sound ungrateful. I'm angry at her, not you. I can't talk now." She gently put the phone down and looked round to see Linda coming in from the laundry with an armful of sheets.

"Who was that?" she asked.

"Social worker, from the hospital. You know. They found my real mother, but she doesn't want to see me." Linda heard the hard edge in Miranda's voice and noticed her white face. It was the same when they were kids; if she got into trouble, she didn't want to cry. You knew it mattered but you knew she'd turn on you if you said anything.

"Don't worry about it, Mandy," she said gently. "You know you've got Mum. She really loves you best. It's only this domestic she's having with Dad." She dropped the sheets onto the floor, picked one up and started folding it. Miranda took the other end and shook it out. They folded it together, Miranda taking the bottom corners.

"What'll you do now?" asked Linda casually, carefully, smoothing the crease in the middle.

"I'm going to pass my exams." Miranda was still hard, but she looked at Linda appreciatively. "That's enough, isn't it?"

Chapter Six

Greenery, grace and order, not overstated, not understated. Refined, but not prissy. Beautiful, but not stunning. Never dramatic. Architectural faults hidden behind the great avenues of trees, gaucheries rendered harmless by the great sweep of the lawns, the banks of azaleas and camellias. It was just how Charlie remembered it. Exactly. He remembered the long walks he and Ginny took towards the end. Down streets like this: tree-lined, houses well back. Not a place where you laugh much, Virginia had said. It was true. You smiled, you exchanged pleasantries, but you didn't laugh, or talk about money, sex or religion, or scream or swear. You didn't make a fuss. Heart-land Protestants: staunch, strong, straight as a die, straight and very narrow.

He remembered this road. Golf course on both sides, the club house on the right, Tudor style. Virginia was driving fast and the images flashed by him, familiar, but new because his way of seeing had changed, not because they were different. Virginia flicked her cigarette ash out the open car window. Charlie grinned. Yeah, she was at home here, she was coming home but it was on her terms, not theirs. With the same defiance she sped up the hill and turned blindly into the driveway of the house. Half way up to the house, she stopped the car, watching Charlie.

It seemed untouched. The garden, mature when he first came, twenty one years ago, was just as magnificent. In the lush shrubbery, you sensed different and exotic plants, all of which had their special time of display. The driveway was the same—raked, red gravel; the lawn—carpet-like, except where it was bare under the jacaranda, with the bareness tastefully obscured by the old garden seat. The house itself, he'd forgotten how pretty it was: white, two-storeyed, Victorian with iron lace and a little Gothic tower on one side. The wide verandahs, the upstairs balcony which had never been used in the months he'd spent there.

"If we park at the front, it says I own it," said Virginia. "If I drive round the back, it says I live here. What shall it be?"

"Let's live here," said Charlie. "Bugger it, you own it anyway."

Virginia revved the Volvo and swung it round the side driveway to the back of the house. Here things had changed. The tennis court had been screened off by greenery and a pergola had been built by the pool. There seemed to be less gravel, more greenery, although the old formal rose beds were still there, cut back to nothing over winter, only a few red tips hinting at their magnificence in spring and summer. Virginia stopped the car, but didn't get out. She stared at the flower beds.

"I can't imagine why we're doing this."

"It's a lovely house, Virginia."

"You sound like a bloody real estate agent. Your Yankee accent doesn't help: 'It's a lovely home, madame. Ensuites in every cupboard and the garages are carpeted.' I had a lovely house at the Bay."

"You needed the money: support your computers."

"I'm hoping the Corpran contract will pay for that now." She looked at the house and shook her head. "It still seems crazy that a terrace over there could be worth more than this."

"Real estate. Eastern suburbs. Prime location. This is only the rich heart of the north shore. We're really slumming it."

"All the money gone into the business. That bloody computer... and the rest. And I still owe two hundred thousand. We're trapped."

"I wouldn't exactly regard this as a trap, Ginny," said Charlie gently. "It is, real estate parlance or not, a *loverly* home."

"Home," said Virginia slowly, considering the word in relation to the house. She opened the car door and got out. "Come on, Charlie. Let's go in. It'll be a terrible shock to you. It's exactly, precisely the same as it was twenty years ago. Even when Mum was in the nursing home she'd ring up the cleaning lady and tell her what flowers to cut. And there was no one living here. She wasn't just a homemaker, she was a preserver. I think she would have hated the idea of me moving back in.

You know, I might make it untidy or not feed the bulbs." She squeezed his arm. "I'm glad you're with me, Charlie." She put the key into the big old brass lock and opened the door.

Charlie stepped into the sunroom and found the same, ugly, silly drawings of flowers in the frames of varnished, yellow wood, the chintz sofas with the antimacassars, the round flowered carpet over the polished parquetry floor, the 1950s bar, padded with white vinyl. But Virginia was right. It was eerie. Twenty one years later, it was exactly the same as when he'd come here as an exchange student from Ohio. Slowly, he moved towards the stairs and remembered the times he'd tackled them drunk, trying desperately to be sober. Now he climbed them, looking at the little lithographs of Paris, one every three stairs.

"Do you mind if we change some of the pictures?" he asked.

"We're going to change the whole bloody thing," said Virginia in a strange voice. "New pictures, new paint, new furniture, new people."

"Not this fella," said Charlie. He stood in the front hallway, in front of the oil picture of Virginia's father in the gilt frame. It wasn't a good portrait, he thought, but it could have been worse. It caught the old man's humour, the light in his eye, his sardonic manner.

"I really liked your old man you know."

Virginia was silent.

"He was a good bloke, good for a yarn."

"Really?" said Virginia.

Charlie didn't notice. "I remember I used to yarn with him. I'd get home a bit tanked but he never seemed to notice. Bloody amazing. Knew everything."

"Yes he did," said Virginia.

"I felt closer to him than my own Dad."

"You would have. Yours was in the States."

"Don't be shitty, Ginny. You know what I mean. You got on well with him."

"Fantastically," said Virginia. "I suppose we would have been closer if he'd remembered my name." She smiled at Charlie. "You know me, poor little rich girl." She started climbing the stairs and held her hand out to him. "I'm going to run up the stairs. I was never allowed to run on the stairs." She ran up, stopped at the landing and ran down again, then up again, right to the top and then down, into Charlie's arms. She started laughing and hugged him tightly. He rolled on top of her and she rolled over again and they wrestled and giggled on the floor, undressing in the process; laughing and fighting, then laughing and kissing, then laughing and making love and then just lying on the floral carpet, tracing the patterns with their fingers, their hands coming together, feeling and touching again.

"I'll tell you what," whispered Charlie, as they lay still and naked on the floor. "I don't feel happy making love in this part of the world with the back door open. One of the neighbours might pop in to borrow scones or whatever it is they borrow."

"I don't feel entirely comfortable making love on my mother's Axminster under my father's portrait," said Virginia.

"Comfort wasn't entirely what we were after."

"No," said Virginia. "It wasn't."

She looked up at her father's portrait. "He really was a bastard you know."

"Coo yah, coo yah." The early morning calls of the currawongs were slow, relaxed and melodious and Virginia listened, looking through the great, gaunt jacaranda at the winter blue of the sky. Her hand, under her silk pyjamas, smoothed over her stomach and she found herself drifting, remembering those kicks, the fullness that had been in her. She thought of one of Charlie's portraits, a girl of about eleven with pigtails that stuck out, spiky. She tried to imagine the same girl, nearly twenty. She couldn't. Yet, in her mind, she knew that was the reality, the truth. She felt panic that the girl was here, in the same city, looking for her. She'd always thought she must be a long way away, but she was here, a real person, not Virginia's image at all.

She felt she must stop it. The idea of the girl scared her. The idea that the girl had a name, that she was someone, someone quite different and separate from Virginia, someone who was looking for her.

The idea grew in Virginia's mind. What would the girl want? Someone to love? Someone to blame? Someone to have a cosy fireside chat with? Maybe she was a sensible girl who liked to get things sorted out. Maybe she was a silly, grossly sentimental girl with an idiot boyfriend. Maybe they wanted her at the wedding. Well, she'd go, she thought. Wouldn't be blamed. But she couldn't love. She knew it. She'd been down that road before. It had brought her to the brink of insanity and she knew she had no business lying in bed on a Sunday morning rubbing her stomach and feeling for babies. Yet she knew one day, when she got the courage, she'd ring Petunia Rice. When the house was finished, when she finished the Corpran contract, when she got her next big contract, when Charlie got sick of her. God knew when.

She put her hands above the bedcovers, straight, by her sides. The cover was a thick, pale pink silk with a pattern of flowers delicately woven into it. It matched perfectly the pale pink pillowslips, pure cotton, Chinese embroidered, lying on the matching sheets, over which Virginia's dark auburn hair now spilled. She felt like the lady of the lake, lying in her barge, going down the river, but she was in her mother's bed, listening to the currawongs, watching the bare jacaranda and the ash tree through the lace curtains. It felt strange that she should even be lying in the bed, let alone have slept in it.

She remembered, when she was seven years old, visiting her friend Margaret Connolly. She walked round one Sunday morning and Margaret had taken her straight into her parents' bedroom, as if it was the most natural thing in the world to do. Virginia remembered standing paralysed with embarrassment, watching the two Connolly parents, in bed together, eating Red Tulip Cherry Liqueur chocolates. No one had to explain to her that it was wrong, she had known that instinctively. Margaret had climbed onto the bed with them and she remembered looking at the three of them beckoning her to come up, laughing at her shyness, holding out chocolates to entice her. They looked like creatures from a fairy story—seductive, but wicked. She'd been tempted for a moment but far, far too scared. She told them she had to go to Sunday school and turned and left.

She had walked home slowly, pondering the mystery. She had known of course that some parents shared the same bed or bedroom, but the Connollys had been so blatant, so public. She had also pondered her own mother's maxim that children should never get into an adult bed because they might suffocate. She realised, for the first time, that it made no sense at all. Margaret Connolly, sitting up there eating Red Tulip chocolates had been in no danger of suffocating. But she also knew it would do no good at all to mention it at home. It was the first time in her life she had realised that there was another way to live. It had both shocked and excited her. It was the same feeling she had now, lying in her mother's own, chaste bed, realising she could do in it whatever she liked.

"Yoo hoo," yelled Charlie. She heard his footsteps on the stairs and sat up, as he walked in with a tray, set with teapot, matching china cups and plates, with two buttered muffins.

"No poofy croissants. A proper breakfast for this part of the world, don't you think?"

"Spot on," answered Virginia. "You look as if you've been up for hours. What on earth have you been doing?" She noticed Charlie's paint-spattered shoes, his grey overalls over which he wore an old blue jumper with the sleeves cut off at the elbow.

"Organising," said Charlie. He lay next to her on the bed and took a great mouthful out of the muffin. "First, I've organised my studio down in the sunroom. I want you to come down and look at it after breakfast. The light's fantastic there. Second, I've thought up some colour schemes for the house, which you can think about at your leisure. Thirdly, I want your permission to remove that bloody rose near the front door." He held up a scratched hand for her inspection.

"Nope," said Virginia. "It's the only really good dark red one for cut blooms." She realised it was exactly what her mother would have said. "You can pull it up and strangle it for all I care."

"Fine," said Charlie. "Just one more organisational detail."

"What?" asked Virginia suspiciously, quickly finishing off her tea and putting the tray to one side.

"I want to share this bedroom with you. I want to wake up with you as they say in the song. You're a passionate woman, Virginia, but you treat sex as if it's a rationed commodity. But it's not just sex. I want to stop this pretence we're having a casual affair. I want to spend my life with you."

"No," said Virginia fixedly. "Not yet." She softened. "Charlie, I do like you—a lot."

He laughed. "Be careful not to mention love."

"I am careful." She was serious and he felt cross with her.

"I get lonely at night," he said. "I get pissed off you're not there. You're a very independent woman, Virginia, and I hardly see that if I share the same bed I'm going to infringe on you any more than if I'm a back room boy. I don't snore, I don't fart all that much and I'll try not to take over your dreams or your mind."

"It's not that," said Virginia. She softened again.

"Have you thought how it makes me feel?" asked Charlie. "Touch inadequate, touch unwanted. And then at times you come on hot and strong."

"I'm sorry. You take it too personally."

Charlie sat up in the bed and looked at the ceiling. "Personally! Too personally? How else could I bloody take it? I'm the only one here aren't I? Of course I take it personally!"

"I'm really sorry, Charlie." She could feel her heart beat faster. "I want to settle in first. I will think about it. I don't think of it as a casual affair, but the less casual it gets, the worse I seem to become." She jumped out of bed and walked round the bed to him, knowing how he liked her in the maroon silk pyjamas. "Come on, show me the studio."

"OK, but I'm not giving up."

In the late afternoon, Virginia went for a brisk walk along the streets, fragrant and smoky from the smell of burning leaves in the street gutters and incinerators. The lawns were smooth and green for Monday morning, the gravel driveways raked into perfect lines. Here, gardening was not simply a matter of bunging palms and other spectacular specimens in terracotta pots or organising pergolas and hanging baskets. It was a serious business of upkeep: lawns, leaves, gutters, weeds, raking, pruning, clipping, fertilising, spraying. It was amazing they still had time for golf.

She walked past the Connollys' house, scene of original sin. Margaret had apparently come out of childhood without any ill effects, married a doctor and gone to live in Edinburgh. Mrs Connolly lived in the old house alone and as Virginia walked past and saw the light go on in the front room, she hoped she still ate chocolates in bed on Sunday mornings. It didn't seem very likely.

She walked back towards her house and saw the light was on in the sunroom. In one way, she would have liked to share her recollection of the Connollys with Charlie, but she suspected he might use it against her. She knew she needed Charlie. She suspected she really loved him, but she felt she must keep him at a distance for her own protection. She walked down the back garden, past the pool to the little tennis shed. She walked in and in the dusky light, found her old racquet, hanging on a nail on the wall. There was a big cane basket full of balls and she picked one that wasn't too spongy and walked out onto the court. She bounced the ball and hit it up against the practice board. It came back to her, faster than she expected, bouncing up at her and she hit at it awkwardly, but managed to get a weak shot up against the board. Gradually, she got her rhythm and hit ten forehands in a row, then ten backhands, just as the coach had taught her. Now, though, she allowed herself to hit the backhanders double handed and was surprised at the new strength of her stroke. She hit with power and concentration, biting her bottom lip, her eyes totally concentrated on the ball in the growing darkness. She finally hit one so hard against the practice board that it bounced behind her, into the dusk.

"Bravo!" boomed Charlie as Virginia walked off.

"It's fantastic, Charlie," she said. "I never thought about the court, but it'll be wonderful."

"Tennis parties every Sunday afternoon," he said sardonically.

"I just might," said Virginia. "What have you been up to?"

"Painting. Come on, I'll show you." He put his arm round her, massaging her neck gently as they walked up to the back of the house and then into the sunroom. This morning, when Virginia had seen it, Charlie had already set it up with easels, canvases and his drawing board. Now, on the other side of the room, arranged in a neat semicircle, on the shelves and window sills, were what appeared to be hundreds of white plaster statues of the Madonna. Virginia jumped backwards against Charlie.

"Christ! What on earth are they? Where did you get them? Charlie, they're awful!"

"An artist never expects to be appreciated in his own lifetime," said Charlie piously.

"Come on, what are they?"

Charlie took her hand. "I didn't get the baked beans contract."

"Oh Charlie, why ever not? You didn't tell me."

"I didn't want to upset you before we moved. I was late

with my submission. The agency said they were lovely baked beans, best they'd seen, but, old McGlynnon implied if I couldn't get a submission in on time, well, they wouldn't trust me with the account. In the kindest possible terms, he told me he was sick of the way I screw them up timewise. Fair enough."

Virginia looked at the madonnas. "You turned to religion?"

Charlie put his arm round her shoulders. "This may seem hard to believe, but this is part of a life plan. Painting madonnas is very profitable and involves almost no creative stress. It will, at the very least, pay the rent."

"There is no rent," said Virginia quickly.

"I'm living with you, not off you. Anyway, painting madonnas is not a lifetime career. I'll do a few cloaks and faces every morning, and then, in the afternoon, I'll work on a series of proper paintings. If the reaction is good, I shall pursue that. If not, I shall get a proper job in an agency and go to work like a proper person."

"Fantastic," said Virginia. "I mean painting, not being a proper person. Why, after all this time?"

Charlie turned to his canvases and equipment. "Partly losing the account, partly the futility of it. And coming back here. I know you never saw much of it, but in the year I lived here, I did some fantastic stuff. Whatever I had then, I still have."

Virginia led the way up the stairs. "I'm really glad. But don't flaunt the madonnas around the neighbourhood. Around here, you're not even supposed to play with Catholics."

The sea was dark, almost smoky grey, like the thin cloud that lay along the horizon. The sky rose up above it to a pale eggshell blue, streaked with flimsy windblown clouds, tinted a delicate bronze by the sunset.

Miranda lay on the blanket, snuggled against Patrick's chest, his arms around her, hers around him. The wall of the bunker protected them from the evening wind and the sand under them was soft and smooth. About two metres away at the edge of the bunker was a sheer cliff, which fell to the rocks thirty metres below. Miranda looked over Patrick's arm at the sea, the line of the furthest breakers just tipped with the gold of the sun. From below, she could hear the pounding of the surf on the beach and make out the long reef stretching out into the sea.

"This is the most fantastic place I've ever been to for a picnic," she said dreamily. "It's the best place I've been to, all the time I've been in Sydney. It might even be the best place I've been to ever."

"Cliff-top picnics are like life," said Patrick, snuggling back up against her, as the breeze flicked sand up against them. "Just don't fall off. And hope like hell nobody hits their golf balls at you."

She looked over the edge of the bunker. All week, she'd worried about her and Patrick. She padded around the house feeling ungainly and lumpish, wanting to change her clothes, worried that if she did, he'd notice and think her vain. When he rushed off to a lecture one morning, she became certain he'd lost interest in her. When she sat at her desk at night, trying to study, she'd be uplifted by the idea of being in love. Over breakfast, it made her shy and diffident and she hid behind the paper. She felt horribly embarrassed by her lack of sexual experience. She wanted to explain all this to him, but was scared he'd think her silly. So she avoided him until he cornered her and talked her into the cliff-top picnic.

Being with him, she'd forgotten herself again, but now, as he kissed her passionately, she was suddenly scared of what he wanted from her. She pretended to respond, looking over his shoulder, fixing on the thin line of gold along the horizon, framed by the blackness of the sea below and the blackness of the sky above. As he stopped kissing her, she neatly disengaged herself, sat up and brushed the sand off herself in a brisk, businesslike fashion. Then she bent over him and kissed him gently. He tried to pull her down, but too fast, she stood up and offered him a hand to his feet.

"We'd roll over the cliff here," she said calmly. "Come on, I'll buy you fish and chips down at Manly." He looked at her longingly and dumbly, but she took no notice of his silent plea. Quickly she tidied everything into the picnic basket, then jumped neatly up the side of the bunker onto the damp grass of the golf course.

Pauline had got up at six, but Kevin was awake before her and she knew immediately that he remembered Miranda's birthday. He'd gone into the bathroom to shave. When she picked up the phone, he came raging out, lather all over his face, the razor

in one hand. "Don't think I'm paying for calls to bloody Sydney."
Louis was there and as his father retreated into the bathroom,
he whispered to her.

"Don't let him stop you, Mum. You gotta ring her." Despite
the obvious physical inequality between him and his father,
Louis had a burning desire to challenge Kevin. His puberty
was beginning, with pimples and a break in his voice. But to
Pauline, the most disturbing thing was his hunger to confront
his father.

"Mum, you know what she's like about birthdays." Miranda
was his favourite sister. He was determined not to let Pauline
bury the issue.

"I can't. He'll be out like a flash if I pick up that phone. And
he's been so stingy with the money that I'm still saving for her
present." She looked at him pleadingly. "She'll understand."

"You should ring her now. Before she goes to uni."

Pauline looked at her son angrily. She didn't like the adolescent, male violence she saw simmering in him. The first
time, there'd been a certain innocence and she'd felt proud of
him. He'd been like a little boy, loving her passionately, innocently. But in the persistence of his hatred, she saw the
meanness of his father.

"Did you send her a card?" she asked him accusingly.

"No, but..."

"Well don't tell me what to do, if you can't even send your
own sister a card."

Louis silently poured cereal into his bowl and started eating.
He never had milk and he sat making loud, angry crunching
noises.

"Louis, getting angry won't fix anything. He'll just take it
out on everyone. You gotta work around him."

Louis said nothing. The crunching continued.

"You gotta remember how mad he gets, love. I don't want
him belting you. We keep out of his way, things'll be okay,
lovey. Really." She watched Louis's face colour, as rage and
desperation flowed through him. She thought of Kevin's love-
less sex that left her feeling violated and felt the hollowness of
what she was saying. She heard Kevin go out of the bathroom,
into the bedroom where she'd hung his ironed shirt. She
lowered her voice. "It's not that bad. We still have fun. You
know, when we get out with Roy."

"It's not fair on Mandy," he said stubbornly. "She's twenty, Mum. It's really being grown up when you turn twenty."

Pauline knew Lou was right. Miranda did care about birthdays, not like Linda, for the presents, but because she needed to feel they all remembered. She thought of her looking for her mother. Her mother—she hated to even think of her—but she had to face the truth, that's what the woman was. She didn't believe two strangers could become mother and daughter after twenty years, but she feared Miranda might abandon her, disappointed in her because of her weakness with Kevin. She sat down next to Louis and put her arm over the back of the chair. He wriggled forward, to avoid her touch.

"I'll send her a telegram," she said. Louis didn't look at her. He got up. "Lou," she said quickly, hearing Kevin in the hallway, polishing his boots. "I'm going to leave him. I don't know when, but I'll get money and a place and we'll get out. Honest. Then things will be really okay."

He stood near the door and looked at her, still stony faced.

"You mean it, Mum?"

"Yep, I mean it." She felt agitated. It had been growing inside her. This was the first time she'd spoken it out loud. It felt almost right.

Louis looked at her, unsmiling still, but his face softer, more childlike. She read the relief in his eyes. "They offered me the station paper run," he said slowly. "Robbo reckons it's worth fifteen bucks a week. I already get ten for the weekends. I'll give you all that, Mum." He looked at her, bright, hopeful, as he picked up a packet of chips and a fruit juice from the dresser and shoved them into his school bag. She smiled at him. "Will you feed the lizard for me, Mum?" His voice squeaked as he went out the door and he gave her an embarrassed grin.

The laboratory smell competed with the smell of the blood as the twenty students made neat cuts in the rats' heads and gently prodded into their brains, delicately cutting and laying pieces to one side as they searched and probed. Miranda loved anatomy, the combination of a technical and intellectual challenge. Of all her subjects, it was the only one in which she still felt her old confidence. But she reminded herself that a credit or a distinction in anatomy would do her no good if she failed everything else. Every time she thought of her marks, particularly biochemistry, she had a feeling of panic, almost disbelief that it could be happening to her. She thought of Geoff's words: "You're passing, maybe just, but you're passing. A few more months and you'll be right." Dr Stone not only haunted her mind, but seemed to lurk in corridors, waiting to catch her. "Well, Miss Darnley, all these problems, eh?" his words making a mockery of Geoff's reassurances.

She looked at her rat's face, which she had managed to keep intact. His eyes were open, staring, but he had a sweet face that reminded her of the naive country mouse in a book of *Aesop's Fables* which she had borrowed week after week from the school library when she had first learnt to read. In dissection, even with frogs or mice, she liked to remember that it was an animal she was working on, something which had been alive and breathing. She remembered when she had worked for the old vet at Uwalla and the great tenderness with which he had fulfilled his council contract for destroying strays. "You poor old thing," he'd say. "Geez, I'm glad I only have to do this side of it. Them dog police are the real mongrels."

She felt a pang at the thought of Uwalla. Logically, she understood them not ringing this morning, but the disappointment ate away at her, as if she were coming adrift, being separated, slowly, painfully and inevitably from her family. Two mothers, one not wanting her, the other one not able to ring her, even on her birthday.

She finished the anatomy exercise and left the lab. Walking through the university, past the banks of jasmine, reminded her again it was her birthday. "Out just in time," her mother had always said. She decided she had better get sensible. Patrick was taking her out and if her family didn't contact her it wasn't really that bad—after all, she reminded herself, she was twenty. She wasn't a five-year-old, she wasn't living at home. She was independent, free and she couldn't spend her life wanting something she couldn't have and was too old for anyway. When she walked in the front door of the house she was feeling strong, grown up and eminently sensible.

"Happy birthday, happy birthday, happy birthday." A swollen Linda danced up the hall, Hazel following her. Linda handed Miranda a telegram. "Happy birthday. Love Mum and the kids." Miranda promptly burst into tears.

"Look what I gotcha." Linda pushed Miranda excitedly into the kitchen, where an elegant "Chez Sleeze" shopping bag lay on the table. "I know you'll say it's not your colour and you can change it, but you've got to try it on first. You've got to, you've got to."

"You must keep it," drawled Hazel, as she held the ruffled, pink silk shirt in front of Miranda. "I know you won't wear pink, but that's only because you don't know what pink to buy. This one, my darling, is pure pink, your pink. Linda, get her a mirror before she has a nervous breakdown."

Clutching her telegram, Miranda let them lead her upstairs. The blouse, she admitted reluctantly, was exactly the colour she should have been wearing all her life. Hazel got out a voluminous dark grey skirt and made her put it on. She also found a wide elastic belt with a jade buckle and then made Miranda lean over the ironing board while she ironed her hair.

"My neck's hurting," complained Miranda as she leant with her hair spread over the board.

"Well that's what you get for wearing your hair in a pony tail," scolded Hazel. "You should use clips, not a rubber band. It's only because you've got such lovely, strong hair that it's survived." She sprayed her neck with Chanel cologne and Miranda shivered.

When Patrick came in, they finally let her stand up and she caught sight of herself in the mirror, looking like someone she'd never imagined she could be. She smiled at her reflection, then walked downstairs and met him in the front hall.

"You look fantastic. Beautiful," he said. He put his hands on her wide belt. He'd last seen her white-faced and distraught at nine o'clock, waiting for the phone call from her mother. "How do you feel?"

"Like a virgin bride," she said, and laughed.

Corpran had refused to extend the deadline for completion of the digital terrain model. Even working the computer triple shifts, the model would not be finished on the due date. Virginia had been sitting in a meeting for two hours with Corpran's chief engineer, Julian Hill, her secretary, Di, by her side. She had marshalled arguments for the extension of the contract. Corpran had been late with the initial contract. Corpran had not provided the information specified in the contract. Corpran, on two occasions, had provided the wrong information. Virginia gave facts, figures and proof, but with as many gracious concessions to the Corpran executives as possible. All she asked was that they did not invoke the penalty clauses.

Julian Hill sat across the big boardroom table as she presented her case, his face betraying no emotion. Four times, Corpran's new interior designer came in, waved apologetically in Virginia's direction and asked Julian what he wanted done with the mini rainforest he was assembling on the executive floor. Julian listened with close, detailed attention and replied soothingly. When Virginia began to speak again, he closed his eyes. When the clock on the conference room wall reached five, he closed his eyes permanently and Virginia decided it was time to wind up.

"Julian," she said persuasively. "I've given you all this in writing. I've been absolutely scrupulous about fulfilling the contract. I suspect the law is on my side, but your legal guns are a lot bigger than mine. Could you tell me, do you intend to impose the penalty clause?"

Julian yawned, shuffled his papers together and stood up. "I'll have to consider the facts, Virginia."

Virginia's tone took on an icy edge. "You asked me here to present the facts, so we could come to an agreement." The interior decorator came back into the room.

"Please excuse me a minute," said Julian. He turned to the designer who was holding out a sketch. "I know those palms look fabulous there, but I want them in my office, up against the skyline, to frame the view." He turned to follow the designer out.

"Julian, I want an answer."

"I'll have to read all this. I'll let you know tomorrow. Goodnight, Virginia. Thanks for coming in."

Virginia turned to Di as he disappeared. "I have a very bad headache and I think I might be going crazy. What was going on there?"

"He had the hots for the designer. Couldn't wait to get him up to the executive suite."

"Julian Hill's not gay, is he?"

Di looked at her pityingly. "You didn't know?"

Virginia shook her head and walked to the lift. "I didn't know there were gay engineers." She pressed the button.

"You should have sent Andrew along," said Di.

Virginia felt exhausted. "He's not gay is he?"

"He's in love with you," explained Di patiently. "But he looks cute."

Virginia felt her head throbbing. She couldn't take much more of this. The actual work was child's play compared to the politics of the negotiation. She began to feel dizzy as she stepped out of the lift and promptly threw up into one of the giant palms intended for Julian Hall's office.

"Spot on," she remarked to Di.

Charlie could not remember when he'd ever worked like this before. He'd painted the living room and had begun stripping back the banisters. The madonnas all had their first coat of paint and the only hitch was that they needed a week to dry in the humid, late winter weather. Each night, he lined them up to amuse Virginia. Last night, they'd eaten at the big dining table surrounded by a great circle of madonnas. At the weekend, he'd scattered them through the front garden, like gnomes. With the first coat complete, they'd formed a scrum on the kitchen floor.

"I think it's very irreverent the way you treat them," Virginia
had said.

"I think the whole idea's highly irreverent," said Charlie. "And they're gaining possession of my mind. I don't like the idea of sending them back. No one to play with." Tonight, he'd placed one on each side of every tread of the stairs.

But his excitement and energy was really coming from his painting. He was half way through a wonderful, lush, riotous still life which Virginia seized upon every evening when she got home. Every night, it seemed perfect, the next night, even better. But she was less enthusiastic about his other work, taken from her school photo, when she had been tennis team captain, sitting racquet crossed with the vice captain, a sign at their feet, "Allendale Girls Grammar. Junior tennis. 1965". This afternoon, he had begun to paint the figure in the foreground, a girl with a double-handed backhand, impressionist, quite different from the carefully posed and detailed team. She had flying red hair, strong legs and concentration. He heard the car come up the drive and found himself feeling nervous about how Virginia would react.

She walked in in a foul mood. "They wouldn't tell me whether they'll enforce the penalty clause."

"They'll let you know when they're ready. They always take time to decide."

"So whose side are you on?" she said aggressively. Charlie knew better than to reply. She hadn't yet noticed the still life. She was staring at the tennis painting.

"Is that supposed to be me?"

"In a way, I suppose. Yes, it's got red hair, your energy." Her face froze and saying nothing, she walked up the stairs.

"Some people would be flattered," he called after her.

She turned, furious. "Well, I regard it as an invasion of my privacy. The least you could do would be to ask me." She looked down at the madonnas on the stairs, paused for a moment and then viciously kicked at one, sending it toppling over the one below, so the whole line collapsed, stair by stair, madonna by madonna, almost in slow motion, as Charlie watched horrified till they crashed onto the sunroom floor. She gave a short scream and ran up the stairs.

Charlie stood in a white hot rage, curbing his instinct to run after her and thump her. Slowly, just in control, he picked up the madonnas. Two were shattered completely but the rest just required a bit of filling. He turned them over gently in his hands, feeling for chips or scratches. "Miraculous," he said softly, then laughed. He looked at them tenderly, almost reverently as he examined the damage. "I won't ever let her near you again," he said to one whose foot was missing. He often talked to them as he painted them and in a strange way, he enjoyed the work. It was simple, almost mechanical, but he knew, when he got to the faces, he'd know them all well enough to be able to give some of them a hint of a smile, others a Mona Lisa look, some slightly sour and disapproving. All the same, all a bit different. He placed the damaged ones to one side and stood looking at the tennis picture. He had known Virginia was sensitive about it—he could tell that, even when he was painting from the photo. There was something she didn't want to remember, or even want him to remember, but he knew, just as surely, to have got her permission would have killed the picture. But she should like it, be proud of it. He walked slowly up the darkened stair, along the black upstairs hallway and into her room.

The street lights dimly backlit the great branches of the jacaranda which stood out bleakly against the dark sky. But the faint light from the window didn't extend to the bed, where he knew she would be, huddled under the covers, cold as ice. He sat on the bed and gently stroked her motionless form.

"Ginny," he said softly. "It's OK, Ginny."

She wasn't crying but her face was still wet and he moved under the blankets and held her. Slowly, she put her arms round him. "Charlie. It's my baby's birthday today. She's twenty. It's such a long time time but when I saw your painting, it felt like it happened this morning. It's been with me all day. Coming home here, seeing that made it so much worse."

He sighed and stroked her hair.

"Charlie," she said hesitantly after they had lain there in silence for a few minutes. She took his hand. "I've done a terrible thing."

"Kicking madonnas?"

"Worse."

"What?"

She was silent again and when she spoke, her voice was high, strained. "My baby...my girl...my daughter wants to meet me. The hospital social worker contacted me and I refused. She probably thinks I don't love her."

She felt his body stiffen. "Reasonable conclusion."

"It's not!" she said fiercely. "I can't go through it all again. I can't stand it again. I want to forget it."

His anger came back and he pulled roughly away from her, stood up and turned on the light. Virginia winced, looking at him fearfully as he stood there in the bright light. He looked at her with a contempt she almost couldn't bear, but she held his gaze.

"Just because you want to forget doesn't mean you can," he said brutally. "It doesn't mean because you want something that you're entitled or due. Some things are painful and we can't get rid of the pain. It's there, it eats into us, it's part of us." He leaned over and rested his hands on the bed. "But if we get the one in a million chance to go back, to make it right, there's something pretty gutless about us if we simper around saying 'I can't, I can't. I'm too sensitive, I'm too fragile.' And that's exactly what you're doing, Virginia." He walked out and slammed the door behind him. She lay there in the blazing light, remembering the finality in his use of her full name. Her jaw set stubbornly, her teeth clenched, she reached over, turned out the light and then pulled the cold sheet over her head. She lay—frozen, stubborn, her anger just containing her despair.

·Chapter Seven·

The cappuccino machine Hazel had bought a month ago had stopped making coffee after Linda filled it with instant coffee. However, the milk frothing attachment continued to work. Miranda sat at the kitchen table with a mug of the frothed milk, trying to cram for biochemistry. She began to feel as if the milk was coating her brain, making it impermeable. She knew she was spending too much time with Patrick, with Linda, with Hazel, too much time preoccupied by her own thoughts, agonising over her studies, but unable to start working. Even when she did study, she felt slow and inefficient. Hazel maintained it happened to everyone over twenty. Linda thought Miranda worked too hard. Patrick told her not to worry so much.

Miranda's mind spun obsessively round and round her anxieties: not being able to go home to Uwalla, the rejection by her real mother, her inability to decide whether to sleep with Patrick, her paralysing insecurity about how he really felt about her. She sat, staring into space, trying to get her mind on to the book in front of her. When the phone rang, she felt relieved.

"Hullo, Miranda here."

"Hi, how are you?" The voice was warm, a hint of a laugh.

"Who is it?" she asked.

"You don't recognise my voice?"

"David." Feeling sick and panicky, she wriggled up onto the kitchen table, nervously pushing her thumb against the ragged, bitten nail of her middle finger. "What do you want?"

"I'm starting a special ed training course. I'm down once a week. Today's our first seminar. I'd like to see you."

"Why?" Her tone became hostile.

"Unfinished business, Miranda."

"Not for me."

"I could tell when I saw you." His voice had assumed that tone of patient explanation teachers reserve for less capable students. "I know I still mean a lot to you...and you do to me."

Miranda tore the nail, not noticing how much it hurt. She clenched her first tightly. "I don't want to see you."

"C'mon." His voice took on a persuasive tone. "That's just because Linda's there, I know. We can meet on neutral territory. Miranda, we never even got started."

There was a hint of deliberation and weariness in his tone that told her he'd said this before, some other time, to someone else. She suddenly understood that what she had thought was their relationship, had simply been her illusion. She had adored him and wanted him. He'd been unattainable, somehow better than other men. With a sickening certainty, she realised she had been nothing more than a year twelve fling, unconsummated only because of her fear. She had endowed his compliance with a highmindedness it never had. All she'd had was a schoolgirl crush.

"Find some other school kid," she said furiously and put the phone down.

Part of her, a dream, had been ripped out. But her anger was turning against herself for being party to the deception. She could hear Linda and Hazel giggling in Linda's room upstairs and she gathered up her books and walked slowly down the hall, into her room. Feeling cold, she put on her big, old navy sweater. Hazel had told her it didn't suit her and she hadn't worn it for weeks, but now it felt comfortable and familiar. She looked in the mirror, saw her cold, pinched face. A wave of self disgust swept over her. She pulled her hair back angrily into a pony tail, knotting it through the rubber band, not caring that it hurt. Desperation and a sense of abandonment engulfed her as she hurriedly started tidying the room. She wanted Patrick, and then, childishly, her mother. She felt empty, a nagging pain, which had been there for a long time, just below the surface. Now it seemed be rising up, taking her over. Savagely, she kicked at a large pile of books that lay next to her desk.

"Mandy, come on, we're going." Linda came clattering down the stairs. "You ready?"

"Be out in a sec," she called out. She sat down on the bed, closed her eyes and breathed in and out, slowly and deliberately, six times. Then, not wanting to think, she jumped up, grabbed her bag and ran out the front door. Hazel and Linda were sitting in the front seat of Hazel's Citroen, both laughing, Hazel playfully shaking Linda. Miranda got into the back seat, pushing aside a mass of clothes, textbooks, cigarette cartons and the half bottle of brandy Hazel always carried. Hazel turned round to her.

"Half an hour's drive, she told me. Now she tells me we're going to the country. I'm not dressed for the northern spring." She rifled through her bag for a cigarette. "It's two hours, at least. You still want to come?"

"Please, Mandy, please come," said Linda. "It'll be so exciting. She's a healer."

"Cures pregnancy," remarked Hazel dryly.

"Yeah, I'm coming," said Miranda. "I can't study today anyway."

"Fight with the lad?" asked Hazel casually, starting the engine. "Lovers' tiff?"

"Not with Patrick," said Miranda lightly. She smiled at Hazel, aware she was forcing it from her contracted misery. Hazel never noticed, Miranda thought angrily. With Hazel, everything was cool. Sympathetic, funny, quick, but never too involved, always cutting you off when it really hurt. Don't get close, don't get involved, was Hazel's prescription for life.

"I'm cold," said Miranda. "Can we have the heater on?"

Hazel put the car into gear and roared off leaving a cloud of black smoke. She glanced back at it. "Give it a moment and we'll be burning in the furnaces of hell."

As Linda's pregnancy progressed she had become intensely preoccupied with her body. Now, as they drove out along Parramatta Road, past the glitzy car yards and then out on to the freeway, she was oblivious to her surroundings, lost in thinking about the changes occurring within her. Pregnancy had become part of her. She thought of herself as "Linda, pregnant" and felt sure the others saw her that way. When she'd left Uwalla, she felt a failure, but she was almost proud of the baby now. She felt smug when she walked down the street and people looked at her bulging stomach. She felt a sort of superiority, having a child when she was so young. "Only seventeen," she often thought to herself, glad she wouldn't be eighteen until after he was born. Phillip liked to feel the baby moving and she allowed him to put his hands on her stomach. Hazel said she found it "spooky", but Linda sensed a certain reserved jealousy in Miranda. She felt a mean satisfaction in that. For once she was first, for once, she was the special one. She'd even talked to her mother on the phone a few times, no longer as a rebellious adolescent, but as a coming equal. "Put your feet up when you can," Pauline instructed her. "Don't wear high heels. No tight pants and don't wash your hair too often." Linda wore tight jeans done up with a string of safety pins across the bulge, bounced round on four centimetre stilettos and washed her hair every day.

But the reminder of Uwalla that came from her conversations with Pauline also brought to mind the penalties of young pregnancy. These had been inculcated into her from an early age. In Glebe, in the city, young and pregnant was young and free, whereas in Uwalla, young and pregnant was getting fat and staying fat. Uwalla's young and pregnant was varicose veins, tight pot bellies, flattened breasts, marbled flesh, stretch marks. Her own pink stretch marks now extended from her thighs over her hips, "Over my bikini!" she'd told Dr Johns, who'd smiled in a motherly way and patted her head.

"I can't promise you they'll go away, but they will fade."

In desperation, after Dr John's dismissive laughter, she'd gone to the local healing centre to see if naturopathy, acupuncture or massage would take away the horrid pink stripes. She'd been seen by a serious young man. "Remedial masseur," he told her. "Bach remedies too." He liked her pregnant earth-mother body. She, in turn, liked the attention, the creams, the ointments and the tinctures he prescribed, that had to be taken at special times every day, according to the phases of the moon. She never took them, but she liked to talk about them. As the young man massaged her with a strange, sweet smelling oil and enthused over her expanding belly, she worried about whether he knew how really important it was that the stretch marks be made to disappear. But as the massages progressed, and she felt more familiar with him, she began to tell him the Uwalla stories: "Mum says the first is agony . . . Mrs Robbins had to get sewn up, thirty stitches. All inside. The doctor got it all back to front. Your muscles split, right from here," pointing to her cleavage, "right down here," pointing at her pubis.

He laughed as if she was making a joke and other people at the healing centre told her to make positive affirmations, to decode her mind, to give the baby instruction in painless birth. Linda finally realised they'd never understand why Mrs Robbins had screamed so hysterically in the labour ward. Attentive, almost obsessive about her pregnancy, they nevertheless persisted in seeing stretch marks as a badge of honour. She felt they were a bit silly in the same sort of way Hazel sometimes was. But when someone mentioned a healer past Wiseman's Ferry who could cure everything, it seemed an easier option than the birth classes and breathing exercises Dr Johns kept advocating. She asked Hazel to drive her there and persuaded Miranda to come with them. Now, sitting in the sun, in the car, Miranda pretending to sleep in the back, Hazel singing along to the radio, she felt good. It must work, she told herself. It must work because she couldn't bear pain or stretch marks or sagging breasts. She wasn't at all sure about the baby, unable to imagine picking it up or changing nappies. She hastily dismissed the thought.

Hazel had turned off the main road and drove along a narrow dirt road, prettily bordered by trees and hedges, an occasional picturesque wooden farmhouse with a sign advertising home-grown vegetables, free-range eggs or local honey.

"I bet she's non-nuclear, home-grown, hand-crafted, vegetarian and herbal," said Hazel as they drove up the steep, unmade road to the healer's house. "Probably deeply spiritual too." She threw her cigarette out the window. "I wish this car didn't smoke so much. I wish I didn't smoke. I'm sure your healer will make me feel bad about it." She stopped the Citroen in front of the small farmhouse. The traditional rose-covered cottage was surrounded by an open verandah, with wind-chimes above a front door with delicate leadlight panels of birds and flowers. As Hazel switched off the engine, a small, pretty woman in jeans and a T-shirt came to the door, holding a small, dark, lively baby.

"What's her name?" Hazel asked Linda. "Or do we just call her Madam Blue Healer?"

"Don't be stupid, Haze. Her name's Alison," said Linda

crossly. "Just be nice to her. She really can cure stretch marks."

"Sure," said Hazel, getting out of the car and walking across to Alison. She flashed her a stunning smile. "Hi, I'm Hazel. This is Miranda and this is Linda." She put her arm round Linda. "She's the one with the stretch marks."

"Do come in," said Alison softly. She had a beneficent smile that never seemed to change and she led the way into the house which smelt overpoweringly of incense and flowers. It was small and dark and looked to Miranda like she'd always imagined a harem to be, with big Indian pillows spread around the floor and a large embroidered rug hanging on one wall. "I'll get you all some herb tea," said Alison softly. "It'll relax you, after your journey."

"I'll take the baby for you," said Miranda eagerly. The baby was small and neat, about nine months old, hanging onto its mother like a little koala, observing the world with dark, intense eyes, that focused momentarily on faces, then were coyly lowered. Miranda held out her arms and Alison passed the baby across to her.

"Sharna," she said. "Her father's Indian."

Miranda sat down on a cushion and held the baby in front of her on her knees. The child looked into her face, serious and intent. Suddenly, she smiled and Miranda smiled back. The child made a grab for Miranda's hair, grunting with satisfaction as she caught a few strands.

"She's wet," Miranda called out to Alison. "Do you want me to change her?"

"The nappies are in the bedroom," called back Alison. "And dry pants if she needs them." As Miranda got up, the baby snuggled against her, one hand on her breast, its solid little legs clasped around her hip. The bedroom obviously served both mother and baby and Miranda gently laid the baby down on the double bed and shook it out of its trousers. She playfully poked its stomach as she undid the safety pin and was rewarded with a wide smile. Nappy off, the baby kicked joyfully then rolled onto her stomach and crawled away, looking flirtatiously back at Miranda. Miranda grabbed her and with a deft movement, put her on her back again, quickly pinning on the new nappy. She tickled the baby gently under the arms then picked her up, smelling the fresh, baby smell, remembering Kerry and Lou.

"Which of your friends is going to be your labour partner?" Alison asked Linda as Miranda came back into the room with the baby.

"I'm her sister," said Miranda automatically.

"Hazel's coming into hospital with me," said Linda, checking Miranda's reaction with a sideways glance. "They only let you have one person," she added quickly, seeing the hurt on Miranda's face. "And Mandy will probably still be doing exams."

"Probably," said Miranda hoarsely. She'd noticed before that Linda had always avoided discussing the birth with her. She stroked the baby's soft, fine hair. "She's a lovely baby," she said to Alison. "Very calm."

Alison smiled at her enthusiastically. "We're together all the time. I feed her when she wants and she sleeps with me. Lots of massage and skin contact." She looked at Linda. "It's called the continuum concept. It really cements the mother-child relationship."

"I bet it does," said Hazel, horrified.

Linda looked doubtful. "Don't you get sick of it?" She looked dubiously at Sharna, pulling on Miranda's hair.

"Oh no. I decided when I was pregnant. You know how they feel part of you. You keep that lovely closeness this way."

Linda placed her hands over her stomach. Even through her sweatshirt she could feel her protruding navel. In some way, she felt attached to whatever was in there, but she wanted her body to be her own again. Miranda sat down on the big cushion and the baby wriggled out of her arms and crawled across to Alison. Like a little puppy, she wriggled up under Alison's T-shirt, searching for her breast, snuffling with an excitement Linda found obscene. Alison lay back on the cushion and bared her breast, the nipple dark, swollen with milk.

Linda was quite sure she didn't want a baby.

They had left Alison, directing energy through quartz crystals at Linda's stretch marks. As Alison launched into a discussion on the difference between the healing properties of various crystals, Hazel's eyes had begun to glaze over and she'd nodded to Miranda, who'd scooped up the baby and offered to take her for a walk.

"Too much eye contact takes it out of me," said Hazel, as they walked outside. "All those caring, sharing, loving vibrations."

"It makes you think though," said Miranda, snuggling the baby against her. "She really is the calmest baby."

"Probably bored out of its tiny mind," said Hazel as they started walking down the hill through a bank of she-oaks. "Not that I'd know. Not familiar with the baby of the species." She turned and looked at Miranda. "Linda would be much better off having you with her when she has this kid."

"She's made up her mind to have you,' said Miranda looking down the hill to the creek. "Her choice."

"It's only because I won't be doing exams."

They were half way down the hill, overlooking the valley. It was green and lush, hazy from the late afternoon cold. The baby snuggled against Miranda as a gust of wind came down on them and she looked at Miranda in wide-eyed surprise as if she'd created it. Miranda stroked the soft cheek with her finger, immersing herself in the child, deciding not to think about Linda's rejection.

"What do you mean you're not doing exams? Is social work all assessments now?" she asked Hazel, picking her way down the rocky path.

"I'm a drop-out," said Hazel. "I stopped going, last week; got bored. Decided to get Phillip to take me seriously."

"Does he?"

They reached the creek at the bottom of the hill. It flowed prettily over the rocks, overhung by willows, but the bank was slippery with mud and the grass was covered with cow pats. Hazel pulled herself up into the fork of a willow and Miranda leaned up against the trunk.

"He's confused," said Hazel. "Doesn't admit it. Doesn't pay to be confused when you're in the army. You know, you might kill the wrong people." She felt for her cigarettes and frowned when she realised she'd left them in the car. "He used to think I was just a lot of one night stands strung together. Now he wants to marry me. I couldn't handle that, but I am crazy about him."

"It's so complicated," said Miranda dreamily. "I always thought you just grew up, fell in love, got married."

Hazel laughed. "Why on earth did you think that? Marriage is terrible."

"Not always," said Miranda uncertainly.

"I know mine would turn out like my parents'," said Hazel.

"Divorced?"

"More the mess before. Mummy got to the stage where she had to drink so much to get herself to a party that she blacked out the moment she got there. Then she had to take so many pills to get on to the tennis court that she couldn't swing a racquet. That's when Daddy left. It was a sensible arrangement. She wanted to be left alone. He was sick of it. Then, it was fights and hassles and shouting." Hazel smiled her beautiful smile at Miranda.

"We had all that too," said Miranda, stroking the baby's head. "But I've always thought I'd make mine different. I wouldn't let all that happen."

"You might be OK with Patrick," said Hazel softly, "if you ever let him near you."

"I might be,' said Miranda. "But I mightn't be. I mean that's the confusing part. You can't tell in advance."

There was a clap of thunder and they looked at the sky, which had turned almost black.

"Going to rain," said Hazel, jumping down from the tree as the first drops splattered down.

Miranda looked up the hill which rose above them, steep and slippery. "How will we keep the baby dry?" she asked anxiously.

"Stick her up your jumper," said Hazel, climbing the bank and reaching her hand down for Miranda. The rain started to pour down and Miranda doubtfully put the baby under her jumper, took Hazel's hand and climbed the bank. They began to run awkwardly up the hill, the rain soaking them, the baby laughing and gurgling as it bounced against Miranda in the dark warmth of her sweater.

Hazel slipped and rose from the muddy ground, her hands and knees covered with mud, her wet hair lying in streaks across her face. She put her face up to the rain, letting it pelt down on it. She looked at Miranda and grinned at the writhing, gurgling bulge under her sweater.

Miranda laughed, feeling her boots squelching with water. She linked her arm into Hazel's to get up the last steep part of the hill. They reached the top and stood for a moment, panting, laughing, arms round each other, faces to the rain. "Maybe we don't have to get married or get through uni. Maybe we should come and live out here," said Miranda, jiggling the baby.

"Don't panic, we're organic, but I think I'd miss my fags," chanted Hazel. "Let's get back and bludge a nice cup of herbal tea."

"Why do you keep your arms folded when I hug you?" asked Charlie. He and Virginia were standing in front of the big French windows in the form al lounge room. Most of the room was covered with painters' drapes, making it look dead and forlorn. Charlie had found her there, after the rain had stopped, still staring at the rain-soaked garden, the wet, lush, dripping greenery.

"I'm cold," said Virginia, not moving in his arms.

"This doesn't exactly warm me either," said Charlie. "But the theory is, that if you press up against the hugger, there's an exchange of warmth between hugger and huggee."

"You know, I don't think you should use that bright pink on their cloaks," said Virginia disengaging herself and looking at the conga line of Madonnas coming from the kitchen. "It makes them look tarty."

"Maybe I'm in need of tarts," said Charlie. "I hate to get personal, Ginny, but are we still having a sexual relationship?"

"Oh Christ, Charlie!" She turned and faced him, her fury cold and contained. "Is that all you think about?"

"Practically all," said Charlie. "It's become a pressing need on account of I'm not getting it."

"Well that's not my problem."

"It's your fault!"

"You think I'm just here for you, when you want. Stuff you, Charlie, I'm just keeping myself together."

"And not particularly well."

"What does that mean?" she asked furiously.

"It means I can hear you when you wake screaming in the night. It means I can hear you when you get up at five in the morning and vomit. It means I hide the knives and check the gas and make sure the drug cupboard is locked and there aren't hoses in the garage."

"Don't be melodramatic."

"I'm not a fool, Virginia. I can see all the signs." His voice rose. "Fuck it, I love you. And I know you love me. But I tell you, you do something about that child of yours, you contact that social worker because I'm not sticking round to see the alternative ending."

She stood by the old velvet sofa, which was covered by a drop sheet. She crumpled down into its folds. "Don't push me, Charlie, don't push me." Her voice was hard, but she looked small and childlike.

He softened and went and sat on the edge of the sofa, his hand on her hair. "Ginny, you've got to do something. You've just got to. I'll help you. You know that."

She moved away from him, along the sofa, swallowed up in the dust cover. Her voice, though high, was strong and hard. "I had that baby on my own, Charlie. I had no one. Not a soul. And I'll do this on my own if you don't mind."

He got up and stood in front of her, leaning over her, his hands resting on the back of the couch. Almost menacing, he looked down at her. "Your problem is that you do every bloody thing on your own. You don't know how to let anyone help you. I think you better decide whether you're having this relationship on your own or whether you'd like to have it with me." For a moment, his anger was so fierce that she was afraid he was going to hit her. He looked at her, trying to get something from her. She wouldn't give. He straightened up and walked through into the big, cold lonely dining room with its crystal chandelier and the long, bare cedar table. He walked out into the kitchen and with all his might, slammed the connecting door. The line of madonnas shook slightly.

Pauline had been in a rage all day, all the more vicious because it was contained. She'd lain awake most of the night, wondering how she'd leave Kevin, how she'd support the kids, doing sums in her head, alternately elated at the thought of freedom, then terrified by what she was contemplating. By early morning, her back was giving her hell and, unable to sleep, she sat at the kitchen table, watching the day dawn, blustery and cheerless. As the family rose after their night's sleep, she'd felt a cold anger against them all. Then, once the kids had gone to school and Kevin had driven off, her rage had risen to a bitter fury, intensified because there was no one to vent it on.

She found herself uselessly scraping the vacuum cleaner back and forth across the worn carpet, viciously stuffing fluff balls into the head, furiously cursing as they dropped out back onto the floor again. By the time the kids came home from school her anger was concentrated against them. They knew her mood and adopted a sullen, compliant silence, hoping to avoid the brunt of it. She slapped Kerry, banged saucepans, yelled at Natalie and made her scrub the bathroom. The more she let it out, the more it built within her, the more justified she felt.

"Get your shoes on," she said furiously to Lou. "We're going to Franklins."

"Why don't we wait till Roy comes?" he whined.

"Don't give me cheek." She didn't tell him Roy was away for three days. The thought of Roy had been forlornly in her mind all day.

"Mum, I finished the bathroom," said Natalie timidly. "Can I go to training now?"

"No!" yelled Pauline. "I'm going out. You gotta cook tea."

"Mum, the trials . . ."

"I tell you, Natalie, I'm sick of this bloody swimming. You do your fair share around the house or I'll cut it out altogether."

The high shelves of the supermarket, stacked precipitously with tins, bottles and cartons crowded in on her. When she saw Lou looking longingly at a two-dollar cricket ball, she pointed out the split in its seam with savage satisfaction. But she softened momentarily and put a cheap packet of chocolate biscuits into the trolley. By the time she got to the breakfast cereals, she again felt a deep resentment, this time towards a slow-moving pensioner blocking her way with a trolley containing a single packet of Jatz. The kids hated Corn Flakes, but she reasoned that if they ate less cereal, she'd at least save some money. She caught Lou's scared look of reproach and realised, almost disappointed, that the energy of her anger was draining away. When she came to the check-out, the bill came to five dollars more than she had. She made Lou take back the Corn Flakes and a packet of peas and paid the check-out girl, making a joke of her poverty, but remembering how Roy sometimes gave her an extra five or ten dollars when he took her shopping. "Nothing," she thought bitterly, "to what Kevin spends at the pub," somehow damning both Roy and Kevin with the same thought.

Outside the supermarket, they packed the groceries into the flimsy plastic bags, fighting the gusts of wind. Pauline picked up three heavy bags in each hand. With studied martyrdom, she waited for Lou to get the rest.

"Mum, we can't carry these all the way home. They're too heavy. They'll burst." She set off ahead of him. He grabbed a trolley and loaded the remaining bags into it. On the front was a sign, "Not to be removed from supermarket premises".

They walked side by side, down the road by the railway. On the other side of the railway was the river, the grids of the oyster leases stretching unevenly out into the water, the old wooden shacks perched on patches of cleared land on the steep, thickly wooded banks, tiny boatsheds and wharves dotted along the edge of the river. Lou looked longingly at the fisherman in the dinghy out in the middle of the current, as he struggled with the cumbersome trolley along the unmade footpath. He knew Pauline was watching him with grim triumph.

"That bag's ripping," he told her, satisfied.

She gathered it in, then, in an admission of defeat, hoisted them all into his trolley. Seeing the scout hall ahead, she turned to him. "Let's have a breather."

As they sat on the warm concrete steps of the scout hall, her mood relaxed, but his became more sullen. Suddenly, he brought his hand down over a tiny lizard which had emerged from the patch of weed at the bottom of the steps. "Got ya!"

"Lou, what ya doing?"

"I'll feed him to Bluey."

"No you don't, Lou.'

"Lizards eat lizards."

"Yeah well, not in my house, they don't. You can give him some of the chocolate bikkies. He likes chocolate."

Lou held the tiny lizard in the palm of his hand. "Wild prey. It'd be better for him."

"He's not a wild lizard any more, you tamed him." She was placatory now.

"He'd still like to eat it."

They bickered like kids until Lou tipped his hand and released the little lizard. Then, he got up, and staring into the dirt at his feet, he mumbled, "Mum, are we still leaving Dad?"

"Yes, son."

"When?" His voice was sullen again.

"When I got the cash. I got a hundred put by. I reckon I'll need five hundred." Pauline's voice had a note of pride. The hundred dollars was a considerable achievement.

"It'll take months," said Lou gloomily. His face was pink and slightly swollen, as if he had been crying. "Dad hates me, Mum, he hates me. He hates you and he hates Mandy. He hates me so much I get scared." Pauline looked at him, not knowing what so say. She walked over to him and put her arm over his shoulders. She couldn't give him an answer, but for once, he didn't squirm away.

She started pushing the trolley. "Come on, son, let's get this damn stupid thing home."

"Hey! hey! You! You! Get offa my cloud! Hey! hey! You get offa my cloud! Don't hang around 'cause two's a crowd on my cloud babe." The Rolling Stones blared out over the "Festival of the Sixties" being celebrated in Glebe Town Hall, packed with couples celebrating the rock and roll of their babyhood. They were dressed in black jumpers and jeans, almost indistinguishable from their everyday clothes. A few girls wore black miniskirts and some had the teased, beehive hairdos of the sixties. Miranda, influenced by her mother's stories of the golden years of Elvis, wore her pink silk blouse and a full skirt, ballooned out by Hazel's genuine rope petticoat. Patrick was watching her, in the same way she used to see the boys at school dances watching Linda. She was aware of other men looking at her too and she felt free, exuberantly female, knowing she stood out from the crowd and liking it. Her full skirt swirled around her as she danced. Slowly, the band geared up to "When a man loves a woman", sensuous, so ridden with emotion that it became a parody. The crowd cheered derisively and Miranda wound her arms around Patrick's neck and pressed against him. As the lights dimmed, she kissed him. "I want to make love to you tonight," she said softly. He didn't reply, but began dancing her towards the edge of the hall, through the slowly swaying crowd. As the last bars of the song ground out, they danced past the bouncers at the door, onto the steps of the Town Hall. The hooting and laughter of the crowd spilled out into the quiet of the street. The night was warm, almost sultry and Miranda looked up at the sky. Only a few stars showed through the clouds. They stood hand in hand. "We're not going back in?" she asked Patrick.

He raised his eyebrows. "You've got to be kidding." He took her hand and led her down the steps.

Her room was lit by a small candle and the red glow of the single-bar radiator. Miranda lay back on the bed, her bare feet against Patrick's chest. He'd taken off her stockings and was gently stroking her foot, sliding his hands down her leg. He kissed her toe.

"Patrick, I'm a virgin, you know."

"Nobody's perfect, Miranda." Patrick leaned down, kissing her legs. "Don't worry, I'm not fussy."

He undid her skirt. "Why do you keep telling me that?" he asked seriously.

She wriggled out of her pink silk blouse and tossed it on the floor and lay against him, naked, shivering with cold in the narrow bed. He lay beside her, stroking her, caressing her gently.

"Virginity's not a social disgrace, you know."

"It's very uncool though. Haze is always teasing me."

"She's desperately jealous."

"She thinks I'm a prude."

"Are you?"

"No." She snuggled up against him. "I'm not. And I don't want you to think so."

"I don't." He kissed her, wanting her desperately. "I want you, Miranda. I really love you."

"I love you too, Patrick." She felt it too, realising it was different from when she'd said it to David. With him, it had been an attempt to extricate herself from the guilt she'd felt about their relationship, an attempt to make it mean something. Loving Patrick was just loving Patrick.

She snuggled down into the bed, warmed and wanting. He began to kiss her and she knew she wanted him as much as he wanted her. She felt the depth of her passion. She felt her neediness and her desire for him. She looked in his eyes, to reassure herself that he loved her. As they made love, her own abandonment and passion surprised her, and she sensed it surprised him too. She indulged herself more, wanting and finally fulfilled. She lay against him, content, secure, her arms twined around him as they drifted to sleep.

She half woke at four in the morning. The candle had burned out and the radiator had overheated the room. The streetlight outside lit the room faintly and Miranda looked at Patrick's face and kissed him, wanting to arouse him in spite of the tired aching of her body. He snored lightly and she was suddenly frightened by the way his sleep separated them. "I love you," she whispered at him desperately. "I love you."

He groaned and kissed her on the mouth, his tongue exploring hers, his arms tighter around her. Then suddenly, he lay back, fast asleep, and turned his back on her in the little bed. She pressed against him, wanting him, even more frightened, needing to feel him embracing her. But he didn't move and she felt rejected. Her heart pounded, her fear swamping her with bitter disappointment. Knowing she wouldn't sleep now, she got out of bed, put on her old blue sweater and a pair of knickers. She went out to the kitchen and frothed up milk in the cappuccino machine. She sat at the kitchen table, not understanding how her loneliness could have replaced the fullness and confidence she'd felt before.

She went back into the bedroom. Patrick had spread himself out, taking up her whole bed. She sat in front of her desk and turned on the lamp, looking round the room, waiting for him to wake.

She saw the green album on her bookshelf and thought back over the way her mother had given it to her; a double-edged sword—gift and rejection. Her thoughts turned to the night Patrick made her look at it; how he'd made her ring the hospital, how she'd been bursting with hope, then the horrible reality of Petunia's phone call. Angry, she pulled the album down from the shelf, feeling that her desire to know her real mother, the wanting and needing had to be expunged. She opened the album and looked at the first page, the hospital photo, her mother's amateurish lettering. She turned the page and saw the flower, pressed under the plastic, the notice written by her mother, "From cot in hospital", the little card, "3 hrs. Lactogen." She peeled back the plastic sheet and ran her finger over the flower. As she pressed it, it wrinkled and she pulled off the fragile stalk. She pushed one of the petals with her finger, grinding it into the page, tears at the back of her eyes, but satisfied by the destruction. The flower stuck to the page and she began to prise it off with her fingernail, determined to wreck it.

"What are you doing?" She turned, guiltily, to see Patrick sitting up in bed, hair tousled, eyes heavy with sleep. She shut the album.

"Nothing," she said forlornly. He looked at her. She was white faced, pinched looking, as if she was about to cry. He got quickly out of bed and came over to her. His nakedness, last night so familiar to her, now embarrassed her. But at the same time she desperately wanted him to take the loneliness away.

He put his arms round her. "Hey, Miranda." She relaxed against him and took his hand. He stroked her hair and kissed the top of her head. Seeing the album on the desk, he opened it, saw the pulled-back plastic sheet, the half-destroyed flower.

He tried to smooth down the plastic sheet, but it caught and wrinkled on the hospital card. He picked up the card off the page and unthinkingly turned it over. On the back was written, "Virginia Nathan. Next of kin phone-JX 3825." He looked at Miranda. She stared at the card, and then looked at him. She got up and gently put her arms round him, aware of her heart pounding hard.

"Patrick, it must be her, it must be her. That's my mother." She picked up the card.

"What are you going to do about it?"

"It'll be all right this time," she said breathlessly. "I'll find her and it won't be like an agency. I'm sure it's meant to happen. Petunia was so nice and everything, but it never felt right. This time'll be different."

He laughed with her, lifted by her happiness. She kissed him, first lightly, then passionately, then pulled him down on to the bed. She rocked herself against him and kissed him again. She looked at him tenderly. "I really want you."

"I want you too."

·Chapter Eight·

Linda clattered down the stairs from the bathroom, her high-heeled slippers clipping against each step. "Miranda slept with Patrick! She slept with Patrick!" she announced triumphantly as she came into the kitchen.

"Linda!" Hazel's admonishing drawl came clearly through the thin partition which separated Miranda's room from the kitchen.

"She did so!"

Patrick groped for his shoe under the bed and finding it, threw it at the wall. The voices in the kitchen stopped and Miranda collapsed against Patrick, her laughter muffled under the bedclothes.

"True or false?" Phillip's voice boomed through the partition.

"True!" screamed Patrick and Miranda in unison.

"I told you so," Linda proclaimed self-righteously.

She poked her head round the door. "Do you want a cup of tea?"

"Yes please," said Patrick.

"I'll get it," said Linda. She looked at her sister's head resting on Patrick's bare chest. "Are you on the pill, Mandy?" she asked censoriously. Miranda turned and looked at her, Linda's ballooning nightdress emphasising her pregnant form. She tried to suppress her giggles and wriggled back under the bedclothes.

"You are a bitch," said Linda. She slammed the door and Miranda emerged from under the sheets.

"My room next time," said Patrick, stroking her hair. "This room's only for certified virgins." Miranda slapped him playfully and then kissed him on the mouth. He returned her kiss then pulled away from her.

116

"Don't tease me," she said pleadingly. "Don't tease me." He kissed her again.

Linda's stretch marks had grown steadily longer and pinker as her belly expanded and she became progressively disillusioned with natural medicine. Nevertheless, she retained the soothing services of the sympathetic young masseur although suspecting his interest in her pregnant body was some form of perversion. But after faithfully imbibing Alison's herbal infusions for two weeks and seeing the stretch marks creep steadily upwards, she dramatically tossed the herbal potions onto the small strip of barren earth between the cast iron fence and the front verandah. The result had been extraordinary. In a month, the bare strip had become covered with bamboo. "Rebirth, reincarnation or something," Hazel commented. "Just look at the stretch marks on that bamboo."

Hazel had ripped out some of the new growth to keep the letter box accessible. In the mornings, sunlight streamed through this strip to warm a small rectangle of the clammy tiles of the verandah.

Miranda sat in the strip of sunlight, towelling her damp hair. She swiped at the cat as he sniffed at the remains of her warm milk. He jumped away, then slunk back guiltily and started cleaning out the cup. Miranda scratched him forgivingly behind the ears. Her attention was absorbed by the writing pad resting on her knees. On it were a list of Nathans, initials, addresses and phone numbers, about half of them crossed off. She'd made the list from the phone book, while lying in bed with Patrick. She'd got up and begun making phone calls. At first, her actions were automatic, a spontaneous response to her discovery of the night before. But after a dozen phone calls, her bravado had suddenly deserted her. She had a shower and was now wondering how best to attack the remaining names. She moved her pen slowly down the list, looking doubtfully at each one. Maybe ringing up hadn't been such a good idea.

Music blared out from inside the house, but Miranda was oblivious to the rich complexity of the Bach fugue. Preoccupied by the list, she began numbering them. She counted the twelve that had been crossed off. Not one of them had even heard of

Virginia Nathan. When a woman had answered for the first time, Miranda had been almost too nervous to speak. "Are you Virginia Nathan?" she'd managed to blurt out, then, "Do you know her?", feeling so agitated that she'd almost been relieved to get "No" for an answer. Yet she had an underlying sense of excited confidence, convinced things would fall into place, filling the emptiness which ached inside her.

"Isn't this fantastic?" Patrick stepped out into the sunlight of the verandah, stretching out his arms.

"It'll be warm enough to swim soon," said Miranda, smiling up at him.

"The music, not the sun."

"You've got to remember we were brought up on Elvis: 'Jailhouse Rock' and the rest. 'Viva Las Vegas' is as sophisticated as you get in Uwalla."

"Philistine!" Patrick picked up the towel, dropped it over her head, wrapping the ends around her, pulling it tighter as she struggled to get free. Screaming with laughter, they rolled off the verandah, into the bamboo where Miranda finally struggled out of the towel. Breathless, she lay back against Patrick, squinting into the sun. She became aware of Geoff Harris staring down at her through the iron pickets of the fence.

"Hi," she said lamely.

"G'day Geoff," said Patrick with patently false enthusiasm, his arms wrapped round Miranda proprietorially.

"I was wondering if you wanted to revise that book today," said Geoff primly. "I'd have time to go over it with you." He pulled at his beard.

Miranda felt guilty at his hangdog look. "Thanks, but I'm going out."

"I thought you said you were still way behind in biochem?"

"I am."

Geoff looked at her pleadingly.

"But I can't study today."

"Oh," he said sadly. "See you round." He disappeared behind the bamboo. Miranda looked guiltily at Patrick.

"He's been so good to me."

Patrick kissed her neck. "He's an animal."

Miranda laughed, picked up the cat and pulled its tail.

"Sometimes I get this awful nightmare that I'll have to go and work for Valentino if I fail." she said. "But then I lose momentum and feel like a cat that wants to lie in the sun."

"You've got the makings of a fine vet," replied Patrick.

The Roger Quarnby Memorial Hospital for Incurables was fifteen kilometres inland from Uwalla, on the flat side of the river, and although the road was bordered by shallow lakes and marshes, it was dry and dusty. Roy's ute sped along it, churning up stones and dust at which Kip, tied in the back, was barking, straining at the rope, as if he wanted to leap on the cloud of dust and rip it to pieces.

"Can't you do something about that dog?" Pauline asked irritably.

"He can't help it," said Roy. "Got into the poison cupboard when he was a pup. Did something to his nerves." He paused, expecting a response from Pauline. Not receiving one, he went on. "Never been right in the head since. Seemed to set off the barking." He paused and looked sideways at Pauline. "I don't know why yer going for this job."

"Yeah, well like I told you, Roy, I don't have a whole lotta choice. There's no jobs in town. If I don't get a job, I can't leave Kevin and look after the kids properly."

"You can come and live with me." Pauline didn't answer and Roy swung into the hospital grounds, slowing the truck as he drove up the tree-lined driveway. He stopped in front of the large, single-storeyed weatherboard house, framed by a wide verandah, its iron roof glinting in the sun. The neat buffalo grass, too short and scorched by the summer sun, stretched out in front of it, intersected by two concrete paths which divided it into four equal triangles. In one of the triangles was a small swing and an iron climbing frame. In each of the others was a single garden seat, facing the squat, concrete wishing well in the centre.

"Grim, isn't it?" said Roy.

Pauline looked at him. "Listen, Roy, if you're going to start telling me how to run my life, I won't ever be living with you. I've had a gutful of that."

Kip barked wildly at Pauline as she got out of the truck. Roy leaned out the window. "I just think you'd be better off at home with the kids."

"And don't start telling me how to look after my kids!" She felt near tears.

"I always thought you were a terrific Mum," replied Roy sulkily.

"Yeah, well I'd heard you used to be a terrific husband to Shirley, like the break-up was all her fault, but just lately I been hearing a few other things," retorted Pauline angrily.

Roy looked furiously at Pauline. Then his face softened and he put out his hand to her. "Listen, I just want the best for you. I do love you, you know."

"OK, Roy." She tried to smile at him. "Thanks." But as she walked up to the hospital she could feel tension across her shoulders like an iron bar. As she walked into reception, a tall woman in white, with an old-fashioned nurse's veil, suddenly appeared from a doorway.

"I'm Matron Fowler. Come about the job, have you?"

Pauline nodded.

"I'll get sister to show you round the wards," said matron. "Then you can come back to my office for a chat."

A sister in a blue overall ushered Pauline into a ward. It was a big, sunfilled room with a line of cots along the wall. In each cot was a child. Some, Pauline noticed, were not really children, but child-sized. Some had clear, childish faces, others looked almost wizened. Each cot had a fresh, knitted pale blue blanket. There were bright posters on the wall and the mobiles hanging from the ceiling moved in the slight breeze. Pauline looked along the line of cots as one child made muttering noises, with a sudden gleam of another consciousness showing in its face.

"Are they very retarded?" asked Pauline softly.

"D ward," said the blue overall sister, as if that explained it.

Pauline gazed across the cots.

"They're all the same, all individuals," said the blue overall sister briskly as she led her through to another ward. Pauline looked down at a little baby who was sleeping. He had a strange shaped head and thickened fingers. She stroked his cheek, swamped by tender and maternal feelings. She squatted down, close to the children lying on mats on the sunlit floor, but the sister motioned to her and led her into matron's office. Pauline realised that she wanted the job very much, far more than a job in town, or a job with higher pay. She searched her mind frantically to find the words to explain to the matron that she could do it and do it well. Straight-backed and rigid, she sat in the armchair opposite the matron's desk. Nurse-like and efficient, Matron Fowler produced a form from her drawer and pushed it across to Pauline. Pauline started looking through it.

"Take it home with you, dear, and post it back," said the matron. "What I want to know now is whether you could do the job."

"I'm good with kids," said Pauline. It was the only thing that came to mind.

"They aren't really kids," matron replied. "This hospital is the end of the road for most of them. We try, but mostly they don't get much past what they are."

"I could cope with that," said Pauline. "I've had five babies." She could feel the tension down her back and wished she could think of something more convincing to say.

Matron Fowler looked at her closely. "Are you feeling all right?" she asked.

"Not quite," said Pauline. She blushed, furious at herself that she could feel tears prickling behind her eyes. She felt overcome with a sense of hopelessness, as if she were being condemned to her present life. Matron Fowler got up and walked over to her. Pauline looked up at her, overawed by her authority. But the matron sat down on the arm of Pauline's chair and gently began rubbing her back. For a moment, Pauline felt scared, wondering what on earth this large, strange woman expected of her. The rubbing continued, down the iron bar of her spine. As the matron's arm slipped around her shoulders, Pauline found herself, her head in her hands, sobbing. Matron Fowler continued massaging, reaching over to her desk for the box of tissues which she put on Pauline's lap. Pauline picked a tissue out of the box and firmly blew her nose, but, to her embarrassment, couldn't stop her tears. Matron Fowler took another tissue, dabbing at Pauline's cheeks as if she was a small child. Then, she got up and walked back behind her desk.

"I like a good cry myself," she said briskly, then coughed. "Now, dear, tell me why on earth you want this job so much?"

Pauline looked at the other woman and suddenly decided it didn't matter that she'd broken down and cried. She didn't know if she could trust her, but she had to talk to someone. The matron, strange as she was, had a calming effect on her. She told her about adopting Miranda and how she'd always wanted kids. Babies were the one thing, maybe the only thing she was good at. She could handle them, and it'd make her feel useful doing a job like this. She was desperate and she'd do anything, but she felt she really could do this job.

"Why so desperate?" asked the matron.

"I'm leaving my husband." She hesitated. "He works hard, pays all the bills," She hung her head, feeling ashamed. Matron Fowler said nothing and Pauline finally looked up. "He won't let the girls home. Always had it in for Mandy, now Linda." She lowered her voice. "She made a mistake, got herself pregnant." She went on, braver now. "I want to leave, get the family together. Then there's Roy. He's just a friend. He said he'd look after us, but it wouldn't be right. It seems the wrong thing, whatever I do."

Matron Fowler listened with careful attention, leaning forward across the desk. "I may have a job available in six weeks. I'll let you know. You seem like a sensible woman."

She smiled at Pauline who smiled back. The phrase, "sensible woman" gave her a warm, satisfied feeling.

Matron Fowler went on. "You want your daughters home and you want to get rid of that dog of a husband." She looked to Pauline for confirmation and receiving it, in the form of a short nose blow, she went on. "You'll have to sort all that out for yourself, of course. But maybe it's time you started thinking about yourself too. It's your life, you know."

"Your life." Pauline wasn't sure if she repeated the words to herself or out loud, but they struck her as terribly important. She sat in the armchair, her expression unchanged, but amazed that for so long she had missed the point. Of course it was her life. It seemed so obvious now. She stood up and picked up her handbag. "Thanks, matron," she said cheerfully.

Matron Fowler smiled briskly at Pauline, then touched her finger to her lips. "Your lippy's a bit smudged, pet. Bathroom's down the hall before you go out there again." She jerked her head towards the window, through which Pauline could just make out Roy, sitting on the tailgate of the sunbaked ute, patting Kip.

"You look a lot more grown-up to me," said Petunia, as she led Miranda outside.

"I've got a boyfriend," said Miranda shyly.

"Well then, you're streets ahead of me," giggled Petunia. She sprawled down on the grass at the front of the hospital. "I feel more comfortable talking out here, seeing as this is sort of unofficial."

"Are you going to tell me which one she is?" Miranda produced the list of Nathans.

"That one," said Petunia. She looked at Miranda's guilt-stricken face. "It wasn't exactly a state secret. You would have found her, you know."

"Yes," said Miranda. She pulled at the grass nervously. "I'm scared now that I do know." She looked at Petunia pleadingly. "Why didn't she want to see me?"

Petunia looked at her steadily. "There's lots of possibilities. You can't know for sure. What's more important is what if she still won't see you?" She turned to look at the ambulance coming down the drive, siren at full pitch.

Miranda took a deep breath and waited until the ambulance passed. "I have thought of that." She half smiled at Petunia. "Like constantly. I guess I just go on, as if nothing happened."

"That's what she's tried to do. It doesn't work." She looked at Miranda. "I run a support group for people in this kind of situation."

"It's not my style really," said Miranda quickly.

"It's got nothing to do with style."

Miranda hesitated. "I don't want to make a big thing of it."

"It is a big thing." Petunia got a biscuit out of her pocket and started nibbling on it. She offered one to Miranda. Miranda shook her head and Petunia noticed how set and white her face was. "Just remember I'm here, OK?"

"OK," said Miranda. "I'll write to her, I think. Not ring her up. Do you think that's better?"

Petunia got to her feet and helped pull Miranda up. "Much better. Less confrontational." They walked back towards the hospital in companionable silence.

"I'll get a bus over here," said Miranda. "Thanks, Petunia, for the address, and the advice. I hope I don't seem ungrateful. I really appreciate you." She turned to go and then turned back, suddenly anxious. "What should I put in the letter?"

"Just a bit about yourself. Maybe a photo. Keep it brief and don't say anything to scare her."

Miranda smiled at her. "Watch out or we'll end up in your support group."

Charlie sat sweating, panting and grey, staring at the line of madonnas, vowing that never again would he jog. He could no longer imagine what early morning vision had left him, now, at midday, with an ominous feeling of an imminent heart attack. He pressed his fingers into his wrist, but the blood was pounding through his finger tips too fast for him to detect the pulse. He looked up and scanned the madonnas on the shelves and then closed his eyes. The cloaks, the dresses, the facial tints were magnificent, but those few faces on which he had attempted to paint features looked silly and empty-headed, like a group of moronic school girls. The only exception was the one whose foot Virginia had broken. Her face had assumed a particularly vicious sneer.

He picked up a turps-soaked rag, determined to wipe the expression from her face and angrily rubbed the rag across her features. But instead of removing the red mouth, it smudged, so that lipstick ran down her chin and what looked like mascara splodged under the eye. "Tart," he muttered angrily.

His tennis painting gave him far more profound pain. In the last few weeks, the face of the girl had hardened and aged. He hated it and suddenly remembered why he had gone jogging. It was a crazy notion, that he would get into shape for Ginny and that their relationship would come back together again. He'd be all right, she'd be all right. He went over to the painting and looked into the face. He wanted to cover it with a black cloth, to mourn it. It needed to die. The thought distressed him. He had given birth to the painting, loved it to life and now it was dying on him. He kicked off his sneakers which were torturing his bunioned feet and lit up a cigarette. He thought of a drink, but the memory of the long lonely days in New York when he'd drunk alone warned him off. Now, he hated to drink alone, even in the evenings. His thoughts came back to Ginny: how happy she'd been going off to Perth with the Corpran contract under her belt but when she rang to tell him of her progress with the new contract, the tell-tale, high-pitched tone in her voice made him sense the emotional distance growing between them.

He almost decided to ignore the knock at the door. Then, as the knocker continued to bang, he decided that it might take his mind off himself to discuss life with a Jehovah's Witness. Treading carefully up the stairs to avoid knocking the tender parts of his feet, he shuffled to the door and opened it. He looked at the young woman on the doorstep. She was unnaturally pale and her hands were thrust into the pockets of her long shorts. She looked around, nervously, past him into the house, along the front verandah, almost as if he wasn't there. She had the same colour hair as Virginia.

"I'm Miranda Darnley," she said. "I'm looking for Virginia Nathan."

The voice made him look at her more closely: the dark red hair, the brown eyes, the firm, full mouth, the same high cheekbones. Even the fear-pinched face, tension packed in the jaw. "I'll bet you are," he said huskily. "She's not here. But come in, I'll talk to you. God, what a turn up. Come in."

He walked ahead of her, along the passageway, to the stairway. Miranda followed him, looking around. He turned suddenly.

"You are her daughter, aren't you?" he asked.

"Yes," Miranda answered, relieved to have been acknowledged. He said nothing more, but continued limping along the passage, picking his way over the tins of paint. There were painting drapes everywhere. The masking tape on the woodwork reminded her of the walls at Uwalla, marked by odd bits of sticky tape. But this house, of course, was totally different: very rich and very grand. Although she'd sometimes fantasised about her mother being wealthy, the reality of the money here made her uneasy. But the man limping ahead of her didn't quite fit the picture: a grey jumper unravelling at the sleeves, black curly hair unfashionably long and unkempt, an American accent.

Charlie turned round again at the top of the stairs. "I'll take you down to my den and make us a strong coffee. You can start firing questions then." He ushered her down the stairs into a room that immediately reminded her of Hazel by virtue of its eccentricity. In one corner was an elaborate sculpture of warped tennis racquets from which dangled a string of balls.

Three easels were set up with uncompleted paintings. Madonna figurines, elaborately painted except for their blank faces, lined the bookshelves.

"I've got a letter," said Miranda nervously. "I was going to drop it in the box, but then I found myself on your doorstep. Maybe I should just leave the letter . . . " She held it out to him.

"God no," he said. "Cross the threshold into the lion's den and you've got to stay here." Miranda put the letter back in her pocket as he went to the small bar and filled an electric jug.

"Coffee?" he said. "We'll sit outside. There's too much clutter here. That great package in the corner is a spa I'm getting installed for Ginny. Have it ready when she gets back." He clattered away busily then looked at Miranda again. She looked back nervously at him.

"Ginny?" she said slowly. "Is that what you call my mother?" She felt her knees trembling uncontrollably and she leant against the bookshelves. The shelves wobbled and the madonnas swayed and clinked against one another. She backed away hastily. "Sorry," she said to Charlie in alarm, almost backing into his painting. "Sorry."

He moved out from behind the bar. "You must be ten times as nervous as I am," he said. "There aren't any set rules on how to behave in this situation, are there?" He was afraid that she would burst into tears from sheer tension. "I'm Charlie," he said quickly. "I forgot to tell you that. I'm not her husband. I'm the resident painter and lover." He felt it was important to explain his position, but it left him with nothing further to say and Miranda still looked blank and white-faced. "It's just as well Ginny's not here."

"Where is she?" asked Miranda desperately.

"In Perth. She'll be back in two weeks' time." The jug started to whistle shrilly and he went back behind the bar and poured their coffees. He picked up the cups and led the way out onto the terrace. "Let's sit out in the sun and talk," he said kindly.

They sat out under the great spreading plum tree with its canopy of dark purple leaves. Charlie pointed out the pile of sand and rubble near the house. "That's where the spa will go," he said, "but at the moment, I like the sandheap. Gives the place a nice slummy feeling don't you think? Needs a few old dogs to pee on it, run a few fights and we'd be in business. Trouble about this neighbourhood is that it's so bloody tasteful and neat." Miranda could see he was trying to put her at ease with in-neighbourhood jokes. But the neighbourhood was so alien to her that she didn't know how to respond. She smiled politely, her head buzzing with the questions she didn't know how to ask.

"How did you find us?" Charlie asked. "Did the social worker tell after all?"

"No," said Miranda quickly. "She just hinted Virginia had really wanted to see me and got cold feet. And she told me she didn't have any family." She looked at Charlie, embarrassed. "She didn't mention you, so I didn't think I'd be intruding."

"Did you actually track us down—do a detective job?"

"It was just luck. Virginia's name was on the back of a card Mum had pinched from the hospital. It's been there all the time, but I'd never thought to look." She paused. It seemed an awfully long time ago. "When I found it, last weekend, I began ringing up all the Nathans. Then I worked out it must be this one and wrote the letter. I was going to mail it, but then I thought I'd like to see the house. Then, I found myself on the doorstep."

"A true foundling," said Charlie, "except its usually someone else who does the puttig on doorsteps."

"Why wouldn't she see me?" Miranda's expression made Charlie decide that desperation was hereditary.

"She was scared. She likes to be in control. Not whatever will be, will be. It has to be signed, sealed and delivered in advance for Ginny."

"Will she be angry at me coming here?"

"Of course not," said Charlie with a heartiness he didn't quite feel. "She'll be relieved. It's been eating away at her for twenty years. She was only fourteen when she had you." He started teasing a dry leaf away from its stem. "So what do you do when you're not tracking down runaway mothers?"

"Student," said Miranda. "Second year Vet."

"Why Vet?" he asked.

"It's hard," Miranda said slowly. "And I like a challenge . . . and I really like animals . . . and there's lots of possibilities when you finish."

"Castrating poodles and sewing cats' ears back on?"

"Even that would be OK," said Miranda. "You'd meet lots of animals and owners. And you're on more equal terms with people than if you're a doctor. I did think about medicine."

"So you're going to settle down to a suburban practice?"

"No way." Miranda smiled for the first time. "I'd love to work in a really outback region. Really hard, really different. Cattle management or something. Or a wildlife vet would be terrific. Maybe go to Africa. I used to dream about Africa when I was little."

Charlie wanted to find out more about her. Although nervous, she was contained and cool. Yet he felt a great intensity. He began to draw her out about her childhood.

"I knew I was different. I always knew. I think that's why I was such a Mummy's girl."

"Did your mother treat you differently?"

"I was her favourite. Me and Louis I think. But that didn't matter all that much. You know, in a big family you're so busy getting the breakfast and doing the washing up that nobody worries too much about favourites or anything like that."

They sat, silent for a while, Miranda looking up through the dark leaves, at the blue sky, wisps of white cloud strewn across it. She looked round the garden, at the tennis court discreetly hidden at the back of the garden. It was very different from the rare back-yard court in Uwalla, where the court took up the entire yard and was used constantly for coaching. In Uwalla, a tennis court was to make money. She had always wondered who lived in these big, grand suburban houses, what their lives were like. Charlie wasn't the sort of occupant she'd imagined.

"When did you meet my mother?" she asked suddenly. She had decided after vacillating between Virginia and "my mother" to call her "my mother". But it still didn't sit comfortably.

"I came here as an exchange student, well, that was the official title. My parents actually wanted to get rid of me for a while. I was too delinquent for a little, mid-west town. Ginny was about thirteen when I arrived. I was eighteen."

Miranda stared at Charlie. "You were here when she was thirteen?" she said slowly. She looked at him, one hand twisting her pony tail. For a moment, he didn't understand the sudden tension. "You were here when . . . ?"

He suddenly realised and shook his head. He leaned over

and squeezed her hand. "No, I am not your father. Ginny and I didn't have that sort of relationship till three years ago. Back then, we were just mates."

Miranda lost her shyness in the moment of intensity. She began to fire questions at him. Where was he when she was born? Who was the father? It was strange. She called him "the father" as if he had nothing to do with her. He was a figure who had never before entered her imagination.

Charlie didn't know or wouldn't tell. "The past, that's Ginny's department. She hasn't even told me a lot: she's a secretive person."

He got up abruptly and went into the house to brew more coffee and Miranda sat alone under the plum tree as the afternoon shadows crept across the garden. She shivered, but she didn't want to go yet. Charlie came back with the percolator and began talking about Ginny, almost as if he was talking to himself. It was not about the past, but the present. He found himself talking about her in a way he didn't even know he felt about her, proud of her achievements, frustrated by her lack of commitment, scared for her, scared for their relationship, realising how fragile it all was. He began to see, although he said nothing of it to Miranda, how isolated he had become in this relationship with Ginny, and now how he was almost depending on Miranda to make it work, while realising how unfair that was. But what if it failed? What would happen to him? What would happen to Ginny? Both of them treated each other so casually, yet they depended on each other almost totally. He had hassled her about her lack of commitment to him. Although he told her that he loved her, he'd always felt he could walk out when he wanted to. Now, he realised he couldn't.

He gathered up the coffee cups and realised gratefully he hadn't thought about a drink. "Stay for dinner?" he asked casually. "I can give you good student fare: baked beans on toast."

"I think I'll go home. It's been wonderful, but I should study."

She opened the door for him. "So what do I do now? About my mother?" Her urgency had come back.

Charlie realised he had been watching her face closely the whole afternoon, fascinated by the similarities to Ginny's.

Her features were softer, less defined except for the forehead which was broader.

"I want to ask you a favour," he said. "I want you to come inside and be a model for a painting I'm doing." He saw a momentary look of alarm flit across her face. "Don't worry," he laughed. "All your clothes on. I only need your face."

"OK," said Miranda quickly. "But you haven't told me what I do—about getting in touch with my mother?" Charlie led her inside and sat her down on a stool.

"I'll tell you while I paint."

Miranda had caught a glimpse of the tennis painting before. She liked its mixture of formal, almost photographic style with the rush of the girl at the front. Now, as she sat on the stool, looking towards the window, where Charlie had put her, she felt the strangeness of the whole situation: sitting, posing for a painting for a man she met only a few hours ago, in the house where her mother had grown up, a house more alien and foreign to her than the wilds of Africa. The Virginia who was her mother, who she had created in her imagination, was assuming a form, a reality—according to Charlie, an uncertain, fragile, sometimes brittle woman driven by achievement and success.

Charlie worked silently for a while and then stood back, looking at the painting. "We'll have lunch, Saturday week, the day after Ginny comes back," he announced. "No time for her to make a fuss. But we won't make it heavy. I'll be here and you bring your sister."

"Is that a good idea?"

"Yes, because we'll have lots to talk about. Less of an up-front emotional confrontation for Ginny. Chance to get to know you gradually."

"OK."

Miranda swallowed, but said nothing more. She had explained to Charlie about Linda, unmarried and pregnant. He'd been interested, so she didn't think he'd forgotten. Yet she felt as if there was something indelicate about Linda coming, a danger that her pregnancy would assume a special significance. She was afraid she'd appear prudish if she objected. And she desperately wanted to be just right.

Charlie put down his brush and palette. "Come and look. You've brought it back from the dead."

Miranda walked across to the painting.

Charlie smiled, stroking his brush over it lovingly, touching up the mouth. "It's only sketched of course, but you're just right. You've been eluding me. I was about to scrap the whole thing."

"I like it," said Miranda politely, staring at herself on canvas, not knowing what to say. "That lunch will be all right... with Linda... won't it?"

"I know Ginny," said Charlie. "Trust me."

"Ron Black's Boxing Gym", the sign said. It was elaborately lettered in red, black and gold, painted on a board, splitting in one corner. The sign was propped against an old Moreton Bay fig tree at the expressway side of the park. Under the tree, a tattooed man in red silk shorts, a grubby singlet and tight boxer's boots was pummelling at a vinyl cushion, being held fast in front of him by a small, frail man. Two other young men lounged against the tree, jeering and heckling, as punches landed dangerously close to the edge of the cushion.

"He'll kill ya, Ron, if he keeps that up."

"Kill! Kill! Go for it, boy!" the old man exhorted, dancing in his excitement, as the frenzy of the punches increased.

"Gawd, look at the poofta," drawled one of the young men as Patrick ran towards them.

"Bloody poofta!" shouted the other man.

Patrick ignored them, swiped at the punching bag that hung from the tree and jumped over the pile of cushions that made up the rest of the training equipment of the Ron Black Gym. It was an afternoon ritual, Patrick making the provocative jump, the Ron Blacks shouting abuse, sometimes even chasing him. It was the only interest in his long daily run. Otherwise, there were only a few dedicated greyhound walkers. Even the drunks favoured the smaller, more protected park up the hill.

This afternoon, in spite of the heat and the drabness of the park, he felt alive and excited, thoughts of Miranda running through his head. From the time he met her, she had intrigued him. Most men who came to the house pursued Hazel and made friends with Miranda. For him, it had been the opposite but in spite of their passion for each other, he was still unsure of her. It seemed as if part of her was quite separate and inaccessible, perhaps even to herself. But he didn't really know. Never before had he felt so strongly about a woman.

The owner of a group of cowering greyhounds pulled the dogs out of Patrick's way as he raced round the edge of the stadium in a burst of energy, a car tooting insistently from behind. He ran on, ignoring the sound until the car pulled ahead of him and he realised it was Miranda, driving Hazel's car. As she drew up at the kerb, he jumped over the concrete wall and still breathing hard from running, got into the car. Puffing, he looked at her—her colour was heightened and he could sense her happiness. He slid across the seat and put his arm round her.

"So you actually found her?" he said.

"I went in. I know I shouldn't have. But I did. Anyway, she's away—for two more weeks. But there's this lovely guy she lives with—Charlie—he's an artist. And the moment she's back, I'm going over there. It's less than a fortnight. I'm so excited...I'll actually meet her. Only a week from next Saturday."

"Did you actually just walk up to the house and say "Hi, I'm Miranda. Is Virginia home?""

"Amazing, but true. But I drove round the block twenty times before I went in."

"So why wouldn't she see you before?"

Miranda waved the comment aside. "Come on, let's walk. I've been sitting and talking all day. Linda and Hazel are over the other side."

They got out of the car and Miranda took Patrick's hand, moving close to him as they walked. "So much happened. I feel like I'm a different person. You know, Charlie was sure she would have got in touch some time. She just reacted badly to being contacted by the hospital."

"Did you get an idea of what she's like?"

Miranda noticed with a childish satisfaction that they were walking in step. "I think she's sort of shy—and soft, but very successful—and that I've been very important in her life."

Patrick brushed a strand of hair off Miranda's face. "Incredible, isn't it? You dominate her life, she dominates yours."

"And we've never even met. Well, not since..."

"Not formally introduced," put in Patrick.

Miranda laughed. "From what Charlie was saying, we've got a lot in common, apart from the same colour hair...but even *that*. I've never met anyone with exactly my colour hair before. All my family are sort of red gold, like Linda. And Charlie says I look like her. He painted me." She paused, and clasped Patrick's arm. "You know what she does? You'll never guess. She's an engineer."

Patrick grinned. "Am I supposed to be pleased? Is that supposed to give me something in common with her—or with you? Anyway, you know what I decided today? I'm not going to be an engineer. One of Dad's old mates offered me a job after I graduate. I had this awful feeling that if I took it, I'd be there the rest of my life. I'd like to pass my finals, but that's it for engineering."

Miranda was shocked. "Isn't it a waste?" She couldn't imagine why anyone would throw away an education. "What'll you do?"

He smiled at her doubtful expression. "I'll go to China in the holidays and I'm going to get a business going: importing art works. I know a bit of Chinese. Language and art. Things I'm interested in. And until it pays, I'll go labouring for the rent."

Miranda thought it sounded crazy.

"It means I won't be here in the holidays," he said ruefully.

She squeezed his hand. "I don't know what I'll be doing anyway. There's Linda's baby for starters. I really want to go home, more than anything, but I mightn't be allowed." An angry tone crept into her voice. "Come on, let's run. I need oxygen."

Patrick started to jog along beside her. "With this air, you're putting it back in."

As they jogged, they saw Linda in the distance, rising unsteadily to her feet. She stood and watched them, stroking her hands down across her belly. She had preferred the baby when it was smaller—a neat, contained, little hump. Now, it was pushing up under her breasts, weighing her down as she walked, taking over her entire body.

"Here's Miranda and Patrick," she said to Hazel who was lying face down in the grass.

"Oh God," groaned Hazel, looking up. "Young love." She lifted herself on her elbows and smiled weakly as Miranda ran up to them. Hazel looked pale and her smile lacked its usual brightness.

"You OK?" asked Miranda.

"I said goodbye to Phillip this morning," said Hazel brightly. "Adieu, not au revoir. He had to go out to the airport to meet an ex-fiancée or his fiancée to be."

"I thought he wanted to marry you."

"He did, but it was nothing personal," said Hazel. "When I told him no wedding, he went back to the other girl. Actually, I'm really glad I'm falling out of love. I hope it never happens again. It's been ghastly." She looked up at Patrick crossly. "It's all right for you men—you don't have feelings."

It was the Wednesday before the Friday that Virginia came back from Perth. Miranda knew, because she'd crossed every day off in her diary. Sometimes, she played games, working out the number of hours, as if that would make them go more quickly.

It was also less than a week until her exams began and so she sat at the kitchen table, staring at the biochemistry text. For the first time in her life she was facing an exam she mightn't pass. But her anxiety was overridden by her excitement. Meeting Virginia, she was sure, would make everything better.

It was midnight, too hot to study, too hot to sleep, especially in Patrick's little attic room where she now slept. From the back yard came the shrill, clear sound of a single cicada blocked out temporarily by the revs of a truck coming up the hill in low gear. From upstairs, she heard the clip of high heels descending, stopping at the bathroom, resuming as Linda came down to the kitchen. Miranda snapped her book shut.

"Mum'll be upset if you don't pass," said Linda accusingly.

"She doesn't care about results," said Miranda scornfully.

"She does so. Yours anyway. You should hear her go on about them." She foraged round in the fridge, breaking off a piece of cheese, wrapping it in a slice of salami and a leaf of lettuce. "I can't sleep," she complained, looking at her stomach. "It's so big. I'm sure my face is going puffy too." She flopped down in the lounge chair and leaned back over the arm, her feet dangling over the other side. "You know what I'd like right now? Emergency caesarian. I wouldn't even care about the scar. Knock me out. No pain. Nothing. Back to normal."

"I thought you were going to send me out for ice-cream again," said Miranda thankfully.

Linda leaned further back, her long hair cascading to the floor. "I'm sick of it, Mandy. Sick of it."

Miranda got up, lifted Linda's head, gently massaging her forehead. "Only four or five weeks and you'll be through. It'll be OK, Linda, really."

"I suppose so," said Linda, grumpily, pulling her head away. "Mandy, will you come to the hospital with me if Haze isn't right by then? I know it's your exams and all, but you know what Haze is like at the moment."

"Sure," said Miranda, stroking Linda's forehead. "I've always wanted to, you know."

"I still mightn't need you," Linda said irritably. But she let Miranda massage her forehead as she looked over to the table. "Who are you writing to?" she asked.

"My mother," said Miranda. "I forgot to leave the letter the day I went out there. Petunia says it'll be easier if she gets a letter from me first. Sort of an introduction." She reached over and picked up the pale blue envelope. "Smell it. I bought specially scented paper, with the embossed butterfly in the corner. It's nice, isn't it?"

Linda sniffed it. "It's OK." She yawned. "But I don't know why you're bothering with her."

"What do you mean?" asked Miranda coldly, her hand lying on Linda's forehead.

"We're your family. I agree with Mum. You can't just go and get another one. What if she's got more kids and you've got brothers and sisters? They wouldn't be like a proper family."

"She hasn't," said Miranda defensively. "I just want to know where I come from."

"Try Uwalla."

"Charlie wants you to come to the lunch too," said Miranda. She hadn't told Linda about the invitation before. Now she felt confident of a refusal. "But you don't have to."

Linda sat up and beamed at Miranda. "I'd love to. I thought we'd never be allowed to see her. You know, all hush hush. One of your secrets."

"Nope," said Miranda casually, but with a sense of unease. "No secrets."

The moment Charlie saw Ginny come into the arrival lounge he knew it was a mistake to come out to meet her. She had that separate "don't touch me" look that made him feel a hopelessness about himself and her. She walked up and kissed him dryly on the cheek. "So why are you here? I thought you hated airports at night."

"But I love you." He hated the insincerity in his voice.

"What else?" she said accusingly, then laughed at her tone. "Did you dig up my mother's rose?"

He took her arm as they stepped on to the escalator, but she moved away from him, lounging back against the side, watching him with a sardonic look. In her dark tailored suit and flaming pink blouse, she looked polished, groomed, completely contained. By contrast, he felt shabby and ill at ease. He looked down at his worn sneakers, the stain on his trousers. It wasn't even an artistic paint splatter, just grubbiness. Looking at Virginia, he knew she was high as a kite on business. He'd seen it before, work acting almost like a drug, making her untouchable and remote.

"You won the contract?"

She smiled at him more warmly. "I got it and another little one with one of the shire councils. And there are some definite possibilities for next year. I'm seriously thinking I could open an office in Perth."

He didn't answer. They stepped off the escalator and stood side by side next to the luggage carousel. "You know," she said confidentially, "even though I lost a little bit on Corpran it was worth it. Everywhere I go, people ask me about the Corpran contract and how a small firm like ours won it. It's really opened doors for me. The company's going to take off!" She was half watching the bags as they came out of the chute. "So what have you been up to?" she asked casually, not looking at him. Charlie didn't know what he could say. Seeing her bag, he pushed through the crowd and picked it up. Never had he felt so distant and remote from her. The feeling of love that had grown in him during her absence had dissipated in the few minutes they'd been back together. He still wanted her desperately, but at the same time, he despised her and himself as well. He wished he could be rid of wanting her, unable to understand what it was about her that made him feel that way.

He showed her the spa first. It was outside, under the stars, the branches of the jacaranda silhouetted against the stormy summer sky. He had heated it and turned it on before he went to the airport and it was bubbling and frothing, lit a weird green by the light at the bottom.

"Does it carry on like this the whole time?" Virginia asked.

"I put it on before I came out. I thought we could jump in and relax. It's going to rain any minute. It'd be wonderful."

"Not quite my style," she said briskly. "But it'll be wonderful for entertaining." She softened a little. "I'm tired. Maybe I'll try it tomorrow. It's a good idea, Charlie."

He caught her as she opened the door to go back inside and turned her round towards him. "Ginny, I really missed you. I got lonely."

She wriggled out of his grasp. "Well, you ought to go out more, Charlie." Only the memory of Miranda's anxious face stopped him shaking her.

They walked up the stairs and into the dining room where Virginia poured herself a small whisky. "Want one?" she asked casually.

"No," he said fiercely. He stood in the middle of the room as she picked up her letters from the sideboard. She looked round the room, then sat down at the table and put on a pair of reading glasses.

"I like the cream colour in this room, Charlie. You really have done wonders, you know." She started sorting through the letters.

He stood his ground. "Your daughter turned up two weeks ago."

For a moment, he thought he saw something flash across her face, but then she smiled gently up at him. He wondered which one of them was going crazy. "What's she like?" she asked.

"Really nice," he said uncertainly. "Her name's Miranda Darnley and she's coming to lunch tomorrow."

Virginia picked up the letter in the baby blue envelope. She looked at the name on the back and then sniffed it. "Fancy that," she said. "She's written to me. The last time somebody sent me a perfumed letter with a butterfly on the envelope, I was seven years old." She threw the letter back onto the table, stood up and walked towards the door. "I must say I think you could have asked me, Charlie." She went out and he heard her walk up the stairs. He waited, standing, listening to her go into the bathroom, taps running, toilet flushing. He could just discern her footsteps directly above him as she went into her bedroom. He walked over to the lamp and turned it off. He stood alone in the dark by the door. Suddenly, from above, there was a bang as Virginia's door loudly slammed shut. Charlie leant against the door jamb and started to cry.

·*Chapter Nine*·

Patrick sat hunched over the piano, which stood in one corner of his room, tucked under the attic roof. It was the only object of furniture which would not conform to the size and shape of the room. The slope of the ceiling forced him to bend his head over the keys as he picked out the notes of the same chord over and over. He swung round on the piano stool, got up and flopped down onto the bed. He picked up a notebook, glanced at it and then threw it down dismissively.

Miranda stood in front of the tiny mirror next to the window. She pulled a few strands of hair from her tightly drawn back pony tail, so her face looked softer and less severe. Two more hours and I'll see her, she thought. All week, Virginia had been on her mind, with a half-formed hope there'd be a phone call, or a letter in reply to hers.

"I bet I get a credit in something this year," said Patrick. "You don't get nervous if you don't care."

She turned round to him. "It's unfair. I care so much I can't think straight." She looked back in the mirror, pulling at her hair.

"You look fine," he said quietly.

"It looks untidy now," she said, turning impatiently away from the mirror. "I keep telling myself it doesn't matter what I look like. Then I think that if I wear something more dressed up she'll like me better. I wish it was time to go." She leaned against the window, her bare, skinny legs emphasised by her billowing white shirt.

"Speaking of dressed up, are you are going to wear something else, besides the shirt?" asked Patrick.

"That grey skirt of Hazel's. Linda's taken it down to the laundromat for me."

"Haze given up washing?"

139

Miranda sighed, then sat down on the mattress. "I wish you'd talk to her. She just lies in bed all day, watching TV and drinking. She never used to watch any TV. She told me last night she knows it's morning when Humphrey Bear's on."

Patrick pulled Miranda down to lie next to him. She moved her head away from him, not wanting to mess up her hair. "Why don't you talk to her?" she said.

"Hazel hates advice, especially if it might work. She's a born self-saboteur."

"She is not," said Miranda defensively.

He resisted her attempt to sit up, holding her down next to him. "I don't know what I could say to her."

Miranda sat up, her hair tousled. "I get scared for her. She's so...I don't know."

"I've mucked up your hair." He smiled at her.

She leaned over and kissed him. "It'll give me something to do until we go." Opening the door, she saw Linda puffing up from the landing, Hazel's grey skirt over her arm.

"I ironed it for you," she said enthusiastically. "I think the baby must be coming soon. They say you get all domestic."

"Does it last?" said Miranda, taking the skirt. She looked at Linda critically. "Are you wearing that?"

Linda looked pleased, as if Miranda was complimenting her. "It's cute, isn't it?" She looked down at her pale blue overalls, embroidered with a pink stork carrying a baby.

Miranda didn't have the heart to reply. She put on the skirt and started walking down the stairs. Linda's overalls were cute, far too cute for the big house with its smooth sweeping lawn and immaculate flower beds.

Linda rattled down ahead of her. "I'm going to ring up Mum," she yelled. "You want to talk to her?"

"Yes, I do," Miranda yelled after her.

All week, Miranda had been struggling to ring Pauline, to tell her about the lunch. She wanted it to be right with Pauline, but she dreaded further estrangement. If she found out from Linda, she'd be even more hurt. She hurried downstairs. "Don't you tell her where we're going," she said breathlessly. "I'll talk to her," as Linda dialled the number.

"Don't get in such a stew. Dad's likely to slam the phone down in my ear anyway." Linda was untroubled by her father's rejection, ringing when she wanted to, ignoring the angry drama at the other end. Miranda, unable to cope with the turmoil it engendered in her, only spoke to her mother when Linda had tested the water or, on the rare occasions when Pauline rang.

"Hullo, Mum," said Linda.

"Oh, it's you. Hullo, love." Pauline sounded tense.

"Is Dad there?" asked Linda.

"He's off with Barney Laurence—a long run—coupla weeks I hope, delivering stuff at the Heads. We got the usual panic on here." She looked out through the back door to where Roy's truck was parked outside the garage. The back yard was dusty, barely any grass, a result of Kevin's constant harassment of Lou to mow the lawns. She could see Roy fastening the "GARAGE SALE" sign to the back of the truck which was piled with old bits of furniture and household bric-a-brac. For some reason, it was the kids' old stroller perched on top that struck her most poignantly. Kip sat on top of a wardrobe, barking at the children who stood in the sunbaked yard, silently watching Roy.

"I gotta tell you something, Mum," said Linda.

"You're not sick, are you? Not swelling up or anything?"

"If I swell any more I'll burst," said Linda. "Mum, that was only a joke." She paused. "No Mum, I'm having the baby adopted. That's all." She looked at Miranda to make sure she had heard. Miranda turned and stared at her.

"Adopted? Your own flesh and blood? Adopted? Linda, you gotta be kidding." Pauline's voice took on a pleading tone. "Honestly, Danny'd have you back, love. He's always asking after you."

"Mum, it's not his baby. But that doesn't matter anyway. I decided to do it. Months ago. I didn't tell you because I knew there'd be such a fuss." She tilted her head defiantly, seeing Miranda's furious glare. "Mum, Mandy's here. She wants to talk to you." She quickly handed the phone to Miranda and started busying herself with the dishes.

Miranda picked up the phone to a flood of indignant protests from Pauline. Her own shock was absorbed in her attempt to calm her mother. "I didn't know, Mum. She didn't say anything...It's the first I've heard of it, honestly...Mum, it is her business...Yeah, I care, but I can't stop her."

Pauline knew Miranda was speaking the truth. When Linda

made up her mind, nothing could stop her. And, perhaps, she thought, it was for the best. "Sorry, love," she said, "it's not your fault. I know what she's like. Never sticks at anything. How are your tests and all going?"

"My exams? They start Monday. I'll be OK I think." Miranda bit nervously at her nail. "Mum, I've got to tell you something."

Roy banged on the screen door, motioning to Pauline. The children stood immobile in the back yard, waiting, shoulders drooping. Pauline fixed her gaze on the old stroller. Why was she doing all this, she wondered. Where was it getting her? Maybe it'd help with money to move, but she still hadn't heard from the hospital and there weren't any other jobs. She wanted to tell Miranda that she'd have things sorted out so they could come home, but she was unsure of it herself.

"Mum, I'm going to see my . . . my other mother this morning." Miranda's voice faded away, on the edge of tears.

Kevin's bees were starting to swarm outside the kitchen window. One buzzed in through the hole in the flywire. In a sudden burst of fury, Pauline leant over and angrily pulled the window shut. "Well that's your business, Mandy. You just shop round and find which mother you like best. She'd probably like to have you there for Christmas. Stay all the holidays if you like. Don't worry about me and the kids. Don't worry about me going to all this trouble. Just forget we're alive!"

She slammed the phone down. Miranda, shaking, put the receiver down. She walked over to the sink and started to fill a glass, almost unaware of what she was doing. Linda looked round at her accusingly. "I don't know why you told her. You knew it'd upset her." She wiped her hands on the tea towel. "I wouldn't have let on, you know."

"Like you didn't let on you're getting the baby adopted?" said Miranda furiously.

"Sort of," said Linda sheepishly.

Miranda poured out the water and ran up to the attic. It had to work with Virginia. It just had to work.

Miranda had given in to Linda's cajoling to practise driving on her L plates during the drive to Virginia's place. She began to regret it. She needed something to do, something to stop the nervousness which was almost overwhelming her as they passed

142

through the cultivated greenness of the suburbs. She wondered why she'd ever trusted Charlie's judgment.

"Next left," she said to Linda, who immediately swerved dangerously over to the left. They had barely exchanged a word. Linda was in a defiant, jaunty mood, dismissive of any hint of criticism. Miranda knew it would have been useless to try to talk about the adoption. Yet the fate of Linda's baby loomed large in her mind, somehow connected with her own. The memory of Pauline's anger kept coming back at her, piled on top of her other insecurities.

She was held together by a single thought: once she saw her mother, it would be all right. Without knowing exactly what the "all right" was, it was a promise to herself, the fulfilment of which would stop the fragmentation inside her. She hunched forward, hands twisting nervously, the seat of Hazel's Citroen hot and sticky against her back. She wanted her shirt to remain pristine white.

"Next right," she said. Linda twiddled her fingers as she always did to tell her right from left.

"Slow down," said Miranda huskily. "That house up there, that white two-storeyed one."

"Posh!" whistled Linda.

"Don't say anything like that! Don't you dare! And don't chatter on. Just... you know what I mean!" Miranda looked at Linda fiercely as they turned into the drive.

Charlie and Virginia were waiting for them, sitting on the old garden settee on the front verandah. Miranda watched as Virginia, small and slim, got up and walked down the steps in front of Charlie. She didn't look like a mother, she didn't look like the person Miranda had imagined. Linda drew the car up in front of the steps, beeped the horn and waved gaily. Miranda sat immobilised, her heart beating, her stomach in a knot.

Virginia walked over to the car and leaned in through the window.

"So you're Miranda?" she said to Linda.

"I'm Linda," Linda replied quickly. "That's Miranda."

Miranda felt her lip trembling, scared she might start crying. The woman looking at her across Linda looked so calm and cool, so normal and controlled, that she bit her lip and breathed in deeply.

"Hi," said Virginia. She smiled at Miranda, an attractive,

self-assured, contained smile.

"Hullo," said Miranda, not trusting herself to smile back, unable to fathom the pleasant, polite assurance. Her own turmoil seemed ill-bred.

"Won't you come in?" asked Virginia. She walked round to Miranda's side of the car and as Miranda got out, she took her by the shoulders and kissed her dryly on the cheek. It wasn't so much an embrace, as a way of keeping her distant, the sort of kiss women who don't like each other much exchange for public display.

"Charlie's made you the most lovely lunch," Virginia said as they walked up the steps. "We'll have it on the side terrace." Charlie came over to Miranda, put his arm round her and squeezed her. He winked at her, a secret signal of encouragement.

Virginia led the way through the house, now free of painting drapes and masking tape. It had become cool, elegant and sophisticated. They didn't go down the stairs to Charlie's studio, but to the other side of the house, into a big modern kitchen and an elegant sitting room, opening onto a large terrace, overlooking the front garden. There was a table set for four.

"No slumming today," said Charlie. "Very best for the return of the prodigal."

"Excuse me," said Virginia. "I'll fix the soup."

"None for me, thanks," said Linda. "I can't eat soup."

"Is that the whim of a pregnant woman?" asked Charlie, as they sat down.

"No," said Linda flashing her most charming smile at him. "I can't stand anything with gravy. But I've improved since I came to Sydney."

"When's your baby due?" asked Charlie. Miranda looked at him. He'd combed his hair down and he was wearing a smart shirt and trousers. She'd preferred him scruffy and unpolished.

"Another few weeks," said Linda brightly. She smiled up at Virginia as she walked out to the table with the large soup tureen. "I've decided to have him adopted."

"Probably sensible at your age," said Charlie heartily. Miranda looked at Virginia. Her eyes were downcast, but for a second, her face had lost its assurance and her hand shook slightly as she ladled out the soup.

"I suppose you're doing exams now," she said briskly to

Miranda, passing her a plate of soup. "Do have some cheese on it. It brings out the flavour."

Miranda sprinkled a spoonful of cheese over her soup. "I start on Monday."

"I used to love them," said Virginia brightly. She turned to Charlie. "Charlie, I think there's a white in the fridge that would be just perfect. I'm sure the girls would love a glass." As Charlie rose obediently, she turned back to Miranda. "I got fearfully nervous, but I'm so damned competitive that I was determined to show everyone. Are you like that?" She sounded combative.

"I was last year, but this year's much tougher. I'll be glad if I pass."

"Second year, are you? Well, that's when they sort out the sheep from the goats."

Miranda looked down at her soup, the remark ricocheting round her brain. Charlie smiled helplessly at her. Virginia took another gulp of wine and casually topped up her glass.

"I enjoyed university," she said, "but it doesn't prepare you for professional life."

"Why not?" asked Miranda, and instantly worried she'd sounded brusque.

"Well, you've earned your degree; naturally you expect the rewards." Virginia's tone was impersonal and dry. "You're not prepared for the backstabbing and underhand methods, the cut and thrust of business."

"I'd say you had that well in hand by now, Ginny," said Charlie dryly.

She smiled at him. "Of course I have, Charlie. I suppose I was just trying to tell Miranda that university isn't the be all and end all." Miranda felt patronised. She didn't know how to answer.

"I'm not at uni," said Linda enthusiastically. "I went straight into business."

"You certainly did." Virginia glanced at Linda's pregnant stomach. Miranda looked at Virginia and received a cool, self-assured smile. She wondered if she were imagining things. Virginia turned to Linda again. "What business are you in, dear?"

"Fashion," said Linda enthusiastically. "Just in the shop, but I'd love to do design. I do a lot of drawing."

Virginia led the conversation off to talk about a friend of hers in fashion design and then made some wry remarks about Charlie's painting. Her chatter induced a sense of almost physical disorientation in Miranda. She turned to Charlie for guidance.

"How's your tennis painting going?" she asked him, hoping to break the spell. "Is it working out?"

He reached over and squeezed her hand. "It's just wonderful. You really made it work." She felt he was reassuring her, and at the same time warning her to go no further with the subject.

"Could you tell me where the bathroom is please?" she asked.

"Back along the hall, on the right," said Virginia. Miranda felt unsteady as she got to her feet and made her way to the bathroom. It was a tiny room, created from an old linen cupboard with a compacted shower, toilet and basin. The walls felt as if they were closing in on her. She turned on the tap and leaned back against the wall facing the mirror. She knew she was on the brink of losing control, of starting to cry, of not being able to stop. Her head was spinning and she saw her reflection, pale faced, dark rings under her eyes, her mouth unnaturally contracted.

"Fuck her," she said under her breath. "Fuck her." She took a deep breath and then plunged her face into the water, taking a great gulp of it, spitting out the taste of the wine. She dried her face and looked at herself again. She wouldn't cry, she wouldn't faint. She'd get through this. That, she told herself, was all she had to do. She took a deep breath and walked back out onto the terrace. As she sat down, Charlie tried to catch her eye, but she refused to return his glance. She picked at the salad on her plate and smiled benignly at Linda.

"I love your garden," she said brightly to Virginia. "Our house in Glebe has a concrete square, with a Hills Hoist and weeds."

"Charlie tells me you originally come from Uwalla," said Virginia. "I'm not sure I've ever been there."

"Hardly anybody has," said Miranda. "It's the most beautiful, fantastic place. It's just terrific." She found herself ably holding forth on Uwalla and its natural beauty, without giving away anything of her life there. She saw Linda looking at her, puzzled. The conversation ranged to places Virginia had been, her recent trip to Western Australia. Charlie contributed stories of hitchhiking through America and Europe. Miranda felt relieved. She was above it all now, playing a game, only the knot in her stomach reminding her it wasn't.

Virginia got sweets and coffee and then liqueurs, managing to consume another half bottle of wine on her own. Linda sat silent and obedient, Charlie, in a sort of slumped resignation. Virginia went into the kitchen again and appeared with a green cut glass bowl filled with black grapes and strawberries. She put it down on the table, took a bunch of grapes and picked one off, holding it delicately between her fingers.

"So you're the oldest in your family?" she asked Miranda.

"Yes," replied Miranda, feeling a glimmer of hope.

"How many more?" went on Virginia.

"Five of us kids." The hope felt stronger.

"Five!" Virginia laughed tipsily. "They adopted five children?"

"No. Just me," said Miranda quietly. "Mum said when she started looking after me, it must have got her hormones going or something. After that, she just kept having kids. Reckoned she couldn't stop once she started. That's why she was so glad to have me." Using her mother's words, Miranda realised she probably sounded naive and childish, but she was beyond caring.

"Fancy, all those children, just from that." Virginia's tone was distinctly mocking as she raised her glass. "Well, here's to fecund and fruitful Mrs Darnley."

Linda tentatively raised her glass. Charlie stared angrily at Virginia. Miranda stood up. "Linda and I are going," she said coldly. "We've got things to do this afternoon. Thank you for lunch." She grabbed Linda's arm and pulled her to her feet. Still clutching the arm of the startled Linda, she walked quickly down the steps of the terrace and across the wide green lawn, under the jacaranda to Hazel's Citroen on the sweeping gravel drive. In silence, Charlie and Virginia watched as Miranda drove the car out through the gate.

Virginia stood up, swaying slightly, glass in hand. "I think I'll go and lie next to the pool." She drained the bottle into her glass. "Thank you so much for arranging luncheon, Charlie."

He watched her walk across the terrace, trim, contained, hard.

"Ginny," he called after her. She turned and looked back at

him, smiling vacantly.

"Ginny, it's been my rule in life that when the going gets tough, the weak and helpless run for cover." He stood up. "I've always done that with the women in my life, Ginny. So I don't know how people behave when they stick around. You're being a real shit, but you know, and I know, we need and love each other. I'm not about to walk off in a huff."

"God, you talk crap, Charlie." She walked off the terrace and disappeared through the lattice gateway.

Miranda drove fast, Linda sitting passively beside her. Linda kept looking at her sister, feeling she should do something. Finally, she reached into the glovebox, got a tissue and laid it on Miranda's lap. It was the only thing she could think of, but Miranda ignored it as they sped out of the green suburb and back onto the expressway. She began to drive more slowly and when they stopped at a red light, she picked up the tissue and blew her nose, loudly, angrily. Linda handed her another tissue.

"I'm OK," she said, her foot pushing down on the accelerator as the lights turned green.

"She was awful," said Linda quietly.

Miranda glanced at Linda. "Can't you see? That's why you can't have the baby adopted! Can't you see how awful she was? You can't just give him away. I don't know why you don't see that."

Linda was silenced by the burst of anger.

"I don't understand you, Linda," snapped Miranda.

Linda looked at her sister, incredulously. "You should be glad she didn't keep you! Fancy having that bitch for a mother. You've got it arse about."

Miranda looked at her coldly. She accelerated into the traffic. "I don't want to talk about it," she said archly. "And I think you should have Hazel there for the birth. I wouldn't be the right person."

Pauline and Roy sat outside the pub, on the edge of the verandah, sipping on schooners. Pauline upended the oyster bottle, using her fingers as a strainer. She held out an oyster to Roy.

148

"Nah," he said and took a swig of the beer. Their silence was companionable. Pauline had taken off her shoes and had rolled up her tracksuit pants. She wiggled her toes in the sand below the pub's wooden verandah. Down at the water's edge, the sand gave way to mud, extending out to the long stretch of water, where old fishing and prawning boats were moored. The afternoon sun glared across the water, making it almost impossible to look past the flat, black mud. From the cool darkness inside the pub, came the sound of the race broadcast, laughter and shouting, the chink of the cash register.

"Are you going to ring the girls and tell them?"

"Yeah, but I'll have to tell Kevin first. I owe him that much." She still felt out of sorts with Miranda and Linda, that both of them had let her down. "When I'm settled I'll tell them. I gotta get a house, you know."

"Not if you live with me."

"Leave it, Roy. I got enough to handle."

Far out beyond the mud, Kip splashed happily in the water, uselessly chasing the seagulls who floated on the water, picking off an occasional sodden chip, or diving for fish. Roy whistled and Kip came bounding out of the water, sliding on the black mud and up on to the sand, panting cheerfully at Pauline, then shaking himself vigorously, showering her and Roy with a mixture of the wet black mud and sand.

"Roy!" Pauline looked disgustedly at her mud splattered clothes.

"It wasn't me, it's the bloody dog!"

Kip bounced around, jumping and barking wildly, throwing more sand up against them. Pauline angrily brushed at the mud on her tracksuit.

"Here boy, here Kip boy, come 'ere." Roy held out his hand to the dog, which slunk gradually towards him. When he was close enough, Roy grabbed him by the scruff of the neck. "Now sit down, and I'll get ya something." The dog sank to his haunches and looked expectantly at Roy. From inside his jacket, Roy got a Mars Bar. Kip pricked up his ears excitedly and Roy released his hand from the dog's neck. He fished in his pocket and produced a bottle of pills. Pauline looked on as he inserted one into the Mars Bar and fed it to Kip, who wolfed it down greedily. "Valium," said Roy. "Quietens him."

Pauline looked at Roy coldly. "I heard stories, you know—but I didn't think they were true—stories about you feeding them things to Shirley."

"Not them. Moggies, Mogadons." He caught the expression on her face. "People talk. Half of it weren't true."

"Well, what I heard was that every afternoon when she got home, you had a cuppa waiting for her, slipped something into it and she was out like a light. That's what I heard."

"Yeah, well, I only ever gave her half a one." He took an oyster, considering how to swing things back in his favour. "She'd go on at me otherwise. Drive a bloke mad."

"Yeah, well, what if I started to drive you mad, eh? What'd you do?"

"Different kettle of fish entirely," he said stroking the dog. He noticed Pauline's fixed expression and looked gloomily at his feet.

She leaned over and patted the dog. "We like to see you, Roy. You'll always be welcome. But it's my life and I won't be rushed into nothing." She folded her arms in front of her. "Shirl does run off at the mouth," she said placatorily.

He looked at her gratefully. "I want to do things for you. I only want to make you happy." But there was a note of hopelessness in his voice.

"The best times we had these last few years been with you, Roy." She frowned. "But if you ever tried anything with them pills . . . if you ever . . ."

He shook his head and grinned. "Shirl was different: pain in the arse." Kip ran off, back into the mud and Pauline moved closer to Roy. He put his arm round her. "I do love you, you know."

"That'll do for now." She wriggled out of his embrace, but allowed his hand to rest on hers.

It was three weeks since the luncheon and Virginia had been careful not to think about it. She kept herself occupied with business, sixteen hours a day, avoiding Charlie and only coming home to sleep. It was an exhausting way to live. Today, she decided to see her parents' solicitor to finalise probate on her mother's will, a task she'd been avoiding. Charlie had said he'd be out all day, so after the solicitor's, she'd go home and sleep. Di, her secretary, had given her three sleeping pills. Now, she sat in the dim, hot office of Harry Thomas looking at the yellowish walls, the walnut panelled furniture which must have dated from when Harry had set up his suburban practice at the end of the depression. The ugly grey carpet, with its maroon roses, swirled out under the door to the tiny reception area, where the ancient Mrs Jacobs seemed to have been sitting forever hunched over an old, whirring typewriter.

Harry ceremoniously handed the probate papers across his desk to Virginia. "If you just sign here, Miss Nathan, and initial in the places I've indicated on the subsequent pages, it will bring this matter to finality." He always spoke in a prim, formal way, as if he believed it was the sort of language a solicitor should use. Intensely shy, he had never achieved any sense of ease with the world. He had been the Nathans' solicitor for over forty years and Virginia wished he wasn't about to retire. Anyone so at odds with the world was unlikely to run off with her money. But what she felt about him amounted to more than that. Harry, she thought to herself, was virtually her last link with her parents' world. She decided not to pursue that line of thought and signed the papers quickly. As she smiled up at him, he drew back nervously.

"You are now the possessor of a considerable amount of property," he said awkwardly. "I don't wish to be personal, Miss Nathan, but have you thought of how you might like to dispose of it in the unlikely event of your death?"

"It's not really that unlikely, Harry. I'm not immortal."

"I...I didn't mean that," he stuttered. "I meant in the unlikely event of an untimely death, before you had, so to speak, lived out the fullness of your life. That you might wish your property to go to...well...to designate it to..."

"I've never thought of it," said Virginia. "I do have a man that I live with."

Harry blushed furiously.

Virginia tried to relax back into the chair, but it was unforgivingly straight-backed. "I'm not sure I'd want Charlie to have it anyway," she said primly.

He nodded sagely, as if she had finally recognised the foolishness of her ways. Virginia sat staring into space.

Harry sat down and fiddled nervously with the pens on his desk.

"Have you any idea of what...er...you would like... done?" he asked cautiously.

"I suppose I could leave it to the Institute of Engineers."

"Of course you could, if that's what you'd like."

"Joke, Harry, joke."

Harry blushed and cleared his throat.

"Harry, I want to ask you a theoretical question."

He spread his hands on the desk and sat up like an obedient child.

"If someone had a child and had it adopted..."

"An ex-nuptial child?" he interrupted anxiously.

"Yes, an ex-nuptial child," said Virginia quickly. She didn't know why she was asking him. She didn't care about it, it didn't matter. She was remembering, without wanting or meaning to, but suddenly there was the picture in her head: the small, almost naked, baby, with its head of fine red hair. Why, she asked herself, why was she doing this? But the words kept coming as the pictures flashed through her head. "And if that child got in touch, later, much later, with its natural mother, would the child be entitled, you know, to the estate?"

"If the parent died intestate?" said Harry solemnly.

"I suppose so." Virgina answered his question vaguely. Miranda was in her head now, Miranda with that hurt look, standing up, walking away. And her own searing hatred of herself, seeing herself, glass raised: "Here's to the fecund and fruitful Mrs Darnley!"

"I don't think it's a question that you would, so to speak, need an intimate acquaintanceship in regard to." Harry was grinding the words out painfully. "My suspicion is that you have a requirement to satisfy yourself as to whom should be the beneficiary of your property, when of course the time arises." He stood up and walked towards the door. "You can contact me then." He sounded almost brusque and Virginia somehow forced a nod, then fled downstairs to the street, to her car.

She unlocked the door, got in and turned on the engine to forestall the scream of the car alarm. She hastily pulled out into the traffic, barely conscious of what she was doing. I'm mad, mad, mad, she told herself. She had to turn off to the right to get home and suddenly, she realised, she couldn't do it, that

152

she was fixed in one lane, the baby, herself, Miranda, all replaying in her mind, flashes of pain through her head. Eventually, she managed to ease over to the left and turn down a side street. She banged into the kerb as she stopped. Her heart was thumping and her hands shook as she fished in her bag for her cigarettes. I've got to do it, she thought. Charlie's right. I've just got to do something.

What she'd left and what she'd taken wasn't quite logical, she knew that. She wanted a bed for herself, but taking the double bed would have seemed to imply the wrong reasons for leaving. Not that it mattered, thought Pauline. It didn't matter what Kevin thought any more. Yet, here she was in the empty house, waiting for him, to tell him she'd left him. She'd expected him early this morning. It was now mid-afternoon and she badly wanted to go. Being alone in the bare house was making her edgy. But whenever she started to write something to him, she stopped before she finished it. A note just didn't seem right.

God knows why, but she'd taken the hall carpet. Now, having no vacuum cleaner, she was forlornly sweeping the dirt down the hall towards the front door. It was strange. She hated him, but she didn't. She was scared of him, not physically, but because of the fear that he might be able to talk her into coming back.

She picked up a blue envelope that had been slipped under the front door. It was addressed to her and she began to shake with excitement when she saw it was from the hospital. The broom fell onto the bare boards as she tore it open..." able to offer you a position as Nursing Aide to commence December 18. We would appreciate it if you could confirm in writing..." She squealed in excitement and hugged herself and began dancing down the hall. She looked to the phone, thinking of ringing the girls, then realised it had been cut off. She danced through the house again and wished she hadn't taken all the mirrors. She would have liked to look at herself, to confirm her happiness. She bent down to pick up the broom at the front door. The door opened. Kevin walked in.

"About time you got the place cleaned up," he grunted and walked down to the hall and into the kitchen. She stood at the front door, still clutching her letter, not knowing what to do.

"Hey, what the hell's going on here?" his voice boomed from the empty kitchen.

She walked slowly down the hall, her heart beating hard. She felt like a small child, but somehow, more certain than she'd ever felt as a child. She stood in the doorway, her letter against her, like a talisman. "I don't live here any more," she said softly. "Me and the kids have gone."

He let out a bellow and for a moment, she was sure he was going to come at her, but he turned his back on her and thumped his fist against the sink. The sound reminded her of the night he'd attacked Danny.

"I'm not coming back," she said firmly. "I wanted the girls home."

He turned and looked at her furiously. "That!" he said. "You make such a bloody fuss about everything. They'll come home some time or another. You make such a carry on about it all." But looking at his face, she could tell he knew. There was even a touch of something defeated and wounded, mixed in with the fury. "Look," he said. "I been trying to pay off the bloody truck all this year. But I kept a roof over yer head, didn't I? I kept the kids fed and clothed. Christ! What more do you want?"

"I'm going," she said, pressing the letter against her. "You can't stop me."

"Jesus!" he exploded again. "Why should I try to stop you? Bloody millstone round my neck: a whingeing wife and five bloody kids who never did a tap of work in their lives. Why should I stop you?" He advanced menacingly towards her.

"Don't you touch me." She stood her ground and he drew back.

"How do you reckon you'll support yourself? Who'll buy the food and pay for the phone? You'll live in some dump, bum end of town. You'll be crawling back here. Don't you think you can come begging me for money."

"I got a job." She half smiled as she said it. "I'm going now. I just wanted to tell you." She started walking down the hall, feeling the terrible futility of the twenty four years, the terrible sadness, the terrible lost dream that it'd be all right, that he'd be nice to her. It was like a force drawing her back into the house, but she kept walking down the hall.

"Who'd give you a job?" he yelled after her furiously.

"I'm working up at the Memorial." She picked up the broom from in front of the door, laid it against the wall in the corner, and opened the door.

"That'd be right," he screamed, his voice hoarse. "That'd be right for you. Lookin' after idiots."

She shut the door firmly behind her and ran down the front path, clutching the letter.

Miranda was at the back of the big hall, where rows of students sat at widely-spaced desks, ceiling fans turning slowly overhead, the sound of the traffic coming in through the open windows. In spite of the fresh air and the fans, the room was stale and hot, and Miranda felt a trickle of sweat down the back of her neck.

"Five minutes, ladies and gentlemen," said the supervisor at the front and automatically, every head in the examination room lifted to check the clock at the front of the room. "Five minutes." Miranda sat calmly, checking her answers, knowing that the late nights of the last three weeks, living on caffeine and nerves had paid off. Scanning through the paper, she realised she would probably get a credit, not bad, when three weeks ago, she'd been convinced of failure. But Virginia's rejection, her mother's rejection, had steeled her and had thrown her headlong back into her studies. Her old ability, her old single-mindedness, had finally come back to her and she felt that she had expunged the emotional upheavals of the past year. Her work acted as a barrier between her and Virginia, between her and Pauline, between her and the pain lurking in her mind. But the barrier was unselective. Her fury at Linda, the coldness between them remained, even though she knew it was illogical. Even with Patrick, she felt distant and remote in a way she didn't understand. When the loneliness closed in, she pushed it away with thoughts of study and success.

Only tomorrow's exam, her last, biochemistry, was a problem. There'd be no credits there, but if she studied tonight, all night, she'd at least be sure of passing.

After the exam, she disengaged herself from the clusters of students dissecting the paper and walked back through the building towards the library to pick up some papers Geoff

Harris had promised her. Outside Dr Stone's room, she felt a certain smug satisfaction, knowing that by tomorrow, she'd be in the position to pass his exam. But when his door opened and he emerged into the corridor, she looked uncertainly at him. He looked back at her for a moment, not recognising her and then smiled dryly. "Ah, Miss Darnley. Good luck for tomorrow." He turned his back on her and walked off.

Miranda felt inexplicably shaken. She forgot about the papers in the library and walked the length of the building, downstairs to where her bike was chained. She squinted as she came into the bright sunlight and hunched over her bike as she pedalled into the traffic of Parramatta Road, cars whizzing past her, a bus almost side swiping her. Feeling suddenly vulnerable, she rode up on to the footpath, got off and slowly walked the bike. She could feel the fierce determination of the last few week ebbing out of her, replaced by an emptiness that frightened her.

She turned into Glebe Point Road. The traffic here, turning and weaving erratically, was more dangerous than on the freeway, but somehow, it felt safer, as if it lacked the vicious intent of the cars on the main road. She got back on the bike and pedalled furiously up the hill.

She pulled up in front of the house, hurried inside and raced up the stairs to the attic room. She could hear Patrick picking out notes on the piano, the beginnings of a piece he was learning. She burst through the door and stood there, not knowing what to say.

"How'd the exam go?" he asked casually, stooping as he came out from behind the piano.

"Fine," she said rapidly. She remained standing next to the door. "Paddy, I know I've been crazy these last few weeks. I know it must seem like I'm using you or something. I got so caught up in the exams, they seemed the most important thing. I don't know, I thought if I did well, I'd sort of prove something about me, to you, to a lot of people, to myself."

He looked bewildered. "Everyone's ratty during exams."

"Oh!" Miranda almost burst into tears, frustrated at herself, and at him for not understanding.

"Anyway, it's your last tomorrow," Patrick said. "Are you nervous?" He walked over and put his arms round her.

"I'm exhausted, that's all," she said listlessly. "I'll stay up and learn two more questions." She leaned against him, holding his hand. She felt like crying.

"You might even come to bed while I'm still awake," he whispered.

She knew she wouldn't. She kissed him and went downstairs.

Hazel was sitting crouched in the big armchair in the kitchen, looking thin and pale. She was dressed in one of Linda's baby doll dressing gowns, somehow grossly inappropriate on her. Her eyes were bloodshot, her skin had an unhealthy yellowish tinge. She caught Miranda's worried glance.

"I got up," she said unsteadily. "I called Aunty Irene and told her my symptoms. She thinks I've had hepatitis." She paused and looked at the empty brandy bottle on the table. 'I guess I've been drinking too much too, so I stopped this morning. I'm going off to a health farm next week. Get myself sorted out." Her tone was listless.

"Sounds like a good idea," said Miranda, knowing it wasn't. "We've been worried about you."

"I've been worried about me to tell you the truth. Aunty Irene says hepatitis is a bugger of a thing. Lays you low emotionally."

"Especially after Phillip," said Miranda sympathetically.

"Oh him!" replied Hazel dismissively. She shifted round uncomfortably in the big chair. "I'm itching all over. It's horrible." She leaned over and picked up her cigarettes from the floor. "I could do with a drink," she said longingly. Miranda noticed her hands were shaking as she lit up. "By the way," Hazel remarked, "your mother called."

"Mum?" said Miranda, her face lighting up. "Mum rang?"

"No," said Hazel. "The other one. The wicked witch from the north shore."

Miranda's face fell.

"She sounded very upset," said Hazel. "She said please, please ring her this afternoon. She needs to talk to you."

·*Chapter Ten*·

"I was fourteen. Only child. Pampered, I suppose. It was all very polite. 'Would you pass the salt, Virginia . . . I've arranged for you to see the orthodontist, Virginia . . . Mrs Parsons has a new pleated tennis dress.' It was so suffocating I didn't know I was suffocating."

Miranda had come, in response to Virginia's pleas, but with a determination to keep her distance. She'd prepared herself by ringing Petunia. "I need a support group," she said. "Instantly."

"Told you," laughed Petunia. "What's happening?"

"Virginia wants me to come over there. It's my final exam tomorrow. If I don't study tonight, I'll probably fail."

There was a pause. "It might be your last chance with Virginia," said Petunia.

"I'm really angry with her."

"That's OK," said Petunia gently. "Go, be as pissed off as you like, but go. If you fail your exam, I'll write to the faculty for you."

"I will go," said Miranda. "I was going to go anyway. I just needed the support group."

Now she had come; a cold reserve, bolstered by exhaustion encased her anger. Her neediness was something she could not afford to indulge, but she recognised the edge of it there. When she arrived at the big house, she had knocked on the door in a businesslike way. Virginia, tense and polite, had led her up to her childhood bedroom to talk. The room had a pink and white girlishness and Miranda immediately sat down in the white cane rocker, refusing to be either impressed or sympathetic. "I need to tell you," Virginia had said.

"OK, tell me," Miranda replied stonily.

"Then Charlie came," Virginia went on. "A sort of unofficial exchange student. His father was some old US Army buddy my father had met in the war. What my parents didn't know was that Charlie had been in trouble in junior college for pinching a car and they wanted to get rid of him for a while. He seemed like the perfect mid-western kid. 'Yessir. Yes Ma'am. Beg you pardon, Ma'am.' Nice clothes, nicely brushed hair. The only odd thing was that he enrolled in art school and they thought that was a really extraordinary thing to do. But they excused it on the grounds he was American and that he'd probably do architecture eventually.

"You can't imagine how different Charlie was! He was eighteen and I'd never met anyone like him in my whole life. I mean he was actually fun. He laughed a lot, kidded around, talked to me, about himself, his life, me and my life. I'd never known anyone like that before.

"His clean-cut image began to wear a bit thin. He got a duffle coat and even though he was super polite, he was a bit noisy. He came home late all the time and you could tell he was a bit drunk. But my parents made an exception for him because he was a visitor and an American. I really wanted him to take me into art school to meet his friends, but he wouldn't.

"'I can't, Ginny, I just can't,' he'd say. Everybody else always called me Virginia.

"One day, I saw him on the train. I was coming home from school, dressed in my school uniform with the hat, the gloves, stockings, blazer, the works. And he was standing up beside the door with this girl. Everyone was staring at her because she wasn't the sort of person who travelled on our train. She had blond hair, all messy, extravagant and very long. She was wearing a long, black jumper that practically came down to her knees, black tights and long black boots. She had great black rings round her eyes and bright blue eyeshadow. Her face was dead white, no lipstick.

"You have to remember, when we went out, we wore court shoes, stockings, pleated skirt, white blouse, Pringle jumper and silk scarf and pearls. Sometimes, we wore lipstick. We wore gloves to church. Maybe the rest of Sydney was more advanced, but that was where we were at in the mid-sixties.

"All my schoolfriends began to talk about the girl with Charlie. They laughed at her and said she looked cheap and sleazy and fancy being like that, and wasn't it disgusting. I didn't tell them I knew Charlie. When we got to our station, I got off at the other end of the carriage, but I saw her lean out and kiss him and he put his hand up her jumper. I was so confused I felt like crying and I ran home ahead of Charlie who came in with his nice college boy manners and his nice college boy chit chat."

Virginia looked at Miranda almost pleadingly. "I never thought about what I was doing. I was too scared. You might find it hard to believe, but I just did things."

"What things?" asked Miranda. Her voice was neutral, her face expressionless.

"I took money out of my savings account. It was supposed to be mounting up to buy me a real pearl necklace when I was sixteen. I'd never done anything rebellious before. I went into town and I bought a long black jumper and black tights and black boots and eyeliner and mascara. It was difficult. I didn't even know the name of some of these things, because I'd only ever shopped at David Jones with Mother.

"Next Saturday, I skipped my ballet lesson and waited on the station. I changed in the waiting room there. I had a lot of trouble with the liquid eyeliner. I knew Charlie would be coming because he went out every Saturday. So when I saw him, I skipped up to him and told him I was coming with him. He looked at me; he couldn't believe it. It was amazing to him that I could look so different. Then he started laughing. 'OK, but don't say it was my fault.'

"We went to a pub, somewhere in the city. At first, I couldn't believe anyone would go to any place so grotty, but it was full of people who looked like me and Charlie. I started drinking, I started laughing, I started talking and I felt as if life had begun. I was like a different person, a real person, not good little Virginia. From then on, every Saturday, that's what I used to do. Sunday to Friday began to seem very unreal, but nobody ever suspected me because I kept playing little Virginia.

"Then my mother and father got an invitation to go away for a golf tournament up the country. They were golf fanatics and they wanted me to come, but I wouldn't. God knows what possessed them, but they left me at home in the care of Charlie. He and I went into the pub as usual, but this time, we decided to invite the crowd home. So all these art school weirdos had our address and they descended on us and we all got drunk. It wasn't even particularly wild, but out of character round here.

"Anyway, this one guy, Trevor, turned up. I'd had this adolescent crush on him for ages, because he was funny and loud, but he'd never taken any notice of me. When he came in, he looked straight at me. 'I want to fuck you,' he said. Ten minutes later he had, on my mother's bed."

Virginia paused, and looked at Miranda as if expecting a comment. "That was when you were conceived." Miranda looked at her coldly. Virginia cleared her throat and went on. "I hated it, but I felt it was very important to be cool, to pretend I had sex every day. I had to belong, be one of them; I would have done anything. And it seemed to work, because Trevor came over and put his arm round me. 'You're my girl,' he said. I really liked that. I had this schoolgirl vision of us getting married, white wedding and all, then leading this super exciting Bohemian life." Virginia smiled wryly. "I suppose I was very immature."

Miranda could see Virginia was making a concentrated effort, but the world she was describing made no sense to her.

"When my parents came back, they realised something had happened. We'd tried to clean up, but neither Charlie nor I was very good at it. All the whisky was gone and half the gin. They didn't say anything, but they phoned Charlie's parents and told them it was time for him to go home.

"Two months later, Charlie went back to America. He didn't go to the pub much in those two months. I couldn't go because my parents were checking on me. But I didn't even want to. I knew it had all been an illusion. It began to feel as if all my life was going to be an illusion. The momentary hope that things could be different had died. Charlie and I went for long walks together, round and round the streets, past all those perfect gardens, past the houses, talking, laughing, just being together. He kept at me in those two months, asking me whether I was pregnant. I told him I wasn't. He told me all the signs and symptoms and I told him I didn't have them. I told myself I didn't have them, although I knew I did. Then about a week after he left, I went into the kitchen one day after school and said, 'Mum, I'm pregnant.'

'Don't be disgusting, dear. That's a very vulgar joke.'

'I am, Mum.'

"She walked out, slammed the door and drove off. She came

back later, but I was up in my room. I didn't have dinner with them that night, but nothing was said. I went to school all that week. On Saturday, Mum packed a bag and told me to get in the car. Dad was in the rumpus room, getting his stuff ready for golf. I knew I wasn't supposed to talk to him, but I went down there anyway.

'I'm pregnant, Daddy.'

'Your mother told me.' He kept looking through his clubs.

'I wanted to tell you.'

He turned round, red in the face, absolutely furious and banged his golf club on the floor. 'I only hope he was clean!' he shouted. I had no idea what he was talking about but I heard Mum tooting the horn, so I ran out. But as we drove down the drive Daddy was standing there. He sort of waved, and smiled in an embarrassed sort of way.

"We drove to this place on the other side of town, an area I'd never been, the Queen Victoria Home for Mothers and Babies, all concrete paths, the lawns all short back and sides and nasty little yellow flowers in the beds. Inside there were vases everywhere, full of the same yellow flowers. The place was spotlessly clean and I had the impression of people scuttling out of the way as we walked down the hall. A nurse in a starched cap ushered us into matron's waiting room and we had to wait there for fifteen minutes. The floor was scrubbed linoleum and you could see everything was just so. There weren't any magazines, just a big clock on the wall with a very loud tick.

"Matron was really nice to my mother, it was all, 'Yes, Mrs Nathan, no, Mrs Nathan, cup of tea, Mrs Nathan?' There was a lot of talk about how this had only happened once, even though my mother didn't know that, talk about supposing young girls could make mistakes, and reassurances I'd be well looked after. Matron explained all the girls in the home were really nice girls. They'd only made one mistake too—she was very emphatic about that—so there was no need to worry that I might pick up bad habits. My parents could come and see me every second Sunday.

"Then the matron looked down her nose at me. 'You've been a silly little Miss, haven't you?' I didn't answer and she kept looking at me. 'Won't happen again, will it, dear?'

"I was furious and I looked her straight in the eye. I said,

'How would you know!' but she looked away and smiled tolerantly at Mum, as if I wasn't there.

"It was a funny place. There was a beautiful Italian girl of twenty four whose family came every visiting day and wept the entire afternoon. Most of the girls were seventeen or eighteen, so I was the youngest. The others had left school and were working in offices. One had even been at university.

"It was very strict. We got up at six, went to the showers and then had breakfast. They were obsessed with what we ate, but the food was horrible. After breakfast we were all weighed and the big thing was that you weren't allowed to put on too much weight. If you did, you were put on a diet as punishment. The girls bitched about it endlessly. I never put on enough weight to satisfy them and they stood over me to make me eat. They were always at you, but later I found out I put on weight if I ate chocolates, so I used to sneak out to buy them.

"After the medical check-ups, we had to work, almost all day. The home was attached to an ordinary maternity hospital and we did all the laundry and the food preparation. I had to wash sheets in a great copper and wring them out on a manual wringer. I had to scrub walls and peel potatoes. Some of the girls who'd been brought up to do housework understood that sort of stuff, but at home we'd always had a cleaning woman and all the mod cons. I felt very demeaned, like being condemned to work in a factory. But there was nothing else to do, absolutely nothing. No books, no paper for drawing or writing, although you were allowed to sew and knit. But I didn't know how to do that. Anyway, I didn't have any interest in it, we'd always had a sewing woman. Some of the other girls knitted like fury. There was one who was determined to teach me, but I couldn't get the hang of it."

"Did you make friends?" asked Miranda quietly. As she listened, she leaned forward in the chair. Her coldness had begun to be overridden by her curiosity. In spite of herself, against her will, she was being drawn into the story. She'd been staring out of the window at the deep blue of the jacaranda and the tennis court beyond, imagining Virginia in the bleak, cold horridness of the girls' home. She couldn't imagine that any mother who created a pink and white room like this for her only daughter could condemn her to such a place. She struggled with the image of Virginia as a fourteen-year-old, but she was still ready to protect herself against the Virginia she knew now.

"I told them I'd been raped," said Virginia. She laughed dryly. "I made up this horrendous story and I kept changing it and embellishing it. All the girls knew it was nonsense, but it became a sort of afternoon entertainment. Matron heard about it and told me to stop it. By then, I was quite popular, but I didn't make friends. None of us did. We were like little mushrooms, growing in the dark, just sitting there, expanding on our own puff. The rest was just backdrop.

"Did your parents visit?" asked Miranda, fingering a miniature white cane basket. The basket had a padded, pink checked, gingham lid.

"Oh yes, religiously every second Sunday. They chatted about tennis and golf and what was coming up in the garden. And they were planning this trip, so they'd be away during the last few months. They always asked whether I was well and sometimes Mum would say I was looking pale or complain that I hadn't brushed my hair. Sometimes she discreetly left a new smock."

"Did you talk about the pregnancy?...the baby?" asked Miranda hesitantly.

"I couldn't be bothered." Virginia seemed dismissive.

"But didn't they?" Miranda persisted.

"Well once, indirectly. My father sat in the car and only my mother came in. She was very agitated and she said some awful things were being said about me in the neighbourhood, presumably that I was pregnant. She had explained to everybody I'd been sick and had gone to New Zealand to stay with an aunt. She couldn't understand why people didn't believe her." Virginia paused, tucked her legs up under her and lit up a cigarette. "Actually, it was worse than New Zealand. At least you can get a drink there."

Miranda got up and walked round the room. The whole thing seemed unreal. The fourteen-year-old Virginia was unbelievable to her. She looked round at the objects in the room: the ballet shoes next to the cupboard, the little china ornaments on the dressing table, the student desk with its globe and tiny bookshelf. It was the sort of room she and Linda had dreamed about when they were little. Impulsively, she opened a cupboard door. There, hung in plastic covers, were a girl's clothes:

simple cotton dresses, frilly white blouses, tartan skirts.

"Shut it," snapped Virginia. Miranda obediently shut the cupboard door and looked at Virginia sitting on the bed. With her legs crossed under her, her hair hanging down loose and a defiant sulky look, she began to see what the fourteen-year-old must have been like. But the room, the clothes, hardly suggested the alienation Virginia described.

"She kept all your clothes?"

"She never threw anything out, except me." She paused and lit a cigarette from the one she was smoking. Miranda noticed the gesture and Virginia picked up her glance. "We used to do that in the pub. It was cool." She drew on the cigarette and seemed to regain her emotional distance from the story. She leaned back on the bed and blew smoke towards the ceiling, stretching up with her hand to follow its path. She looked at Miranda, sensing her doubts. "So that's the story," she said abruptly.

Miranda looked out of the window again. She bit on her lip. She was silent, almost completely still for a few moments, tempted to leave, to bury it forever. But she remembered what Petunia had said, that it might be her last chance.

"That's no story," she said. "That's just the beginning."

"OK, it went on for months and months. I had you. I went home. You went to Uwalla. That's the story!"

"It's not our story," Miranda said icily. "It's your version of your story: poor, pathetic fourteen-year-old. Very sad. It wasn't easy. Poor little rich girl." Her voice rose. "What about me? What about you and me? What about our story? You know what you make me feel? You make me feel like I've always felt. A dreadful mistake. And my mother picked me up and told me I was her darling and her favourite and I wasn't a mistake. And she had to do that because she knew I was. And then my father told me I was. He told me I was your mistake." She looked at Virginia, terrified by her own anger, but unable to contain it. "I hate you! I hate you!"

Virginia almost cowered from Miranda's fury.

"What about us?" shouted Miranda. "What did you feel when I started to move around? What did you feel when you were giving birth? What did you feel when you saw me? What did you feel when you gave me away? You gave me away, you know. You gave me away." Her voice came out in staccato sobs, but stopped suddenly as Virginia looked up at her. She thought she had never seen a look of such deep, wounded pain in anyone. Virginia's pain was devoid of tears. It was dry, deep, cold pain and, looking at her, Miranda saw that the pain had always been there, in every fibre of Virginia's body, in the way she tilted her head and lit her cigarettes, in her every movement. It was the mirror of her own pain. Miranda moved towards her, but she stepped back as Virginia got up off the bed and walked stiffly to the dressing table. Miranda watched as Virginia opened the drawer. She watched as Virginia's hand felt for something, her eyes fixed on the little china dogs and horses on the table top. She watched as Virginia's hand closed round an old blue and white flowered handkerchief. She held it out to Miranda, still not looking at her.

Tentatively, Miranda took it from Virginia's outstretched palm. It lay in her palm now and she unfolded it carefully; fine strands of baby's hair, red hair, against blue flowers. Miranda's hand trembled as she looked at it. She looked at Virginia, now lying on the bed, foetal, arms around her head. Miranda put the handkerchief back on the table and then walked over to the bed and looked down at Virginia. The pain, it seemed to Miranda, threatened to shatter them both and suddenly frightened, she reached down and put her hand over Virginia's. Virginia sobbed, with a drawn out desperation, and pulled Miranda down on to the bed. Their arms were around each other, feeling and holding.

Virginia felt Miranda's hair, ran her fingers through it, cupped her hands over the top of Miranda's head and suddenly began to sob, deep, heaving, releasing sobs. Miranda lay against her, crying quietly, feeling her own hurt, her need, until they lay quietly. After a long time, Virginia spoke, her voice soft and muffled.

"The first time it happened, I didn't know how it would make me feel," she said.

"The first time?"

"We were at an exercise class. Stupid, they were. Breathe in, breathe out. Bend your knees, relax, as if that was how you had a baby." Virginia's voice was still shaking. "And I felt this little flutter, like a little wave inside me." She looked at Miranda. "You."

"What did you feel?"

166

"I felt incredibly happy." A smile passed over her face. "Incredibly. It was the first time I had ever thought of the baby, ever thought of you." She gave Miranda a shy look. "So, being the smart arse I was, I called out, 'I've got something inside me.' Of course everyone laughed and the physio giving the class went very red and said, 'Enough girls.' And from then on, I was one of them. Even though I wouldn't knit or sew, I was growing my little mushroom just like the rest of them, watching my weight, feeling it move, having it, being it. I can't describe it, but you know, I got into bed that night and for the first time since Charlie left, I cried and cried, but I thought, 'It's mine, it's mine. I've got something of my own. Inside me, safe, secure, warm.' I loved it when you grew so big. I loved it when you kicked. I loved it when it got uncomfortable, because it proved you were there."

"So how did you feel when the other girls went off to have their babies?"

Virginia took Miranda's hand and held it in hers. "We all got sort of excited and we all wanted to know how long it took and how much it weighed and whether it was a boy or a girl. But once they went into the hospital, that was it. We weren't allowed to see them any more. We got it from the nurses or the cleaners who'd tell us, really crossly, as if it wasn't our business. And we'd say things like, 'Wasn't it lovely, she wanted a girl', or whatever." Virginia paused and looked at Miranda. "You know the worst thing was when the girls came back for their check-up six weeks later. We didn't want to see them, didn't want to know them, because that was reality. They didn't have their babies. They were looking for jobs or at home with their families. It didn't fit in with our fantasies."

"What was your fantasy?"

Virginia blushed. "I was going to call you Leticia. I always knew you were going to be a girl." Miranda smiled at her. "And I was never very specific about the practicalities, but we were going to live in a little house together. I was going to have a wonderful room for you, with a white cane bassinet and all sorts of frills and fripperies. And an open fireplace. I'd eat scones in the afternoon, in front of the fire, sitting on the floor, which I was never allowed to do here. And you'd lie on a little rug next to me and you'd smile. And I'd tickle your tummy and you'd sort of laugh. And we'd go for walks, and you'd be there in the pram, with that funny little laugh. People would stop and say, 'What an exquisite baby. Is she really yours?' Virginia laughed and squeezed Miranda's hand. "I'll tell you what though. You weren't going to have red hair. Blond. Big blue eyes." She laughed again, as if there was a lot of laughter in her now.

"Did you know it was all a fantasy?".

Virginia was silent for a moment. "I certainly knew it, but I couldn't think about it. I couldn't actually think about things till I was about twenty five. And because I'd learnt to think—you know, sort of self-taught—I learnt not to think about you. That's why all this has been so hard for me." She drew away from Miranda. "You do understand that, don't you? I mean, you don't think I'm just a shit?"

"No, I don't." There was silence between them. "I did before."

"I know." Virginia looked at her. "I was before—not really—I've been very frightened."

Virginia sat up on the bed, intent on clarity, intent on finishing. "I was working in the laundry when my contractions started. The fantasy ended. I knew they were going to take you away from me. So I didn't say anything. I just kept working. But I had to keep bending over this boiling copper because eventually, I couldn't stand up straight when a contraction came. One of the girls told the sister. I told sister I was feeling a bit tired and she believed me. But as she was leaving, there was this great rush of water onto the floor from between my legs and she turned and looked at me. 'You're a naughty girl. I'll have to take you up to the hospital at once.' They wheeled me up on a trolley and the first thing she did when I got there was to say to the labour sister. 'You'll have to watch this one.'

"But they didn't. I was left alone for hours with these terrible contractions, crying and crying, so frightened, and, I don't know, really angry too. Once I started screaming and the nurse came back and looked at me, then said, 'Don't you dare do that. There's a mother in there having a caesarean,' as if I wasn't a mother.

"I was there all night and, finally, they came back in the morning when I was beginning to push. The sister from the home came in because they were short-staffed. She didn't have much experience in deliveries and she told me that I must stop bearing down till the doctor arrived." A look of fear flitted across Virginia's face. "I couldn't stop. And they said, "Stop, you'll hurt the baby," and they held back your head. And I was so scared I'd hurt you, but there was this push, push, push in my body. They were all so angry." Virginia put her head between her knees and wept. Miranda put her arms round her.

"But you didn't hurt me. You didn't."

Virginia wiped her eyes on the bedcover and looked up. Her eyes were puffy with dark circles underneath, freckles showing through where the tears had washed away her make-up. "I didn't know that. And it always scared me. And I thought perhaps I had done something—you know, some sort of damage." She looked up at Miranda. "I didn't," she said emphatically.

"The doctor came and he abused the nurse for not calling him and he abused me for holding back because all my push had gone and you were stuck there. He said it was lucky you weren't dead and he used forceps. And you cried right away when he pulled you out, but he held you upside down like some poor little rabbit and slapped you. I remember I sat up and said, 'Give her to me!' but they wouldn't. They gave me some tranquilliser and started hooking me up for a transfusion and stitching me up. All the time I was screaming, 'Give her to me, give her to me,' until I passed out.

"I was unconscious for most of the next few days, but the moment I came to, I screamed, 'Give her to me, give her to me.' The sister came in and told me you'd already been taken. I screamed and screamed and they injected me with something to knock me out."

"So you never saw me?" asked Miranda. She looked over to the handkerchief. "So how did you get my hair?"

"The most wonderful thing happened," said Virginia. "I woke up in the middle of the night and I was sobbing. I felt broken. I couldn't scream any more. The nurse came in and she was a really nice young nurse with the kindest face, I'll never forget. And she sat on the edge of the bed and she stroked my hair and she kept saying, 'I do wish you'd seen her.' And she told me she'd had a baby four years ago, a little boy. She still thought of him and she was sure he knew how much she loved him. She felt he must know, because she felt it so strongly. I think if she hadn't been there that night, I would have really gone mad. I mean loony-bin crazy. Anyway, she stayed with me till she thought I was asleep and then she went out. About five minutes later, she came back in, turned the light on and shook me.

"'Virginia, she's still here. She's still here. Sit up and I'll bring her in.'

"I struggled to sit up in bed and she was back in no time. I was so weak that she had to sit with me and help me hold you. And the tears were pouring down my face while I looked. This little baby, with long, wispy red hair, and apple rosy face and bruise marks on your skull from the forceps. But perfect, absolutely perfect. And she unwrapped you for me and showed me all of you. I remember when I rubbed the sole of your foot, you stretched your arms out and your head back. I stopped crying. I could feel milk coming out of my breasts, leaking down my front and you must have smelt it and started nuzzling in towards me. And all of a sudden I started having these terrific contractions and blood started pouring out. I couldn't hold you because I was blacking out. So I kissed you and the nurse took you back. The next day you really were gone.

"But that nurse came in the next night and she had that little handkerchief with the bit of hair. She'd put one of the flowers in your cot and she told me you'd gone to a lovely young couple. She had red hair and was really pretty and he was a very clean-cut young fellow with black hair. I hated them, passionately."

Miranda had tears in her eyes as she looked at Virginia. "My poor little mother," she said softly.

Virginia squeezed her hand. "I did want you. I did love you."

"I know." Miranda nodded. "What happened to you after that?"

"My mother came three weeks later. I'd been ill and I stayed in hospital. My mother beamed at me and said it had worked out well because they'd been able to stay an extra week in London. She never mentioned the baby, but she made it clear she was prepared to be very forgiving. And, you know, I think she really tried. She felt she'd failed as a mother because she'd had a pregnant daughter. When I got home, she'd bought me a goldfish. It was the first pet I'd ever had because mother thought animals were dirty. So the goldfish was a big step. But it annoyed her that I sat at the dinner table and cried. I couldn't help it, but it was embarrassing to them because they'd made this big gesture with the goldfish and were prepared to let bygones be bygones.

"Anyway, I wasn't home long. One morning I found the goldfish floating belly up, all white in its little weedy pond and I felt the baby was dead. In fact, I was sure of it and I thought it had happened because I hadn't pushed you out properly. And my crying stopped and I packed a bag and I stole two hundred pounds out of my mother's purse and took her DJ's credit card and left a really abusive note and went back to the pub. I found a man who wanted me to live with him. I got a job waitressing and I got myself back together. I did my higher school certificate at night. I did brilliantly. I went to university and did engineering. I finally got back in contact with my parents and told them I was sorry about all the bother I'd caused them. I saw them on birthdays and Christmas and they were really pleased and believed everything was wonderful. I went out to work and I did very well. I got married to a man and it didn't work out. I got married to another man who turned out to be gay, but gave me good contacts. My father retired and I took over his company. I sent it bust and I'm building it up again now. That sort of success is very important to me. Charlie came back to Australia and I thought maybe he could bring me alive again. He tried, and I help him with his art and he certainly gets me through the day.

"But I died with the baby. And since I found out you were alive and real, I've had to come alive. And it's been so hard. But I'm glad I did, because I love you, Miranda. I've always loved you, always, always, always."

Tears started pouring down Virginia's face. She held her arms out to Miranda. As Miranda held her, she felt Virginia against her, soft, warm, somehow motherly. She felt a soft inner centre in herself that she'd never known was there. "Oh Mum."

"Do you really feel comfortable calling me Mum?" asked Virginia handing Miranda a mug of coffee. They had come outside and were sitting beside the dark green, still wintry pool, leaves swirling into it with each gust of wind. "I should get it cleaned," remarked Virginia, "but I like it green, don't you?"

Miranda looked at her dreamily and took a sip of coffee. "I can't think of it as a swimming pool," she said. "In Uwalla a pool's fifty metres long, with chlorine that makes your eyes water, full of kids. They have the town louts for guards, all wearing tight yellow stubbies. This is more like a pond. Leave it green. Get some ducks."

"And have shooting parties," said Virginia. She slipped in and out of her new intimacy with Miranda, sometimes assuming her old facade, but without its cutting coldness, sometimes stroking Miranda's hair or squeezing her hand. It had been two hours since they had come down from the upstairs bedroom, almost shy, after the passionate tears, the embraces, the outpouring.

"Do you feel comfortable calling me Mum?" repeated Virginia.

"No," said Miranda. "It makes me feel disloyal. Do you mind?"

"No, it makes me someone I'm not. I'm your mother, not your Mum."

"You don't want me to call you 'mother', do you?" asked Miranda in alarm.

"Certainly not. I want you to call me Ginny. But I want you to think I'm your mother, to know I'm the one that gave birth, that even though I didn't bring you up, that you were mine. You know, fruit of the womb and all that," she added hurriedly.

"I do know that," said Miranda. "That's what I wanted all the time I guess...I wanted it. I needed it. I guess I felt more desperate than I realised."

"I'm sorry."

"It's OK," said Miranda slowly. "We've got time...it still feels strange doesn't it?"

"It does and it doesn't," said Virginia. "What does your real mother think about this?" she asked suddenly.

"She doesn't like it. She's a very motherly person, almost too much—it stops her understanding."

"Would you like me to meet her?" asked Virginia. Then she looked embarrassed. "It wouldn't work. I'm such a snob."

Miranda laughed. "So am I." She started tearing at a large oak leaf and throwing the pieces into the pool. "It'd be awkward. Now, anyway." She thought of Pauline, longingly, sadly.

"You'd like her, though." She watched as a piece of the leaf sank into the murky depths. "You know, she's bright and she's pretty and she laughs a lot. People do like her. She's a real stayer, everything she puts her mind to— babies..." Miranda looked at Virginia. Virginia smiled ruefully. "Sport," went on Miranda. "Marriage. She wants things to work. She doesn't think about things, she just does them. Half the time she doesn't know when to give up."

"Did she push you to go to university?"

"No, she didn't really want me to go. She thought it would take me away from her. In a way, she's right. But she's got this sort of inverse pride that I made it. You know, I couldn't be a tennis champ or a swimming champ like Natalie, but I've made the best of what I've got."

"So why did you go to university?"

"Rather than work on the check-out?"

"Well, rather than do a tech course somewhere up there, something like that?"

"I knew I had a really good brain by the time I was about twelve and I suppose I wanted to use it. And then, when I was fourteen, I had a big fight with Dad and we didn't speak again, ever again, really. I knew I couldn't stay. I had to find something for myself. I like animals and I like really difficult academic problems; it sort of keeps me on an even keel. So I threw myself into getting good enough marks to do vet science."

"Much the same way I felt when I left home."

It was getting dark, the wind lifting the leaves on the lawn, sending them scuttling along the path against the wire of the tennis court fence. The sun glowed against the smoky grey of the clouds and the jacaranda was outlined against the sky as Miranda and Virginia walked up to the house.

Charlie jumped as he walked up the driveway. He jumped and gave a little, mid-air, Fred Astaire kick. He whistled and jumped again, nearly dislodging the bottle of champagne he carried under his arm. He clutched it to him, but kept whistling as he walked up to the front door, unlocked it and walked in, pausing for a moment to kiss the sweet-faced madonna with the broken foot which he had placed on the front table. "Ginny, Ginny," he yelled. "Guess what? Sold the painting. It's a big painting.

Big time. Big money." His voice took on a sing song tone. "They like me. They think I might be the new Charlie Evans and they didn't even know the old one. They want more paintings. Ginny!"

The house was in darkness downstairs, except for the front hallway. But there was a light on upstairs, in Ginny's old room. Charlie saw it and groaned, deposited the champagne on the hallstand, bounded up the stairs and threw open the door. Someone had been there, lying on the bed, opening cupboards and drawers. Charlie felt his balloon of happiness deflating. He didn't want to cope with a depressed, angry Ginny with her water-tight excuses for doing sweet fuck-all. He started to go through the house, room by room, expecting to find Ginny prostrate on a bed or floor. As he searched the house, his fear of her suiciding surfaced and he remembered the grey, cold body of the friend he had found in his New York apartment. He felt his anger, a knot in his stomach. Suicide was a hostile act. Fuck her, for even letting him think of it. Fuck her; he was neurotic and sensitive too.

He searched downstairs with increasing panic, then reassured, went upstairs again to change his coat. He went back into Ginny's old room and sat down despondently on the bed. He'd always disliked the room, with its good, good taste and its pink, pink girlishness. It was, of course, everything that Ginny wasn't, but he understood why her mother had done it. He thought back to the Nathans, shadowy figures in his mind. He'd liked the old man—he'd treated him well and always talked to him—not like his old man who'd start reading the riot act the moment you opened your mouth. He remembered his surprise at discovering the depths of Ginny's discontent when he'd returned to Australia. Being raised on violent confrontation over minor domestic issues, he still had trouble understanding that silence and politeness were weapons, just as deadly. Jesus, years of living with Ginny should have taught him that. He decided he was getting maudlin and walked downstairs again.

He got his champagne and went into the kitchen, determined to drink enough to get drunk. And happy too. He wanted to be happy. He got himself a glass and gradually eased the cork out of the bottle. He turned the radio on and Handel's water music blared out.

"Up the lot of you!" he toasted himself. "To art, to love, to me, to Ginny and everybody else." He swigged down his first glass and poured a second with the horrible feeling it wasn't going to work. And he did really want to be happy. He wanted to feel his success, to share it with Ginny.

"Charlie, Charlie, is that you?" He heard Ginny's voice faintly from the studio. He leaned his head over the stairwell.

"It's me!" he bellowed. "And I want you to come up here and drink champagne with me."

"Come down here!"

Ginny suddenly appeared at the bottom of the stairs, clad only in a pair of knickers, covered in soapsuds. She was laughing and smiling: a proper laugh, a proper smile. "Come down here. I've got the spa working and I've filled it up with shampoo and it's bubbling everywhere. Come on, Charlie."

Charlie grinned. This was more like it. He got some plastic tumblers and grabbed the champagne and went down into the studio. The madonnas were lined up, in double schoolgirl lines leading towards the spa. A couple of them had washers, draped like towels around their shoulders and one had a toothbrush under her arm. Charlie laughed. It was the first time Ginny had ever played with them. He wondered what had happened. Outside, the spa was steaming fiercely, too fiercely, and the shampoo bubbles were spilling out over the edge. In the steam and the green, half light from the bottom of the spa, he couldn't even see Virginia, but he heard her humming and giggling to herself.

"I'll get my gear off," he yelled as he stripped. "Be right in." Ungainly and shivering, he rolled over the side of the tub and plunged into the hot, steaming bubbles and came face to face with Miranda, sitting, grinning. Ginny sidled over to him and put her arm round him.

"Just Charlie and me and baby makes three," she sang.

·*Chapter Eleven*·

Charlie groaned, struggling to free his left leg. It felt as though the woman had speared something through it. He couldn't think why they allowed women to wrestle on the campus. There was something terribly wrong about it. She was so big, big enough for a life drawing class. There, he appreciated flesh and muscle, but this was unfair. If he won the match, he'd say something in his victory speech. But the immediate problem was to get her off his leg. He tried to get her in a head hold.

"Jesus! Charlie! Let go!"

His eyes flew open to see Ginny's face directly above his. His brain shuttled between the gargantuan female wrestler of his dream and the slight form of Ginny which was actually lying on top of him.

"I'm getting old," he muttered.

"You must be," she whispered. "I can remember when you wanted to wake up with a woman on top of you."

"Two women," he said. "I always wanted two women." He kissed her tenderly. "But I'm glad you're here, Ginny. If you're going to make a habit of it, I may invest in a double bed."

Virginia sat up in bed. She was naked and he looked up at her breasts. They were so lovely, he thought he'd like to draw them from this angle. "Breasts in flight." She leaned towards him. "Breasts landing." He put up his hand to caress them, and for once, she didn't draw back. "I hate to admit it, Charlie, but you were right. I had to get it sorted out—about Miranda."

He knew something deep inside her had changed. It wasn't just that she had slept with him, but she had lost her characteristic prickliness and defensiveness.

"She's an OK kid, isn't she?" he said.

"She's lovely," replied Ginny warmly. "It's funny—I don't really know her yet, but I feel as if I know her intimately. I

176

never thought I'd feel like a mother. I never thought she'd feel like a daughter, but in a funny way, it's exactly that. Look." She showed him the underside of her breast.

"Lovely," he groaned.

"Stretch marks," she said, running her fingers over the tracery of fine white lines. "I've always hidden them. But when I was pregnant, my breasts got enormous."

"You going to keep talking dirty?" he said.

"We could have a baby," she said. "We're not too old." Her voice was excited. She'd been thinking about it all night, wondering if she should say anything to him. Now, it had just come out. She wasn't used to that. She felt different from how she'd ever felt before, more childlike, but as if she could do whatever she wanted.

Charlie lay still. "Ginny, a baby's very serious." He was silent for a while and she snuggled against him. "I take the madonnas back today," he said.

"Do they want a requiem mass before they go?"

"It'd be a friendly gesture," he said, "but not necessary. Anyway, I pick up another lot—babes in mangers—Christmas orders."

"We'll light candles for them," she said, biting his nipple.

"Well, it would be appropriate—to make a baby while they're here. Part of the rich religious pageantry of the north shore. Before the crucifixes come in for Easter."

She sat up again. "I'm not having a baby till next year at least. I was just asking you how you felt about the idea. But not till I've opened my Perth office."

"Not till she's taken over the world," he groaned. "Ginny, Ginny, Ginny." He buried his face in the pillow. "You know why this really is serious? Because I need to know you love me. Not so I can give you a child or because I'd be a wonderful father or because I happen to be here. But do you love me, for me? Really?"

She looked round his room. It was the tower room, formerly her mother's sewing room, and it was very small. Through the window, she saw the trees against the intense blue of the summer sky. Charlie had painted a fake window with a harbour view, boats, ferries and sailboards skimming across the water. It had a lyrical, silly quality that made her laugh. She looked at it and turned back to him.

177

"Yes, I do love you."

He pulled her down on top of him. "Just as well," he said. "Because I'd be here even if you didn't."

Miranda pedalled up the road, heady on the combination of the hot summer day, elation and exhaustion. She and Ginny had sat talking till four, when she finally confessed she had an exam in five hours. Ginny had offered to drive her to the university in the morning, but Miranda, suddenly panicky about her lack of study, left immediately. She had arrived back at Glebe at five, snuggled into bed with the sleeping Patrick for a few minutes and then studied till eight thirty. Even now, she could hardly believe the paper had been so easy. For the first time in her life, she had a sense of being lucky. She wanted to sing and put her feet up on the handle bars as she'd done as a child on the dirt roads of Uwalla, before her father had told her harshly that she looked like an idiot.

Valentino's shop was a shadow of what it had once been. All his bric-a-brac was stacked and marked "Closing sale—less than wholesale price". The remaining flowers were sadly wilted. There was a smell of decaying greenery even though the real ivy had long since been replaced with sun-yellowed plastic ivy. Since Miranda had doused him, Valentino had shown her a new respect, but until now, she had pointedly ignored him. Now, as she wheeled the bike past the shop, she saw him behind the counter, gloomily packing a life size dalmatian into a crate.

She walked in. "Sorry you had to close."

He looked at her in surprise and then grinned slyly. "You got skinny. Skinny, but a lovely body still . . . Ohh, iron legs."

"Valentino . . ." She stopped, realising the futility of saying anything.

"You no throw water." He retreated behind the counter and took four dripping bunches of fading pink carnations and began to wrap them. "They worth thirty six dollar." He handed them to her. "Free for you."

She grinned at him and took them, pausing at the doorway. "I'll take it off what you owe me," she said. She jumped on the bike, cramming the flowers into the front basket. "Thanks," she shouted back at him.

He stood, hands on hips outside the shop, watching her. At the top of the hill, she turned and waved at him, then coasted down the other side.

Miranda raced up to Linda's room and burst in, expecting to find her at her desk, drawing, as she did every morning since she'd finished work. But the room was empty and Miranda remembered she'd probably gone for her appointment with Dr Johns. She sat down on the bed and looked round the room. The beloved soulful puppy picture, Linda's first purchase, had long since gone.

The room had taken on a new character, with a huge notice-board over the sewing machine table which was draped in bright, glittery material. The noticeboard was covered with drawings of slim, elegant models in slinky, elegant clothes. For the first time, Miranda noticed how professional they looked. She put Valentino's flowers on Linda's pillow and ran upstairs to the attic. It was empty and she felt a stab of disappointment at Patrick's absence. Slowly, she walked downstairs, deflated, no one to share her happiness with. She wanted Patrick, to lie in his bed in the hot attic room, recounting the events of last night, to re-establish their intimacy.

She decided to go down to the kitchen to ring Petunia. As she walked into the kitchen, her exhaustion caught up with her and she leaned against the doorway. Hazel was at the sink, leaning over it, dabbing at her face with a dirty Wettex.

"Where's Linda?" Miranda asked.

"I hurt myself," said Hazel angrily, trying to put her head under the tap. She turned and looked at Miranda. An ugly gash extended from above her eyebrow, into her hair, which was matted with blood. Miranda gasped, grabbed her and led her to the armchair.

"What happened?" she asked anxiously.

"I don't know," said Hazel blankly. "I woke up on the floor and something had happened to my head." She looked at Miranda with the first real sign of recognition. "Is it bad?" she asked, frightened.

"Yes," said Miranda gently. "You'll need it stitched. I'll clean you up and we'll get you to a doctor." She searched for a clean towel and got a basin of water and began to wash the caked blood away, mopping gently at Hazel's forehead. "You don't remember?" she asked.

"I had terrible nightmares last night and I remember Patrick saying something about the car and I was going to get a coffee and then I woke up on the floor." Tears suddenly spouted from her eyes. "Did someone attack me?" A tremor went through her body.

"I think you had a seizure," said Miranda matter of factly. She put down the cloth and took Hazel's hand. The flesh around the gash was raised and purple, distorting Hazel's beauty. The fear in her eyes seemed to be engulfing her. It affected Miranda, but somehow hardened her too. "How long since you had a drink?"

Hazel looked at her, her eyes pleading. Miranda remembered back to her father, drinking, always drinking. Normally, he'd been a controlled drunk, driven by a cold aggression. Once, when she was twelve years old, he'd chased Pauline and fell, smashing his head on the table. She remembered the purple bruise on his head as he lay on the floor, screaming drunken abuse at her mother and her. Now, she stroked Hazel's hair, almost afraid to touch her.

"I haven't had a drink since yesterday," said Hazel. "So it couldn't be the booze."

"It is the booze," said Miranda trenchantly. "You had too much and..."

"I didn't have enough," interrupted Hazel.

"And you came off it too fast," finished Miranda. "That's what caused the seizure." She stood back from her. "Haze, you'll have to go to hospital; dry out properly."

"I didn't even mix my drinks," said Hazel defiantly.

Miranda went to the phone. She started searching through the book, as much to hide from Hazel's wound, as to find help. She felt nauseated by the smell of blood. She could hear Hazel's sniffles. "I'll ring your aunt," she said.

Hazel moaned what sounded like a protest and Miranda turned round. Hazel was shaking, her body wracked with sobs. "Miranda don't be angry at me. I'm sorry. I'm sorry. I never meant to be like this. You know, Mummy tried so hard to be good and I tried so hard to be bad and we both ended up the same. But I can't stop, I can't stop drinking."

Miranda's anger dissolved. She went back to Hazel and put

her arms round her. She held her, rocked her, frightened to let her go.

She was still holding her when she heard the front door open. As Patrick walked into the kitchen, she felt a surge of relief, looking up at him with wide, frightened eyes. "She's had a seizure and cut her head," she said, holding Hazel. "We'll have to take her somewhere."

Patrick walked over and looked at the gash. "Jesus," he said. The two girls looked up at him, white-faced. He squeezed Hazel's shoulder, looking anxiously at Miranda. "We'll take her up to casualty." He lifted Hazel gently to her feet and looked at Miranda. "You've got to go to the hospital anyway. Your kid sister's having the baby."

Patrick had stuffed a chocolate bar into her pocket. He'd wanted to come with her, but Miranda could see the fear in Hazel's eyes and insisted he stay. "She needs you," she'd whispered to him. "You'll have to find some place where they can treat her, stop her drinking."

"Does she want to?"

"Don't be so hard on her. Make her try."

Miranda felt oppressed by the heat as she walked up to the maternity wards on the other side of the main road. It was so hot that the tar was shiny on the road. She seemed to have no energy left, yet she wanted to be able to help Linda. Thinking how she could do it made her feel confused and a little desperate, not knowing what she should do or say to heal the rift between them. As she stood at the crossing and waited for the lights to change, a hospital orderly came up beside her, pushing an old woman in a wheelchair, a drip suspended above her. Miranda noticed her artificial leg, complete with a slipper and sock, held across her lap. The slipper and sock matched those on the leg emerging from under the hospital blanket. As the lights changed, the woman grinned up at Miranda. "Cheer up, love," she cackled. "At least yours are attached." Miranda smiled, fortified. She got Patrick's chocolate bar out of her pocket, but it was already melting through the silver paper. She threw it away, licking the chocolate off her fingers as she walked in through the big double doors of the maternity section. As she walked along the scrubbed corridor, the urgency of the situation struck her and she began running down to the nurse's station.

"I'm Miranda Darnley," she said breathlessly to the nurse behind the desk, who was busy filling in charts. She didn't look up at Miranda until she'd finished ruling a precise line on a graph. "Linda Darnley, my sister, she's having a baby. She needs me. Can you tell me where she is?"

The young freckled nurse looked up at her calmly. She wasn't any older than Miranda, but she was obviously someone who had been competent and responsible since childhood, knowing they have to go through life putting up with the foolish, ungoverned emotions of others.

"She's just gone into the labour ward," she explained.

"So can I go in with her?"

"You'll need a cap." Miranda felt her head and the young nurse looked at her patronisingly. "A sterile cap, boots and a gown." Then, without explanation, she got up and walked away. Uncertainly, Miranda followed her along the corridor until the nurse acknowledged her again. "I think she's a way off, but doctor says you can never tell with these young ones. We popped her into theatre." She turned round to Miranda. "She kept complaining she was hot back in the ward," she said censoriously.

"It's very hot," said Miranda loyally.

"They all complain," said the nurse, handing her the gown and hat. "It goes the other way round."

"Maybe it's because they're having babies," said Miranda. She felt fiercely protective of Linda.

"In there," said the nurse dismissively. "That door."

The labour theatre was bright with light from the big clear window, through which was a distant view of the other wing of the hospital and, above, the deep blue of the hot summer sky. The room was white, with a slowly revolving ceiling fan. Linda sat on a high bed, a small hunched figure in a white gown, her red hair the only colour. Her stomach ballooned under the surgical gown, but her legs stuck out, thin and white, even against the sheet. Her arms looked fragile and her face had almost no colour.

Suddenly her face puckered in pain. "One's coming, it's coming." Miranda grabbed her hand. Linda clung onto her and Miranda could feel Linda's body tensing as the contraction built. "It hurts, Mandy." Linda's eyes clouded over and she lay back on the pillow, her eyes clenched shut, her grasp on Miranda's hand tighter and tighter. "Oh, oh, oh," she moaned.

Miranda leaned in close to her, her face against Linda's, one hand massaging the top of Linda's head. "Relax," she said, trying not to get enmeshed in Linda's fear. "Breathe in, don't hold your breath, now breathe out, breathe out, that's it. That's the girl," as Linda relaxed and lay back on the pillow. She pushed Linda's damp hair off her forehead.

Linda looked at her accusingly. "How did you know to do that?"

"I read the book," said Miranda and laughed.

Linda looked shamefaced. "I didn't."

Miranda stroked her hand. "We'll manage OK."

"Mandy?" Linda's tone was tentative.

"Yes?"

But Linda's body contracted again, her legs drawn up, her hands clenched. "I'm getting another one. Oh God, not yet."

"Breathe." Linda breathed in. "Slowly...slowly. Now hold it. Out now." Linda turned on her side. Miranda rubbed hard against the small of her back. "In again, in, slowly." She felt her own body moving with Linda's, in and out of the contraction, in and out with the same breath, in and out, with Virginia's story last night. "That's the girl." Linda looked at Miranda and smiled.

"It was OK that time," she said. "It hurt, but it was OK." She lay back on the pillow, her head pressed against Miranda. Miranda felt infused with energy.

Linda lay looking at her, eyes shining. "I didn't think I could do this."

"You can," said Miranda. "I saw your drawings."

Linda groaned, but the contraction passed this time, only a tiny shiver across her body. "Are you still mad at me—for adopting the baby?"

"No, not at all," said Miranda quietly.

"Really?!"

"Yes, now breathe, in, in, that's it. Now out again."

Linda looked at Miranda. "Why have you changed your mind?"

"I know keeping him wouldn't work for you." Miranda played with Linda's hand, folding her fingers down as they had when they were little girls.

They worked through the afternoon. "I miss Danny sometimes," Linda said. The pain got worse and with each contraction Linda breathed the painkilling gas in greedily.

When Linda's feet got cold, Miranda rubbed them and put on her socks. "You were right, I am a Darnley," she said to Linda.

"But Ginny's my mother," she added to herself.

Linda was hot again and Miranda gave her ice to suck through a washer. They went through each contraction, Miranda leading, plunging through them like great waves, with increasing confusion as to where they were coming from. "I want Mum," wailed Linda.

Dr Johns came. She had a hurried conference with Miranda at the door about Hazel. "They sent her off to an alcoholic hospital. A public one. I think she's better there." Concern crossed her competent face. "Her mother's been in and out of five-star psychiatric clinics all her life. It never helped."

She walked over to Linda and stroked her forehead. "You're doing beautifully, but we don't want you in pain. I'll give you a shot if you like."

"Please," gasped Linda.

Linda dozed in and out of the contractions, the pain dulled by the injection, her mood heightened. "Rock a bye baby, on the tree tops," she sang quietly. "When the wind blows, the cradle will rock."

The dark blue sky turned to a fierce gold. They watched it together, until the nurse came in, turned on the lights and pulled down the blinds. "Oh," moaned Linda. "I can't take it any more, Mandy. I want to go home."

"Give her another shot," said Miranda fiercely to the nurse.

"Baby face, you've got the cutest little baby face," hummed Linda, as the injection took effect. She turned to Miranda. "Oh," she breathed, as the contraction took hold of her. "I really want to see this baby."

"No damn parking," thought Patrick furiously as he drove past the house. He drove on, around the corner into the laneway. He parked the Citroen, then sat hunched forward across the steering wheel.

They'd given Hazel an injection that had made her drowsy, but she'd begged him not to leave. A counsellor came in and started talking to her, as she lay in the darkened room.

"How much do you drink?" the counsellor asked.

"You'd have to ask Donny Dial-a-Drink. I was his best customer." The memory of Donny Dial-a-Drink upset Hazel and she'd buried her face in Patrick's arm.

"Do you know you're an alcoholic?" the counsellor had asked.

There was a silence in the room and they could hear distant voices, pots clanging in the hospital kitchen.

"I sometimes stop drinking on my own," Hazel said at last.

"And then start again?"

"Well, yes, but I'm hardly in the gutter, am I?" There was a touch of arrogance in her voice.

"You're twenty two, your head's split open, you're a drop-out, you're in a detox unit because you've had a seizure," said the counsellor matter of factly.

Hazel looked scared. "I want to stop," she said softly. "But I don't know how."

The woman didn't answer and Hazel had started to cry softly, the tears spurting out of her eyes as she lay back on the pillow. The wound on her forehead was raised and purple, the surrounding skin almost black. She'd stared at the ceiling intently. "Is that all that's wrong with me? That I'm an alcoholic?"

"It's enough," said the counsellor.

Hazel had turned to Patrick. "You can go now," she said. "Thanks for bringing me here."

As he got out of the car, he thought of Miranda and Linda. As he neared the house, he glanced with annoyance at the truck parked in what he considered to be their parking place. He couldn't see it properly in the dark, but as he approached, a dog in the back started barking hysterically at him. He hoped it wasn't going to be there all night. He put the key in the front door, switched on the verandah light and turned to see a woman come out of the truck, up the stairs, followed by two children.

"Does Miranda live here?" she asked anxiously. "Miranda and Linda Darnley?"

"Yes," he answered. "They're not here right now..."

"I'm their Mum," she said, grasping his arm. "And this is Louis and Kerry." She pattered down to the footpath and hauled a bag out of the back of the truck, slapping the dog to get at it. "It's the place, Roy," she shouted into the truck. "We're right. We'll see ya tonight. Good luck in the trials, Nat."

Good luck, Natalie," chorused the kids from the step. Pauline puffed up the step to Patrick. The dog barked crazily as the truck roared off down the street.

"Miranda said it was OK to stay here. Only tonight. Natalie's swimming in the state trials in an hour. Only Roy can get in because he's coach. Won't let us in. Shocking, isn't it, considering we drove all the way down?" She looked at him critically. "You the new boyfriend?"

"Yes," said Patrick dumbly.

"Handsome Harry," she said, grinning at him, as she dragged the bags in. "Come on kids." She turned to Patrick. "Where are those girls?"

"Linda's having the baby," said Patrick.

Pauline stopped in the hallway. "Gawd!" It was almost a scream. "I'll hafta get up there." She took him by the arm. "Would you keep an eye on the kids for me?" Patrick nodded a confused assent. "You're a doll."

Linda's freckles showed against the paleness of her face as the theatre light beamed fiercely down. Dr Johns stood at one end of the bed and Linda sat propped up on pillows, Miranda holding her from behind. But now, it was Linda who led with each contraction, pushing every ounce of energy into a relentless bearing down.

"I can do this," said Linda fiercely. She sat up, holding her thin ankles in her hands, as if to give momentum to her efforts. "It doesn't even hurt." Miranda marvelled. Linda seemed womanly.

Dr Johns took her hand as she lay back. "Beautiful, dear, but the next few are tricky. The head's crowning, we're nearly there. You'll have to stop pushing."

"I can't," said Linda, panicky as the contraction came.

"Pant!" said Miranda. "Pant. Huh, huh, huh. Pant."

Linda panted. "Look, look," screamed Miranda. "It's coming.

Linda, look." She held her sister forward as the baby's head emerged.

"Little push," said Dr Johns, and the baby slid out into the world, at first blue, then suffused pink, gasping for its first breath. Linda watched, laughing, gasping, her hands childishly over her mouth. "Oh, oh, baby," she panted, reaching forward.

"A girl, Linda."

Linda moaned. "Let me see, let me see." They laid the wet, pink baby on her stomach and Dr Johns secured and cut the cord. Linda pulled the baby towards her, as the nurse wrapped her. Linda gazed down at the baby's face, and touched the wisps of wet black hair. "A girl," she smiled at Miranda. "We got it wrong."

"I'll bathe her for you," said the nurse, approaching the bed.

"Take her," said Linda. She gave her the baby and burst into tears on Miranda's shoulder. Miranda could feel her trembling and held her, to comfort them both.

"It's not final, Linda," said Dr Johns gently.

Linda disengaged herself from Miranda and sat up. "I didn't think it would be like this. I thought it'd be awful. I didn't know you felt like this." She hesitated. "I didn't know you felt so . . . so, sort of strong about the baby." She looked over to the nurse, wrapping the little baby back in her rug. Her eyes were open, her hair fluffed after the bath. She moved her mouth, searchingly. Linda stared at the baby. The nurse looked back uncertainly.

"Do you . . . ?" she began dubiously. "Do you want to keep her . . . till you go back to your room? Till she goes to the nursery?"

Linda turned to Miranda. Her voice cracked. "Take her. You take her to the nursery. I haven't changed my mind." Miranda squeezed Linda's hand and stepped forward to take the baby. But she carried her back to Linda. Linda lay back on the pillows, arms folded, but looking at her baby, taking in every detail. Then she leaned forward and kissed her on the forehead. "I love you, baby," she said and buried her head in her pillow.

Miranda stood in the nursery, rocking the baby, as the nurse prepared the cot. She watched as the nurse wrote out the pink card. "Darnley, Linda Joy. 2.265 kg." She stood, feeling the baby against her, watching the tiny soft spot of skin at the top of her head move in and out, feeling the tiny feet, moving inside the blanket. She watched as a young couple came up to the viewing window. The nurse wheeled their baby up against the glass. Behind them, a bed was being wheeled along the corridor. Miranda saw Linda's red hair against the pillow, and then, her mother, walking beside the bed, holding Linda's hand. Pauline's attention was fixed on Linda, as if she were a tiny baby. Neither of them noticed the viewing window or saw Miranda standing there with the baby. Miranda watched through the glass as they disappeared from view.

Miranda handed the baby to the nurse and watched as she tucked her into the cot. "Dear little thing," said the nurse.

"She's my sister's," said Miranda.

"Adopting out, isn't she?"

"Yes," said Miranda huskily.

"Best thing really, for the baby. They choose them lovely parents now. You tell your sister that."

"I will. I hope she'll be OK," said Miranda.

The nurse patted the baby solicitously, then picked up a restless baby from the next cot. "They have counselling and that now," she said briskly. "She'll be right as rain."

Linda had slid into a stupefied sleep. Pauline looked only briefly at the baby as she and Miranda were leaving. "Poor little thing." Then, as they stood in the dark, waiting for a taxi, "Well, Linda will have to put it out of her mind." Miranda didn't reply.

"It's been a big day, love," said Pauline as they sped down towards Glebe, but her tone was stilted and unnatural.

"Yeah." Miranda stared out of the window, not knowing what to say.

When they got home, Patrick had gone upstairs and was tinkling on the piano, leaving Lou and Kerry to their own devices. Kerry was wearing Hazel's feather boa and an excess of lipstick. She greeted Miranda casually.

"Patrick's a real spunk," she said, "but I don't think he likes us much." Miranda's heart sank. "Do you sleep in the same bed as him or just the same room?"

"Same bed," said Miranda, looking sideways at her mother.

"I wasn't born yesterday," said Pauline tartly.

"Did Linda have the baby?" asked Lou shyly.

"Yes, she did, a little girl." Pauline looked at the children severely. "I don't want you lot gabbing about it all the time. She's having it adopted and it's very hard for her. She'll be coming back home with us, just for a rest. You lot better be nice to her."

"You're almost taller than me, Lou," said Miranda as she filled the kettle. "Like a big brother."

"You know we got a new house?" he said, pleased and embarrassed by her compliment. "You coming home for Christmas?"

Miranda turned and smiled at him. "I want to." She looked at her mother nervously. Things still felt strained. "If that's OK, Mum?"

"Of course it is," said Pauline impatiently. "That's why we got it, love, so you and Linda could come home." Miranda wanted to ask more, but stayed silent as Pauline chattered on. "We've only got the sleepouts for you and Linda, but they're real nice, proper flywire and all. Linda will need company." She looked at Miranda uncertainly. "I asked Mr Gardiner if you could have your old job back at the kennels. He'd be that pleased if you do. He needs a break."

Miranda's face lit up. "Oh Mum! I could stay the whole holidays. I'll give you board and everything."

"You don't have to,' said Pauline. "I can see you don't live rich." She looked around the kitchen. "We manage real well now. There's my wage and Lou brings in fifty dollars a week."

"Fifty!" said Miranda.

"I do two paper runs and collect trolleys at the supermarket." Lou beamed with pride. "I give Mum forty."

"I put twenty away," said Pauline. "He's smart like you, Miranda. Reckon he'll go to uni too."

Lou did an imaginary bowl down the kitchen to show that Pauline's academic ambitions hadn't swamped his cricketing dreams.

Miranda poured a cup of tea for herself and her mother and fruit juice for the children. She ruffled Kerry's hair. "How are you, kid?"

"Sooky sook!" Lou chanted viciously.

"I'm not," whined Kerry.

Miranda sat down at the table next to her mother as Kerry scruffed on the floor beneath her feet. Lou kept taking imaginary wickets, as he pranced round the kitchen.

"Handsome Harry come up with you for Christmas?" Pauline asked casually.

"Patrick?"

"He's nice; one of your high-up types though." Miranda laughed. "You probably terrify him. No, he's going to China for the holidays."

"Ching-chong, ching-chong," chanted Kerry, pulling her eyes into slits.

"God, you can pick 'em, Miranda," sighed Pauline.

"Lots of people go to China, Mum."

"Maybe." Pauline sipped her tea and brightened. "You know Nanna's changed her will. She's leaving me the house."

"I wish she'd die quick," said Kerry. Pauline aimed a slap at her. "Then we could have an inside dunny," she added defiantly.

"Don't say that!" Pauline scolded. "Would be nice though. Your Dad's mad as hell of course."

"Did he care when you left?"

"Not much," said Pauline shortly. "He tried to get the Elvis clock off me, that's all." She chuckled. "Roy set him straight about that."

"Mum," asked Miranda, twisting nervously at her hair. "He wasn't ever any good, was he?"

"Don't talk about your father like that," said Pauline automatically. She looked irritably at Louis. "Lou, for God's sake sit down and stop jumping everywhere."

"But was he ever nice, Mum?" persisted Miranda.

"Not really," said Pauline slowly, sipping her tea. "I married too young. Fell for the looks, then I thought it was all my fault. Thought a baby would fix it—that was you. Then one of our own—that was Linda. Then a boy—that was Louis or a house or a car or a business. Or me doing forward rolls down the front drive." She sighed. "I tried too hard. And he weren't worth it."

They sat in silence until the doorbell rang. Miranda got up to answer it and found Roy, swaying slightly, his arm round Natalie. "Champ!" he said triumphantly, "Gotta champ! Shut up!" he yelled at Kip who was whining piteously from the

190

back of the truck. "She's in the state finals," he continued, walking into the kitchen. "On her times tonight, it'll be the nationals too." He produced a bottle of Star Wine from under his arm. "Toast to Natalie and we'll wet the baby's head." He turned to Pauline. "What'd Linda have?" he asked, popping the cork.

"A girl," said Pauline shortly. She hugged Natalie. "This mean we keep getting up at five every morning?" Natalie nodded and beamed.

Roy raised his glass. "To Natalie...and what's the baby called?"

"She's giving it away, Roy," said Pauline patiently. "She hasn't changed her mind." She looked at him fiercely. "And don't you go giving her a hard time."

Miranda picked up a glass of wine. "I think we should toast her anyway."

"She's adopting out, Mandy," said Pauline.

Miranda turned to her mother. "That doesn't make it nothing," she said emphatically. "She had the baby; she loves her; she'll never ever forget her." She raised her glass. "To Linda and the baby." They raised their glasses uncertainly. Miranda turned to Natalie who was standing tense and white-faced. Miranda took her hand. "And to Nat."

Everybody relaxed. "To Nat!" they chorused.

Roy had heard the sounds of the piano in the attic. "A piano?" he'd said delightedly. "A piano?" making for the stairs. Miranda winced as the family thundered up to the attic behind Roy. When Miranda got there, Roy had upturned one of the neatly packed plastic crates of Patrick's clothes and pulled it alongside the piano stool. Patrick had assumed what Hazel always referred to as his "old school tie" look.

Roy nudged Patrick. "What songs you got?" His hands moved impatiently over the keys. Patrick reached onto the top of the piano, searched through the sheet music and brought down a book of songs.

"Here's a good old one," he said, deadpan, pounding out the opening chords of "Land of Hope and Glory". Miranda shrivelled and tried to quieten the children.

As Patrick played, Roy began to improvise on the high

notes. A smile flitted across Patrick's face and he began to compete on base. Roy looked at him sideways and increased the tempo. Patrick reached across him and added another improvisation. The children tittered. Casually, Roy lifted his leg in a high kick and began playing under his leg. Patrick played faster, forcing Roy to follow. The children burst into laughter and Miranda grinned at her mother as Patrick began to play Chico Marx style, with his head. Suddenly, there was a triumphant finish from Roy. Patrick and Roy raised their fists in salute and grinned at one another. Miranda cheered and Lou gave a piercing whistle.

"Know any Elvis?" winked Roy.

"Like what?" asked Patrick.

"Hound Dog?"

"You mean Big Mumma Thornton."

"You know your stuff, boy," said Roy appreciatively and began to play again. "You ain't nothing but a hound dog . . ." he sang.

"Crying all the time," caterwauled Patrick.

"You ain't ever caught no rabbit," they chorused. "And you ain't no friend of mine."

Roy grinned at Patrick and as they finished the song, he nudged him. "Give me something soppy," he said loudly, sliding off the crate. "So I can crack on to this sheila over here." He winked, nodding towards Pauline.

Roy took Pauline's hand and pulled her to her feet. He was no dancer, but Miranda saw a new softness on her mother's face as she leant up against him. Trust had replaced the hard defences of her body, although she pulled away from him teasingly when she saw Miranda watching them. As the piece finished, the doleful sound of Kip's yowl could be heard from the truck outside. "Your dog and my kids; we'll be lucky to ever get it together." But she smiled at him, tenderly, then sat down on the mattress next to Miranda, as Roy went back to the piano.

"You're exhausted," she said censoriously to Miranda. She softened. "You were good with Linda today, love. She couldn't have done without you."

Miranda felt like bursting into tears, exhaustion and excitement engulfing her. Pauline looked at her carefully. "Well, what was she like?" she asked suddenly.

"Who?" said Miranda.

"Your mother."

There was a silence until Kerry appeared between them, wide-eyed. "Is she rich? Linda said she's rich!"

Miranda laughed. "Yeah, she is."

"Kerry's going to get rich," said Lou. "She charges thirty cents for a kiss behind the wash shed."

"Fifty cents for sloppy ones," said Kerry unrepentantly and kicked Lou.

"Go and watch TV downstairs, you kids," yelled Pauline, looking at her watch. "Nat, you go to bed. Don't want to hear a peep out of any of you..."

Patrick and Roy were still picking out tunes and improvising, concentrating totally. "What's she like?" Pauline asked Miranda as the children filed out.

Miranda looked at her mother steadily. "I guess Linda told you about the first time we went?"

"Yeah," said Pauline. "I was going to ring you. Tell you not to worry, but I was half mad with everything going on up home. And it's been hard for me. I always wanted the right thing for you, but I've been scared for you and scared for me. Thought I might lose you." She bit her bottom lip.

Miranda put her hand on her mother's. "No chance."

"I'm sorry it didn't turn out for you. Well, sorry and glad."

Miranda looked at her mother steadily. "It did turn out. I went back there. Just last night. I mean, she asked me to. She told me all about it. You know she was only fourteen?"

"Fourteen. My God."

"It's been very hard for her, Mum."

"I can see that," said Pauline. "You know, with what Linda's facing." She looked at Miranda. "Not easy for you, either."

"She couldn't let go of it, like I couldn't." Miranda paused and began nervously picking at her nail. Pauline held her hand to stop her, as if Miranda was a little girl. "It's like I had this picture in my head, and when I got depressed or upset, I'd think about her and it made me feel better. You know how I've always been...sort of...?"

"Jumpy," put in Pauline. "Nervy."

"Yeah, I suppose that's it," said Miranda. "I had it in my mind that finding her would fix me. Then I met her and she's just like any other person. But she is my mother. She told me about the birth." Her voice sounded muffled. "That she loved me."

"Of course she did." Pauline looked at her. "I'm sorry I've been hard about it. I can see it more now." She hesitated. "And do you feel different, you know, about us?"

"I've always felt different," said Miranda. "And I hated feeling different. But now, it seems all right to feel like that." She could see Pauline struggling to make sense of what she was saying. "I feel more like I belong with you now." She shrugged. "With you, and the kids. Even though I love her and she's my mother, you're my family."

"I could a' told you that, Mandy."

Miranda grinned at her. "That's the trouble. You never stop telling me." She hugged Pauline and felt Pauline hug her back tightly. "I love you, Mum," she said tearfully.

Pauline pulled away, but Miranda saw that her eyes were wet. "Don't carry on, Mandy. You've always been such a one for carrying on."

Miranda lay collapsed on the bed in the attic after Pauline and Roy had finally gone downstairs. Patrick tinkered on the piano for a while and then came over to the bed. He took off Miranda's shoes and shook her out of her jeans. "Thanks for looking after the kids today," she said.

"That's OK," he answered. "Are you going to sleep right now?"

"Almost."

"I've been practising a piece, on the piano—for you."

She pushed him playfully off the bed. "Then you'd better play it for me, before I fall asleep."

The first notes were quiet, haunting. It built, a simple, soft, slightly mournful tune. Miranda could feel her eyes, her whole body, heavy, drifting into sleep, against her will, the music pulling her back, the events of the last day crowding in. Virginia, the birth of Linda's baby, were confused and mixed in her mind. But she still had the sensation of the tiny baby in her arms, that extraordinary feeling at the moment of birth, the feeling of arms embracing her, Virginia's, her mother's, Linda's. Her own were around them as the last notes of the music faded, still reverberating in her mind, contentment and wholeness took over her exhausted emotions. Patrick lay down on the bed and put his arms round her. For a moment, they lay silently, staring at the sky through the slit of the attic window.

"That was lovely," she said.

"It's called 'Condolences', by Chopin."

"I don't really need them now." She moved closer, up against him. "But thank you." She kissed him and fell asleep.